HOPE
and
FAITH

ELIZABETH WOODRUFF

PAGE PUBLISHING, INC.
New York, NY

First originally published by Page Publishing, Inc. 2018

ISBN 978-1-64424-373-2 (Paperback)
ISBN 978-1-64424-374-9 (Digital)

Printed in the United States of America

Chapter One

She was a tall, slender woman, about five feet eight inches. Her curly brown hair went down to her elbows like a waterfall. Her bright hazel eyes now lit up a room when she smiled. She was twenty-one years old. At the moment, she stood in front of the large house—practically a mansion—dressed in a pair of blue jeans and a red blouse. A taxi waited behind her, its meter running.

Sunlight peaked out from the sky behind the house, lighting it up in a light golden glow, which was a sign of hope to most people. She took a deep breath as she started walking up the steps leading into the house.

Knock. Knock.

She could hear footsteps from within, hurrying to the door. She looked to her left wrist where there were two words tattooed: *Hope. Faith.* She closed and opened her eyes as the door opened and a maid stood in front of her. The maid was about thirty years old and had long blond hair that was currently pulled up into a tight bun on top of her head. She had caring blue eyes, and her body seemed rather built for a woman.

"May I help you, ma'am?" the maid asked.

"My name is Alexandria Hawthorne. I have come to speak with Elizabeth Rhodes," the girl said. She straightened her back, not willing to let these people see how weak she felt, having to return to the house she had grown up in.

"Come in," the maid said. The name immediately sparked a memory in her, and she knew that Elizabeth would wish to speak with her. She allowed the woman, Alexandria, to enter the house and closed the large doors behind her before walking down the hallway.

She led Alexandria to the drawing room in which a woman, about fifty, sat behind a large desk. Her hair was a light brown although gray hairs could be seen throughout her roots. Her brown eyes were hidden behind glasses. "Ma'am."

"Yes, Bridget?" the woman said. She looked up, and then her mouth opened in shock at the sight of the woman in front of her. "Alexandria. Hello. It has ... it has been awhile."

"Yes, it has, Elizabeth," Alexandria said, nodding her head.

"You may leave, Bridget. Thank you," the woman, Elizabeth, said. She stood up and Alexandria could tell that she was about five feet five inches. Bridget nodded and then left the two women alone in the room. The pair was silent for a moment. "You have changed a great deal since the last time I saw you, Alexandria."

Indeed, she had. It had been eleven years since the women had seen each other. "Eleven years does that to someone," Alexandria said. She did not want to go into great deal about what had happened in the last eleven years, at least not yet. Not until she was comfortable with her surroundings and the people around her.

Elizabeth stared at the woman in front of her. She was no longer the girl that she had known and cared for as a child. This Alexandria in front of her was very different. The little girl had been caring and gentle. The woman in front of her seemed distant and rough. It was like a complete flip in her personality.

"How have you been?" Elizabeth asked.

She knew that she wouldn't be able to get the explanation from Alexandria right away, but she wanted to know what had happened. She knew that something had to have happened for her to have such a drastic change in personality.

"I have come for a place to stay," Alexandria stated.

She knew that Elizabeth was going wild trying to figure out why Alexandria was in front of her. But she still didn't dare tell her the truth yet.

"Why?" Elizabeth inquired.

Elizabeth ran a house for people who needed a place to stay; it was an orphanage for all ages. Alexandria had been dropped off as a baby in a basket with only a note to "take good care of Alexandria" and attached was a ring, and Alexandria had lived there until she had found a family at the age of ten. Elizabeth had always wondered how Alexandria was doing; she had not heard word of her since the family had adopted her and taken her away from them.

"Joseph and Marie are dead," Alexandria stated coldly.

On her right hand, she twisted a ring: it was a simple gold band etched with small vines and flowers; it was the ring that she had been dropped off with as a baby. Until the ring fit her, she had worn it as a necklace. Now it fit her finger perfectly, and she constantly twisted it when she was nervous.

"I am so sorry," Elizabeth said.

"They left me with nothing. Their debt was too high for me to be able to keep the house," Alexandria said. "I … I did not know where else to go. You were the only one that I knew would take me in."

"I am glad you still considered this place," Elizabeth said, smiling. "I will have Bridget prepare you a room. Do you have any baggage?"

"Yes," Alexandria said. "It is all in the taxi I have waiting in front."

"Then go and fetch it, and I will have Bridget waiting to show you to your room," Elizabeth said.

"Thank you, Elizabeth," Alexandria said.

She stood up and left the room, going outside. She paid the taxi and got her luggage—only two large suitcases and a duffel bag—out of the trunk and wondered at first how she was going to get it all up to the house. Bridget appeared beside her and picked up one of the suitcases.

"Follow me, ma'am," Bridget said. They were silent as they walked through the house. Alexandria was slightly disappointed when it was not her bedroom from her childhood although she did not let anyone see the disappointment. Instead, the room she was taken to was a large room and had a queen four-poster bed with gold sheets and a red comforter on it. There was a large armoire in one corner; on a dresser in the center of a wall was a television, and there was a vanity also. A door led to what she assumed was the bathroom.

It was a simple room, and Alexandria hoped to be able to make it home, at least for a little while.

"Here you are, ma'am. Is there anything else I can get you?" Bridget asked.

"No, thank you," Alexandria said. "Thanks, Bridget."

"Of course, ma'am. If you need anything, there is a bell just outside your room. Ring it only once and one of the maids will be with you immediately," Bridget said. "Breakfast will be momentarily, if you would like to join everyone in the dining room. Lunch is served at noon exactly, and dinner is served at five thirty."

"Not much has changed in the schedule, I see," Alexandria said.

"Not at all, ma'am," Bridget said.

"Thank you, Bridget," Alexandria said.

Bridget curtsied and left the room, closing the door quietly behind her.

Alexandria thought for a moment before putting all her luggage on the bed and then going down to the dining room. The house had not had much change done to it within the last eleven years. The same paintings lined the hallways and the lights had been upgraded, but the layout was still the same. Alexandria was partly glad about it. It meant that she did not have to have a tour of the entire place, like she had seen numerous people have given to them as a child.

Alexandria was the second person to the dining room; the only other person there was Elizabeth.

"Is there any place in particular that you would like for me to sit, Elizabeth?" she asked.

"Not usually, but today, you may sit to my left. I will introduce you when everyone is here," Elizabeth stated.

"Are you still married to Duncan?" Alexandria asked.

Duncan had been Elizabeth's husband when Alexandria was here when she was young, and he had been like a father to her.

"Yes," Elizabeth said. "When everyone is here, there are eight of us, including myself and Duncan. Everyone is civil to one another."

"Good," Alexandria said.

The next person to enter the dining room was Duncan. Alexandria saw his mouth drop, much like Elizabeth's had when she first saw her today, and then he walked toward her. He was surprised when she did not move to hug him as she had done all the time when she was a child. He knew then that the woman had changed a great deal in the last eleven years.

People then began to enter the room. The next to enter were two men: one, a twenty-two-year-old with black hair that fell right above his blue eyes, he was rather muscular and he looked at her in surprise and sat beside Duncan; the second was a twenty-two-year-old with blond hair that was cut somewhat short with green eyes, he was rather slim but seemed muscular. He sat down beside her after asking if anyone was sitting there in which she simply shook her head.

Then entered a girl about fourteen years old with long blond hair and bright blue eyes; she was rather thin and seemed extremely well maintained. She sat on the other end of the large table, away from everyone else. After that was a ten-year-old girl who had short brown hair and brown eyes; she sat beside the blond boy that had sat down beside Alexandria. The last two came in a pair: one man and one woman. Alexandria could instantly tell that they were twins; they were both about sixteen years old and had the same facial features, as well as the same black hair and brown eyes. They looked familiar to Alexandria, and she then recalled twins that were brought into the house just a week before she had left.

"Good morning, everyone," Elizabeth said with a smile to get everyone's attention.

"Today, we have a new member. Well, she is not necessarily new. She was adopted eleven years ago, and now she is returning to us."

"Why?" the fourteen-year-old girl asked.

"Joseph and Marie, the people who adopted me, died," Alexandria stated. "My name is Alexandria."

The boy beside her spoke, "Welcome back, Alexandria. My name is Mark." He then looked across the table to the boy that had entered with him.

"Colton."

Alexandria could not keep her eyes off him. He was handsome, that was for sure. But something inside of her was pulling her toward him; she just wasn't sure what it was.

Beside him was the twin boy. "Collin."

The fourteen-year-old girl was beside him. "Jessica."

It then went across from her to the twin sister. "Carlee."

And then it left the ten-year-old girl who reminded Alexandria a little too much of herself already. "I'm Anna."

"Welcome back, Alexandria," Elizabeth said. Bridget then came in with another maid, and they began to serve breakfast—scrambled eggs, toast, hash browns, and pancakes.

"Thank you," Alexandria said. She felt like Elizabeth was making a big fuss about her return, and she wished that she wouldn't. She wondered what everyone's story was; she wondered when they had all come to Elizabeth's warm arms.

"I am sorry about your adoptive parents," Mark said from beside her.

"What made you return here? Shouldn't you have your own apartment or something?" Colton asked from across the table. He could tell that Alexandria had an attitude, and he wasn't happy about having another person around them.

Alexandria glared at the man diagonal from her. "I do not believe that is any of your business. And besides, you're my age, if not older."

"I have been here since I was sixteen. You left and came back. There is a big difference there," Colton said with a smirk.

"Colton, be nice," Mark said, staring at the other man. He was appalled at what Colton was saying to Alexandria. "She hasn't been here for a while. And if she doesn't want to tell us, then she doesn't have to tell us."

"You're no fun, Mark," Colton said.

"So you have said many times," Mark said, rolling his eyes. He then turned to Alexandria. "I apologize for his behavior, Alexandria. Colton's extremely curious."

"I'm used to guys being … jerks," Alexandria said, making note of the ten-year-old at the table and the glare that Elizabeth was giving her.

"I can tell," Colton said.

Alexandria glared at him. She hated how arrogant this man in front of her seemed. She didn't bother replying. She just continued to eat. The table was quiet as they all ate. When they were finally done, Alexandria headed back to her room and began unpacking; she put her headphones on and was listening to her music when there was a knock on the door. She turned to see Anna standing there.

"Hi, Anna," Alexandria said, pausing her music and pulling her headphones out.

"Hi, Alexandria," Anna said. "Can I come in?"

"It's a little messy, but sure," Alexandria said. There was a chair at the vanity that Anna sat in. "Is there something I can help you with?"

"No, I just always come and visit people," Anna said, shrugging.

Alexandria smiled slightly. She had done the same thing as a child.

"I used to do the same thing," Alexandria said.

Anna smiled at Alexandria, glad to get to know the older woman more.

"I've been here for five years. My parents were killed in a car accident, and none of my family was able to take me in," Anna said.

"That's too bad," Alexandria said.

"I've accepted it. It's better than having my family abandon me," Anna said.

"And at least you know," Alexandria said before she knew what she was doing. She trusted this little girl. She saw so much of herself in her. "I was dropped off here as a baby. I was adopted when I was ten."

"I'm sorry," Anna said.

"I've come to accept it," Alexandria said.

When she was a teenager, she found her birth certificate and then tried to get ahold of her birth parents. It had been a tough meeting. Neither parent knew what to say or do, and neither parent wanted to take her from the parents who had adopted her. She wished that they had; her adoptive parents were not as good as many people thought.

There was a knock on the door. Alexandria was getting tired of people knocking on her door already. Alexandria looked over and saw Bridget standing there.

"I am here for Anna," Bridget said. "Elizabeth wishes to see her."

"Okay," Anna said and walked toward Bridget. She turned around and smiled at Alexandria. "See you later, Alexandria."

"See you later, Anna," Alexandria said, and Anna and Bridget left. She immediately put her headphones back on and let the music blare everything else out. As she unpacked her things into the room, she was dancing around. She had taken dance classes in high school—from ballet to hip-hop to modern to lyrical. Her favorite had always been lyrical, so it was easy to dance to music blaring in her ears. She twirled and then looked in the doorway to see Mark standing there, staring at her with a small smile.

"Can I help you?" she asked rudely as she stopped the music. She found it rude that he had been standing there, staring at her. She was slightly creeped out and hoped that he hadn't been watching for very long.

"Continue dancing. It was beautiful," Mark said. "I'm sorry, I didn't mean to startle you. I was just walking by and looked in out of habit and saw your dancing. It's beautiful."

"Thank you," Alexandria said. She could feel herself start to blush but pushed it down. She couldn't let anyone know that they were affecting her. She was only going to be staying for a short while, and then she would be gone.

"Did you dance before you came here?" Mark asked. He was now leaning against the doorframe.

"Yes, I took dance classes in high school," Alexandria said.

"You have a lot of talent," Mark said. "I haven't seen much dancing, but I know that it was beautiful."

"You can stop complimenting me now," Alexandria said. She hated compliments; she rarely got them, and so she never knew how to accept them.

He was about to say something when his name was called, and Colton walked over.

"Hey, are you ready to spar?"

"Yeah," Mark said. He turned to Alexandria. "See you around, Alexandria."

"See you," Alexandria said, and the pair of boys left. She then shut her door and put her music back on. She really did not feel like being disturbed again.

She continued to unpack until it was about eleven forty-five, when there was a knock on the door. She opened it and saw Duncan standing there.

"Hey, Duncan."

She allowed a small smile to escape her lips. This man was the first man to treat her with love and to care for her; he was the first man she thought of in a fatherly way. He was the only man that she truly felt like she could let her barriers down with.

"There's a small smile," Duncan said, his own lips turning into a grin. "I was beginning to worry that I wasn't going to see my favorite little girl again."

"I'm not the same," Alexandria said sighing. "A … a lot of stuff happened in the last eleven years, Duncan."

"Do you want to talk about it?" Duncan asked.

"No," Alexandria said, shaking her head. "Not right now at least. With time, maybe. But right now, I don't want to. I don't trust these people yet."

"But you trust me still," Duncan said. It was partly a statement and partly a question; he wanted to know that his little Alexandria— his little Lexi—was still in this woman.

"Always," Alexandria said. "You and Elizabeth are the only two people I truly trust, and that is why I came back here."

"I am glad," Duncan said. "Are you going to come for lunch?"

"Yes," Alexandria said. "I'm almost done unpacking, so the rest can wait until after lunch."

"Wonderful," Duncan said. "Remember when you were younger, and we used to go out to dinner together every week?"

"Those are some of my best memories," Alexandria said with a smile. She stepped out into the hallway with Duncan and closed the door behind her.

"Would you like to continue it?" Duncan asked.

"Let me think about it. I … I don't know how long I am going to be here," Alexandria said. "So I don't want to start anything if I am only going to be here for a short while."

"You are welcome to stay as long as you would like," Duncan said.

"Yes, I know," Alexandria said. "Another reason why I came."

"We missed you," Duncan said.

"I missed you too," Alexandria said. Around everyone else, she was going to be a tough girl, someone you didn't want to mess with. Duncan was the only one she was willing to let her guard down, at least for now.

They were then in the dining room, where everyone was sitting. The two seats beside Elizabeth were free, and so they sat down where they had sat at breakfast.

"So do you go to college, Alexandria?" Mark asked from beside her.

"I just got my bachelor's degree in accounting," Alexandria said. "I graduated a few months ago."

"That must be a hard course load," Mark said.

"It wasn't too hard," Alexandria said, shrugging.

She wondered why this man was trying to make conversation with her. She just wanted to eat her food and then go back upstairs, but she knew it would be far too rude to ignore him.

"That's good," Mark said. He was trying to get to know this mysterious woman beside him; she was beautiful, and yet something seemed wrong about her. It seemed like she was hiding something dark. In some ways, she reminded him of Colton.

Alexandria didn't reply, simply going back to eating her lunch. She didn't really want to make conversation. She just wanted to be able to eat peacefully. She didn't want to get close to anyone here. She would probably be leaving soon anyways; she couldn't count on Elizabeth and Duncan's charity all the time.

"Alexandria," Elizabeth said.

"Yes?" Alexandria said. She looked at the woman she had always considered a motherly figure.

"I want to speak with you in the drawing room after you are done unpacking," Elizabeth said.

"All right, I should be there shortly after lunch. I only have a few more things to unpack," Alexandria said.

"Okay," Elizabeth said.

"Are you thinking about getting a job?" Duncan asked.

"Definitely. I still have bills to pay and student loans to pay off," Alexandria said.

"If you need any help, just let us know," Duncan said.

"You are helping plenty with just giving me a place to stay," Alexandria said. "Thank you for taking me in again."

"You know you are more than welcome here," Elizabeth said. "You always have been."

Alexandria nodded and continued to eat. She had grown accustomed to silence while eating. She didn't like to talk and eat at the same time, but it seemed that everyone there was used to it. She would have to get used to it eventually.

Chapter Two

After she was done with lunch, Alexandria immediately finished unpacking and then went to the drawing room, where Elizabeth and Duncan were.

"Hey," Alexandria said, smiling. These two people were the only people she truly trusted, the only two people that she could really be herself and relaxed around.

"Hey," Duncan said.

Alexandria walked over and sat down in the chair across from the pair.

"You seem more relaxed now," Elizabeth stated.

Elizabeth had not missed the cold attitude that Alexandria had when she first entered the house, and now she was much more relaxed; she was finally smiling.

"I was able to dance for a while as I unpacked, and it ... it feels good to be home," Alexandria admitted. A faint blush fell over her tanned cheeks.

"You dance now?" Elizabeth questioned. She remembered how clumsy Alexandria had been as a child, so imagining her as a dancer seemed something so different.

"Yes, it really helps me relax," Alexandria said.

"At least you found what relaxes you," Duncan said.

"So what did you want to talk about, Elizabeth?" Alexandria asked.

"We just wanted to know how you have been since you left. You ... have changed greatly," Elizabeth stated.

"Yes, I have," Alexandria said. "I ... I cannot lie to either one of you, and you both know that. Life was hell with Joseph and Marie."

"What do you mean? They seemed so good for you," Elizabeth said. She was shocked at Alexandria's statement and wasn't sure what to think of it at first. "Everything came up clean with them." They did extensive background checks to make sure that the people who adopted from them were all clean and that nothing came out wrong with them. She didn't understand what could have gone wrong.

"They were not. They … abused me, kept me shut up in a bedroom in the basement, and acted like they hated me when no one else was around. They did and dealt drugs. It was … not good," Alexandria said.

"How did they die?" Duncan asked.

"Other drug dealers killed them," Alexandria stated as a matter-of-factly.

"I am so sorry, Alexandria … I wish I had known the truth," Elizabeth said. A tear rolled down her cheek, and Alexandria put her own hand on Elizabeth's on the desk that separated the pair.

"It has made me stronger," Alexandria said. "And I am home now, and that is what matters."

"Still," Elizabeth said. Her heart broke for the younger girl in front of her, the younger girl who had been a daughter to her, whom she had raised for the first ten years of her life.

"Do not tell anyone else the truth," Alexandria said. "I have come a long way with putting it behind me and not degrading myself because of the way that they treated me."

"We will not," Duncan said. "I am so sorry, Lexi."

"Please stop apologizing," Alexandria said. Duncan noted that she did not correct him calling her Lexi. "I have come to terms with everything. I am here to start my life over again."

"And we are here with you," Duncan said. "Lexi, it is amazing that you are still so strong."

"Yes, it is," Elizabeth said, "Out of all the people that have stayed with us, you are the one that I am most proud of."

"Me too," Duncan said.

"Thank you. That means a lot to me," Alexandria said. She could feel the tears threatening to fall, and she closed her eyes, trying to get them to stop.

The door opened, and the three saw Colton enter the drawing room. "Oh, sorry, I didn't realize you guys would still be talking."

"Is there something we can help you with?" Elizabeth asked, drying the tears that had fallen.

"Anna isn't doing well," Colton said. "Bridget asked me to send for you while she got her to bed."

"How bad is it?" Elizabeth inquired, walking toward Colton.

"Pretty bad," Colton said. "She's coughing up blood."

Elizabeth was immediately out of the room, followed quickly by Duncan. Colton stood there, staring at Alexandria.

"What are you staring at?" Alexandria asked.

"You were just crying," Colton said. "Why?"

"It is none of your business," Alexandria said, glaring at Colton. She brushed the tear away that she felt on her cheek. "What is wrong with Anna?"

Colton paused for a second, unsure if he could trust Alexandria with Anna's health condition. "She has lupus."

"Oh gosh," Alexandria said, putting a hand on to her mouth. "She looks so healthy though."

"It comes in flares," Colton said. "She usually doesn't like people to know, especially new people here."

"I won't say anything," Alexandria said.

"No, it's not about you saying something. It's about you acting differently around her," Colton said. "Even though she is a little girl, she doesn't want to be treated like one."

Alexandria smiled slightly; this little girl really was a lot like her. "I won't."

"Good," Colton said and walked away.

Alexandria found herself following Colton out, not entirely sure what else to do. "Colton."

"Go back to your room and finish unpacking or whatever. I'll tell Elizabeth and Duncan that you went there," Colton said.

"I don't have to listen to you," Alexandria said, stepping toward him. Colton surprised her by turning around swiftly and appearing directly in front of her in three long strides.

"You will do as I say. Even though you were in this house eleven years ago, it does not mean that things are the same. Anna is *dying*. She will not want you around, and Elizabeth or Duncan won't either. So just go back to your room," Colton said.

Alexandria glared long and hard at him, the same way that he was glaring at her. "I will be in the library," she stated and walked away. Colton ran a hand through his hair and walked in the opposite direction of her.

He couldn't help but wonder why it was that Alexandria drove him crazy. He wasn't sure if it was because she reminded him slightly of himself or if it was because she just drove him crazy with her attitude. She seemed like a complete bitch, and he couldn't help but not want her around because of that.

"What has you looking so angry?" Mark asked, walking over to Colton.

"Alexandria," Colton said.

"Why? She seems like a nice girl," Mark said.

"She seems like a bitch to me," Colton said. "She acts stuck-up like she's better than the rest of us when she's actually just like us."

"Did you ever think that it was you who was causing her to act this way? You do have a way of getting people around you angry," Mark said.

"Shut up," Colton said, glaring at his best friend.

"Hey, it's a possibility," Mark said, shrugging. His voice then got lower, a dark tone taking control. "How is Anna?"

"Not good," Colton said, shaking his head. "She was coughing up blood last I knew."

"Colton! Mark!" Elizabeth shouted down the hallway. The two men turned to look at her. "Anna is asking for Alexandria."

"What?" Colton questioned. He wasn't sure if he had heard her correctly.

"Go and get Alexandria!" Elizabeth said. Both men immediately started walking the other direction.

"She's in the library," Colton said. "Can I just not go in since she drives me crazy?"

"No, come on," Mark said. "How do you know she's in the library?"

"I told her to go to her room since Anna wouldn't want her around, and she said that she was going to the library," Colton said.

"Which would also explain why you are in a bad mood and why you don't want to go to see her," Mark said and shook his head. "You have to be nice to her, Colton."

"She's hiding something from us," Colton said.

"And you're hiding something from her and everyone else besides me," Mark stated.

Colton glared at his best friend, not really believing that he had just played that card.

"Whatever," Colton said.

"Besides, if Elizabeth and Duncan trust her, we should trust her too," Mark said.

"I still don't know," Colton said.

"Well, I am going to trust her," Mark said, and they entered the library. He spotted Alexandria in the fiction section rather quickly. "Alexandria."

"Yes?" Alexandria said, turning. She glared when she saw Colton standing beside him.

"Anna is calling for you," Colton mumbled.

"What did you say?" Alexandria asked. She had a feeling what Colton had mumbled, but she wasn't positive what she thought was what he had said.

"Anna is calling for you," Colton said. His voice had a hard tone to it, and Alexandria knew he didn't want to admit that he had been wrong.

"Oh," Alexandria said. She put the book in her hands down and then walked to the two men. "I hope you'll lead me to the room."

"Of course," Mark said, smiling. "Sorry for Colton's attitude."

"I'm used to an attitude like that," Alexandria said, shrugging. "I wonder why Anna was calling for me."

"Who knows? I sure wouldn't call for you," Colton mumbled.

Alexandria shocked them both by twisting around quickly and grabbing his shirt collar tightly in her hand.

"You don't know the hell I went through the last eleven years. I'm done being degraded. I got it enough the last eleven years. I don't need you trying to push me down too," Alexandria snapped. "So if you challenge me one more time like that, I will punch you so hard it makes you a soprano."

"Understood," Colton said. His question had been confirmed. Something had happened with the couple who adopted her. Now he was just curious as to what exactly it was that happened that made her so angry.

Alexandria released him, and they walked down the hallway to Anna's room. Alexandria was shocked to find that it was her old bedroom. Nothing had changed in the small room.

"Anna needs her rest. Everyone besides Alexandria needs to leave," Bridget said.

"All right," Mark said. The entire room—filled with Elizabeth, Duncan, two maids, Colton, Alexandria, and himself—filtered out except for Alexandria. She immediately took a seat directly beside Anna.

"You … came," Anna said. Her voice was soft and frail. Alexandria almost wished that she was not there at that moment.

"Of course," Alexandria said. "When a friend calls, I always come."

"Friend," Anna said softly. "You … seem very hard on the outside … but sweet on the inside … like a hard candy."

Alexandria laughed at the analogy. "Yes, I am like that. My adopted parents weren't that great to me, so I became hard to the world. But I was raised mainly by Elizabeth and Duncan here, and so I still have part of that sweetness that they spread to everyone."

"They are … wonderful," Anna said.

"Yes, they raised me as if I was their own daughter. It was why I came back here. I knew that they would still love me and that they would let me stay as long as I need to," Alexandria said. She twisted her ring in her hand, trying to push out the worry for Anna.

"I think … you can help us," Anna said.

"Why do you say that?"

"We are ... a distant group ... I think that ... that you can bring us closer together."

"I ... I do not know, Anna."

"Please, for me, at least try."

Alexandria bit her lip and then met Anna's eyes and felt terrible. "For you, I will do anything, Anna."

"Thank you," Anna said.

"Of course, Anna. You remind me of myself quite a bit actually," Alexandria said. "I used to walk around these halls, finding people to talk to and hang out with. And I was always very quiet and kept to myself when I wasn't trying to find someone to play with."

"Take care ... of Colton. He ... he may seem mean, but he's ... he's actually really nice," Anna said. "You just ... have to get to know him."

"I will," Alexandria said.

"I am going to fall asleep now," Anna said. "I will be okay, I promise. This ... this won't win that easily."

Alexandria nodded, trying to keep the tears at bay. Anna fell asleep moments later, and Alexandria started bawling. This little girl acted a lot like her when she was young—always looking out for other people, always worrying about everyone else. But this young girl was so much better than Alexandria could ever dream of being; she was worrying about everyone else when she had a disease that could easily kill her.

A few minutes later, Alexandria stopped crying and went outside to see everyone staring at her. Elizabeth walked over to her and hugged her tightly. Alexandria did not resist her as her own energy had been spent on crying.

"She's going to fight this," Elizabeth said.

"Yes, I know. She's a tough girl," Alexandria said.

"Is she awake now?" Elizabeth asked.

Alexandria shook her head. "She went to sleep."

"Good," Duncan said, nodding. "She needs to rest."

"I'm going to the library," Mark stated.

"And I'm heading to the gym," Colton said.

"Come on, we still need to talk," Elizabeth said. Her arm was around Alexandria's shoulder, and she led her to the drawing room.

Alexandria sat down on one of the chairs, her energy spent. She had barely slept the night before, and now it seemed to be catching up to her. She found herself wanting to lie in bed and cry all night long.

"May we ask what Anna wanted to talk to you about?" Elizabeth asked.

"She asked me to bring the group together," Alexandria said. "And to take care of Colton."

"She and Colton are rather close," Elizabeth said, nodding.

"Well, she's close to everyone," Duncan said.

"She's a sweet girl," Alexandria stated.

"She's much like you used to be," Duncan commented.

"Yes, I have noticed," Alexandria said. "Hopefully she does not have what happened to me happen to her."

"She probably will not. Lupus could kill her," Elizabeth stated.

Alexandria bit the inside of her lip, trying to stop the tears from coming. She was not sure why this girl that she had just met had such a strong control over her. "She is a strong girl."

"As are you," Duncan said. "We need some help, Lexi."

"Doing what?" Alexandria asked.

"We are hosting a fund-raiser here on Friday. We are holding a dinner party and dancing in the large room we have on the third floor that we call the ballroom," Elizabeth said. "I was hoping you would be able to help us decorate."

"Sure," Alexandria said. "Um, I don't have a dress though."

"The other girls may need them too," Elizabeth said. "So later this week, we'll all go to the mall and pick out dresses. We probably will wait until Wednesday, just to see if Anna could come with us."

"All right," Alexandria said.

They were quiet for a moment until Duncan spoke, "She's right, Lexi. You can bring the group together."

"What do you mean?" Alexandria asked.

"Anna was right. You're just what we needed right now. The children are very distant from one another. If you are willing to help everyone, you can make us all a family," Duncan explained.

Alexandria was quiet for a moment before responding. "I am not the same little girl I was when I left. I … I do not trust people easily. I do not believe in people as much as I used to."

"We understand that," Elizabeth said. "Just … try … please."

"I already promised Anna. I told her I would do anything for her," Alexandria said.

"She has a way with people," Duncan said, smiling. "Just like you used to."

"Is there anything else I can do? Or can I return to my room?" Alexandria asked.

"Before you return to your room, have Colton show you to the ballroom," Elizabeth said. "In the last eleven years, we had some work done upstairs, so I do not want you to wander there without someone else yet. Have him give you a full tour right now actually."

"All right," Alexandria said and stood up. "Any idea where he would be?"

"He said he would be in the gym, which we had added down to the basement. Do you remember how to get there?" Duncan said.

"Yes, thank you," Alexandria said and walked out of the room. She went down the hallway where a set of stairs was. She was grateful when the light was on. A memory of her childhood here struck her as she recalled slipping on the stairs and falling down all of them because the light had been turned off.

"Colton!" she called as she headed down the stairs.

A few stairs from the bottom, she slipped and started to fall down when strong arms grabbed her, keeping her from falling and hitting her head against the stairs.

"I've got you," Colton said softly.

It was the gentlest voice she had heard him use all day. It made her feel safe. She could feel the blush starting to creep up on her cheeks. She straightened up and was standing about two stairs ahead of him, making her his same height.

"Thank you," Alexandria said. "I hate these stairs. I fell down them from the very top when I was young."

"That had to hurt," Colton said.

"I broke my ankle," Alexandria said, nodding, "I had bruises all along my body. I was only seven when I did it."

"That would really make you not want to come down the stairs," Colton said.

"I didn't have a choice though," Alexandria said, running a hand through her hair. "Elizabeth and Duncan wanted me to have you give me a full tour of the place since they've done some remodeling in the last ten years apparently."

"Yeah, they had the whole third floor redone, had the kitchen expanded, and had another room added onto the first floor," Colton explained. "Let me just put some stuff away and then I'll show you around."

"Thanks," Alexandria said. "Do you want any help?"

"No, but come on, I'll show you where things are down here too," Colton said.

"All right," Alexandria said, following him.

The basement was larger than she remembered; it was mostly a gym now, with mats along most of the floor and weights in the corner, three treadmills, an elliptical machine, a bicycle, and a stair-stepper machine. There was a large storage box in one corner that Alexandria saw Colton putting a medicine ball and some other things in. She saw a target on one wall and realized that Colton had been putting knives in a black bag and put it in the storage box.

"They made this really extensive," Alexandria said. "When I was here when I was younger, this was half gym, half family room. There was only one of each of the workout machines, and then there were some couches and stuff on the other side."

"That was the way they had it when I got here. And then Mark and I asked for a more extensive gym, and they added on the other family room and made this the gym," Colton said.

"You've been here, what, six years?" Alexandria said.

"Yes," Colton said. "Elizabeth and Duncan used to speak of you."

"They did?" Alexandria asked. She had known that she always held a special place in their hearts, but hearing from another person that they had spoken of her surprised her.

"Yeah, when we did poorly in school, they used to mumble that they wished all their children had been like you. A blow to the stomach, if you ask me," Colton said.

"Is that why you don't like me?" Alexandria questioned.

"I just don't like people, period."

"That seems to be the case with people nowadays."

"Especially when they lose their family."

"At least you had one."

Colton stared at her, wanting her to elaborate but not sure how to ask it. He knew how sensitive people were to discuss their families. She was leaning against one of the walls, staring at the one right across from her. She was debating whether to actually tell him the truth about what had happened to her birth parents or to keep it a secret from him. She figured that he would find out what had happened to her someday anyways.

"My parents abandoned me. They dropped me off at the doorstep here with only this ring and a note saying to take good care of me," Alexandria stated, twirling her ring. "I spent ten years here, and then I was adopted. As a teenager, I tried to find my parents. They didn't want me."

Colton just stared at her, not sure what to say or do. Alexandria wiped a tear from her eye and then looked at him. "If you tell anyone what I just told you or that I cried, I'll kill you."

"Of course," Colton said. "I know how rough it can be. My parents used to fight all the time when I was younger. I had a sister. She died the same time my parents died. They were killed in a car accident. I was with my friends."

It wasn't exactly the truth, but it was a lie that he had told everyone, besides Mark.

"You have no idea," Alexandria said, shaking her head. "You don't know what it's like to be abandoned, not just once but twice. You don't know what it's like to finally see your birth parents after they just gave you up and then to find out that they don't want you and that they've had three kids since you."

"I don't," Colton said. "But whatever, let's just get on with the tour."

"All right," Alexandria said.

"I'll let you go up first in case you start to fall backward," Colton said with a smirk.

"How about you just not tell anyone about anything that happened since I came down for you?" Alexandria said, glaring at Colton.

"As long as you don't tell anyone that I caught you rather than let you fall," Colton said.

"Agreed," Alexandria said. She found it strange that he didn't want anyone to know that he had caught her, that he had spoken to her in such a gentle tone. She shook the thoughts away and headed up the stairs with Colton behind her.

Colton couldn't believe this woman in front of him; one minute she had an attitude toward him and everyone else, and the next minute she's spilling her guts to him and crying. He didn't think he would ever understand the woman in front of him although he did have to admit that she had a good body.

There was not that much that had changed in the house, except for the addition to the first floor and the change in the basement and that the third floor had been changed from a meeting room and a playroom to a single large room that had hardwood floors. Alexandria had no idea how much it must have cost.

"This is where we have most of the fund-raisers," Colton said, leaning against the wall closest to the door. "We go pretty crazy with the decorations and everything, but so far, we've been able to pay all the bills, so I can't really complain."

Alexandria stepped out onto the hardwood floor, standing below one of the chandeliers. She couldn't help it when she started to dance, thinking of what was going to happen this Friday. She pretended to be dancing with someone and was surprised when Colton joined her after a minute of her dancing by herself. They began to dance together, stepping as one without music playing at all.

"Looks like you'll be ready for it on Friday," Colton said.

"I danced in high school," Alexandria stated. "It's my way of relaxing."

"Do you want me to step away so you can relax then?" Colton asked.

Alexandria smiled at him—a genuine smile—and shook her head. "I'm actually relaxed right now. I think the conversation with Anna and then again with Duncan and Elizabeth helped me a little."

"What did Anna want?" Colton questioned.

"She wants me to bring us all together," Alexandria said after thinking for a moment. She wasn't going to add in the fact that she was supposed to take care of him. "And that's the same thing that Duncan and Elizabeth wanted."

"I don't understand why they want that," Colton said, shaking his head.

"They want what is best for us," Alexandria said. "If we actually care about one another, it helps us to know that we're not alone, that we can get through life."

"I don't need anyone," Colton said.

"I used to think that too," Alexandria said. "I used to think that I was the strongest person ever. I used to think that I could handle anything that came my way. And then ... Joseph and Marie died, and I found that I need Elizabeth and Duncan. They're the only people I really trust."

"Same here," Colton said. "When I came here, I was immediately welcomed by them. They treat us all like we're their own children."

"Yeah, they do," Alexandria said, "They are wonderful people."

"They are," Colton said. "And if you tell anyone I have said that, I will kill you."

"How about we just not tell anyone about how we've been nice to each other and go back to hating each other?" Alexandria said.

"Sounds good to me," Colton said.

They stopped dancing and just stood there, staring into each other's eyes. Colton leaned down, his face getting closer and closer, when they heard someone clear their throat. Mark stood there, smirking at Colton.

"What do you want?" Colton said.

"It's dinnertime," Mark said.

"All right, thank you," Alexandria said. She could feel her face was starting to get red. She didn't know why; it's not like anything had really happened with Colton. "I have to go back to my room really quickly, so I'll meet you two in the dining room."

"All right," Mark said, and the two men left. They were quiet for a moment. "Do I want to know what was going on with you two?"

"Nothing, Mark," Colton said. "She's stuck-up and only thinks about herself. Elizabeth needed me to show Alexandria around and mainly to show her the ballroom for the fund-raiser this weekend."

"It looked like you were about to kiss her," Mark said.

"No way! I would never kiss her," Colton denied.

He was not the best at lying to Mark about things like that, but he had to make him believe it. Colton could see the way that Mark looked at Alexandria, like she was some sort of goddess or angel or something. He couldn't do that to his best friend. Colton couldn't take Alexandria from him, if she were to start liking Mark. The only reason why Colton had wanted to kiss her was because she was good-looking. At least, that was what he kept telling himself.

"Would you mind if I asked her out then?" Mark wondered.

"Did you not just hear everything I said?" Colton replied. They were then at the dining room, and Mark smiled at Colton.

"Where is Alexandria?" Duncan asked as Colton sat down beside her.

"She had to go to her room. I gave her the tour and everything, just like you wanted," Colton said.

"Where is Anna?" Jessica asked.

"She's ill again," Elizabeth said. "If she is well by Wednesday, all of us ladies are going to the mall to get you gowns for this Friday. Well, we're going on Wednesday either way, but she will hopefully be able to join us."

"All right," Carlee said. Alexandria entered the room then.

"You're late," Elizabeth stated.

"I had to get my cell phone from my bedroom," Alexandria said. Actually, she had just needed a few minutes away from Colton to figure out what was going on in her head and in her heart. But she was not about to let anyone at the table know that.

"All right," Elizabeth said, and then they began to eat dinner.

Chapter Three

When Alexandria woke up the next morning, she had almost forgotten what had happened the day before. As soon as she recalled Anna, she jumped out of bed and immediately went toward Anna's room in her pajamas—a pair of sweatpants that hung tight to her hips and a tank top. She saw Bridget walking down the hall and jogged over to her. "Hey, Bridget, how is Anna doing this morning?"

"Better then yesterday. She still isn't well enough to leave the room, but she may be tomorrow. It's a lot of waiting for the meds to kick in right now, unfortunately," Bridget said.

"Can I go see her?" Alexandria asked.

"Sure," Bridget said. Alexandria smiled and then went into Anna's room. She was shocked to see Colton sitting there, holding Anna's hand.

"Morning, Alexandria," Anna said. Her voice was stronger than the day before, and Alexandria was grateful.

Alexandria knew she had to be careful with Colton sitting there, and she was suddenly grateful for having slept in her bra the night before.

"Morning, Anna, morning, Colton," Alexandria said.

Colton made a mumbling sound, and Anna smiled before speaking. "Colton isn't really a morning person."

"I'm usually not either," Alexandria said. "But this morning, I woke up and remembered you, so I was wide-awake pretty fast."

"See what I meant, Colton. She's hard on the outside, but sweet on the inside, like hard candy, and just like you," Anna said, smiling.

Alexandria blushed when Colton looked to her.

"Yeah," Colton said. The door then opened and Mark entered the room. He was surprised to see Alexandria and Colton there together.

"Morning, everyone," Mark said.

Colton grumbled again, and Anna and Alexandria both said good morning to him.

"I'm actually going to get ready for the day. I'll see you later, okay, Anna?" Alexandria said.

"I'm going too," Colton said.

"Bye," Anna said, and the two left the room.

"You tell anyone what she said—" Alexandria began.

"And you'll kill me, I got it," Colton interrupted. "And the same here."

"We'll be civil to each other in front of her only," Alexandria said.

"Deal," Colton agreed.

Alexandria changed into a pair of nice blue jeans and a blue shirt and put her hair into a half ponytail before going to the dining room, where everyone else was already seated for breakfast.

"I'm going to go job hunting today. Do you have a printer I could print my résumé off on?" Alexandria asked.

"Yeah, in the library," Duncan said. "Do you know where you're going to apply?"

"No idea. I was just going to walk around and try different places," Alexandria said.

"I work at the grocery store, and we're always looking for help," Mark said.

"All right, I'll look in to it," Alexandria said.

"The library is looking for help too. I'm not sure about the dance studio," Elizabeth said.

"Where is the dance studio?" Alexandria asked.

"It's about a fifteen-minute walk away. I have a class today at seven," Carlee said. "You can come with me. My teacher is the owner."

"All right, thanks. What dance are you taking?" Alexandria asked.

"Lyrical right now," Carlee said.

"Oh, that's my favorite," Alexandria said.

"You dance?" Carlee questioned, raising an eyebrow at the older woman.

"Yeah, I have danced since I was eleven," Alexandria said. "I learned a lot of different types. It helps me relax the best."

"Me too. It just calms me down somehow," Carlee said. "My favorite is probably jazz though."

"That's my second favorite," Alexandria said. "That and tap are tied for me."

"Tap is my third," Carlee said. "But the studio is usually looking for people, so you might have a chance."

"All right, thanks," Alexandria said.

"Would you like someone to show you around town?" Mark asked.

"No, it's fine. I'm not weak," Alexandria said. She couldn't let Mark get close to her.

"I wasn't suggesting that," Mark said. He had no idea how she came to that conclusion, and Colton glared at Alexandria as Mark gave her a confused look.

"I'm heading out now," Alexandria said when she finished her plate. "I'm going to print off those copies and then go into town."

"All right," Elizabeth said.

Alexandria went to the library and somehow wasn't surprised when Colton showed up a couple minutes later.

"You didn't have to be so rude to Mark," Colton stated.

"I know," Alexandria said. "But it's the way I am."

"He doesn't deserve to be treated that way," Colton said.

"Then why do you treat him that way?" Alexandria retorted. Colton stared at her for a moment in complete shock at what she said. "Look, I don't need anyone's protection here. I took self-defense classes in high school as well. I'm not weak."

"Mark wasn't saying that at all. He was just trying to be a nice guy," Colton stated. He was wrestling with himself in his head; he could either tell Alexandria why Mark had really wanted to walk around with her, or he could let Mark tell her.

"So that he could get into my pants," Alexandria said.

Colton laughed at that comment. "Don't flatter yourself so much, Alexandria. Mark wouldn't want to have sex with you."

"Excuse me?" Alexandria said, appalled at what he had said.

"Mark isn't that kind of guy. He wouldn't hook up with some random chick. He's a good guy," Colton said. "He would want to take you out on a few dates first."

"Whatever," Alexandria said and grabbed her copies of the résumé from the printer. "And now if you would excuse me, I have to go into town."

"You can treat me like shit all you want, but you need to stop treating Mark like that, especially if you promised Anna to bring us together," Colton said.

Alexandria froze in her spot. She had told Colton what Anna wanted but not that she promised she would fulfill it. Colton smirked at her response. "Anna, for whatever reason, thinks that you're the greatest thing to happen to this place. She told me that you promised to bring us together and that you promised to take care of me. And just so you know, I don't need to be taken care of."

"I know," Alexandria said. "I know that you don't need to be taken care of. But what was I supposed to do? Argue with a ten-year-old girl who reminds me of myself and who is suffering from a disease that will kill her?"

Colton was quiet, and Alexandria spoke again, "And I know that she thinks that I'm great, and I don't understand it myself. And it's an expectation that I don't think I can meet. But I'm going to try because the one thing that Anna deserves is hope."

She looked down at her wrist, and it was the first time that Colton realized she had tattoos on her wrists. Colton was quiet again, and Alexandria walked out of the library, leaving Colton standing there in shock.

"You really need to stop getting to her," Mark said, appearing in the aisle of some books near Colton.

"Did you hear everything that just happened?" Colton asked.

"Yeah," Mark said. "Thanks for defending me. I had come here to talk to her about it and then saw that you were here already."

"She needs to stop thinking that she's the best thing in the world," Colton stated.

"Actually, I think that she believes the opposite. I think she thinks that she's the worst thing in the world and that people shouldn't want to be around her," Mark said. "And you need to see her point. If Anna were to ask you to go jump off a bridge, you would do it for her. You would do anything for her and so would Alexandria, apparently. Alexandria was right. Anna does, at least, deserve hope—hope that she'll be healed, hope that we'll all be a family, hope that you'll actually smile at someone other than her, hope that you'll break the shell."

Colton had never wanted to punch his best friend more in his life. He hated it so much because it was the truth—he would lay down his life for Anna; he only wanted the younger girl to be happy for once.

"Why do you always have to be right, Mark?" Colton said.

Mark just smiled at the other man in front of him, "One of us has to have a solid head. And we all know it's not you."

"Yeah, yeah," Colton said.

*****

Alexandria had applied to about ten different places before she took a lunch break at the local diner. She sat down and was filling out an application when she looked up and saw Colton and Mark walking in. Mark smiled and she gave him a half smile. Mark took it as a good sign and walked over with Colton.

"Do you mind if we sit down?" Mark asked.

"I guess not," Alexandria said. The two men sat in the booth across from her.

"So how is the job search going?" Mark inquired.

"Okay. I have already applied to about ten different places," Alexandria said. "So hopefully I will find something soon."

"Are you really hoping for a job at the dance studio?" Mark asked.

"Yeah, I am really hoping I get that job. If not, then I hope to, at least, be able to take some classes for pretty cheap," Alexandria said. "I don't know how long I can last without dancing."

"Well, you'll be dancing on Friday at least," Mark said.

"Not that kind of dancing though, dancing just for the heck of it, letting the music flow through my veins and take control of my body. I want *that* kind of dance," Alexandria said.

Colton was surprised at how she had described it and couldn't help but find her beautiful. She had closed her eyes as she described it, and she visibly relaxed at the thought of dancing like that. Her hair fell around her face, surrounding her face with dark curls. It was the first time Colton really thought that she was absolutely beautiful, except for when he had seen her dancing by herself on the dance floor.

"You could always use the ballroom," Mark said, snapping Colton from his thoughts as he stared at Alexandria. "I'm sure Elizabeth and Duncan wouldn't mind. I'm sure for you they would even build an all-new room that was a dance studio."

"I don't know about that," Alexandria said, biting her lip.

"You don't realize how much those two love you," Mark said. "I came only a short while after you left, and they always talked about you. You really were just like an actual daughter to them. How young were you when you came here?"

"I was dropped off as a baby. I never knew my birth parents," Alexandria said quietly. She was surprised when Mark reached over and put a hand on hers. She squeezed it gently and gave him a half smile. She hadn't really expected to tell them the truth yet, but it seemed she didn't have a choice.

"Well, at least you're smiling now. That's better than yesterday," Mark said, smiling. "You have a beautiful smile. It makes you almost look as peaceful as when I saw you dancing yesterday, both times."

Alexandria blushed at his comment. She wasn't used to compliments like this so often. "Thank you."

"You two are making me puke. Would you just ask her out already, Mark?" Colton said.

"Colton!" Mark said. Alexandria started blushing more and could see a faint pink going across Mark's cheeks as well.

"What is he talking about, Mark?" Alexandria asked. She had a feeling that the man in front of her liked her, but she was hoping that it wasn't true.

Mark glared at Colton and took a deep breath before staring into Alexandria's eyes. "I was hoping to get to know you a little more before asking, but I was hoping that you would go out on a date with me." He hated that he couldn't get to know her a little better to make sure that she really liked him first and that he didn't like her just for her body but rather liked her personality as well.

"Mark, I would prefer to get to know you better first," Alexandria said. She could see how uncomfortable this was making him. And she wasn't sure if she was ready to start a relationship or not after her past with her adoptive parents.

"Good," Mark said. A waitress walked over and took their orders. He spoke again when the waitress left. "So where did you apply?"

"I applied to the library, the grocery store, the pizzeria, the sub shop, the floral shop, the ice-cream store, this diner, and then I have to apply to the convenience store online when I get back," Alexandria listed. "And there's still the dance studio."

"Well, hopefully, you'll hear something quickly," Mark said. "Did you work in high school?"

"Yeah, I have worked since I was sixteen. I worked at the pizzeria and the floral shop," Alexandria said. "And the shoe store there. But I really do not want to go back to a shoe store."

"Why not?" Mark asked.

"Retail just isn't my thing really," Alexandria explained. "There are times when I really don't feel like dealing with people, which happens often." She sent a pointed look at Colton, who rolled his eyes. This caused Mark to smile. "And so I really do not want to have to deal with people all the time."

"That's exactly why I don't have a job yet," Colton said. "I can't stand people."

"Yeah, but if I have to, I'll go back to retail. I just don't want to be in Elizabeth's and Duncan's way for very long," Alexandria said.

"You won't be in their way at all," Mark said. "It's like I said, they love you, Alexandria. They raised you as if you were their daughter. You are more than welcome to stay there for as long as you want."

"Yes, I know," Alexandria said. "But I don't feel comfortable doing that. It's the way that they raised me."

"Good point," Mark said with a smile. "That's a good thing. Hopefully, we can all learn a little bit from you." He pointedly looked over at Colton.

"You really need to lay off the nice-guy act. It's really making me want to puke," Colton said. "I know you're a great guy and you're trying to flirt, but it's really disgusting to the rest of us." Alexandria couldn't help but agree; she liked when a guy was nice, but Mark was almost pushing the line to too nice.

"Oh, shut up," Mark said, rolling his eyes. Their food was already there, and they just made small talk as they all ate their lunches. Mark's cell phone went off, and he grabbed it and then immediately grabbed his wallet. "We've got a problem back at the house. We all need to get there now."

"It's Anna, isn't it?" Alexandria said, getting into her own purse.

"Don't worry, I've got the money to cover all three of us," Mark said. "But yes, it is Anna."

"Shit," Alexandria cursed. She immediately started moving out of the booth, ignoring her food.

"I wasn't done yet though," Colton complained.

"Anna is *dying*, Colton!" Alexandria screamed, making others stare at her.

"You didn't have to scream," Colton muttered. He grabbed the rest of his sandwich and then got out of the booth.

"Do you want a to-go box?" the waitress asked as she saw Colton holding his sandwich.

"We don't have the time, and he's going to be eating it on the way anyways. Do you have an estimate about how much it will be?" Mark asked.

"Probably about fifteen without tax," the waitress said.

Mark handed her a twenty and three ones.

"Here, keep the change," Mark said. He knew he was giving the waitress a large tip, but he didn't really care. All that was going through his head was that something was wrong with Anna, and it was not good. "Alexandria, get in the car with us. We drive."

"All right," Alexandria said. She followed the two men to a black car and got into the back seat as Colton got into the driver's side. "Is it safe to have him drive?"

"He'll be able to maneuver the streets and traffic better and get there sooner," Mark said.

"What did the text message say?" Alexandria said.

"It was a text from Jessie saying that Anna needed us home ASAP," Mark said. "Alexandria, do you have your seat belt on?"

"Yeah," Alexandria said.

"You still may wanna hold on," Colton said. "I drive like a maniac when Anna is in trouble."

"You care about her," Alexandria stated. It was not a question.

"She reminds me of my sister," Colton said. He slammed on the gas at that moment. They were silent the rest of the ride back to the house.

Chapter Four

When they parked in front of the house, they immediately all started running up the stairs. Alexandria opened the front door quickly, and they all ran toward Anna's room. They said nothing as they did all this. They knew that saying anything would make them think the worst.

"What's going on?" Alexandria asked. She was slightly out of breath when she saw Bridget standing outside Anna's room.

"Anna started having seizures," Bridget said. "We don't know why or what happened. The doctor is looking at her now."

"You guys have a doctor that makes house calls?" Alexandria said, raising an eyebrow at this fact.

"Only for Anna," Mark stated. "Can we go see her, or is it only Elizabeth and Duncan?"

"She's been calling for all three of you," Bridget said. "Elizabeth and Duncan are in there, but everyone else is in the library."

"All right. Is it okay if all three of us go in together?" Mark asked.

"Yeah, go right in there," Bridget said.

Mark knocked on the door before going into the bedroom with Colton and Alexandria. The doctor was an older gentleman, and Alexandria could recall him from her childhood here. He was the same doctor who had always done their physicals for school and always taken care of them whenever they were sick.

"My, my, is that Alexandria?" the doctor said as he noticed the people enter the room.

"Yes, Dr. Rizzoli," Alexandria said, smiling slightly at the older doctor.

"It's been a really long time," Dr. Rizzoli said. "How are you doing?"

"Fine," Alexandria said. "How is Anna doing?"

Dr. Rizzoli sighed. "It's debatable. She's not doing too well, but she's still alive."

"Can you keep us up to date on what has happened?" Colton asked.

"She had a seizure, and they called me, and she had another one when I got here. I don't know what is causing it, and I won't unless I get her to a hospital," Dr. Rizzoli said. "Her lupus has started to come back, and so her immune system is weakened. I just really need to get her to the hospital and look her over there."

"Do you want us to drive there?" Mark asked. Alexandria and Colton were smirking at the thought of Colton driving around the town with Anna in the back seat.

Dr. Rizzoli smiled. "I have seen you drive when Anna is in danger, Colton. As much as I would rather have an ambulance take her, you're going to get there faster. I just ask that you have someone in the back seat with her."

"I'll sit in the back," Alexandria said.

"Lexi," Anna said softly. Alexandria stepped forward and kneeled beside Anna.

"I'm here, Anna," Alexandria said, her voice lightening. "Don't worry, you'll be okay."

"I know," Anna said. "Is Colton driving?"

Alexandria smiled. "Yeah, he is. I'm gonna be in the back seat with you."

"Thanks," Anna said.

"I would do anything for you, Anna," Alexandria said, and she could feel tears threatening to fall. She wiped the first one away immediately.

"Don't cry," Anna said. "I'm gonna be okay. They'll heal me. They always do."

Alexandria just nodded, and Mark put a hand on her shoulder. "And Anna's a fighter. She won't give up that easily."

"Yeah," Anna said. "Can we go to the hospital now?"

"Of course, sweetheart," Elizabeth said. "Duncan and I will be in another car right behind you guys, okay?"

"Okay," Anna said, nodding.

"If you don't mind moving, Alexandria and Mark, I'll pick her up and take her to the car," Colton said.

Alexandria stood up and was surprised when Mark stood beside her and put his arm around her shoulders. She was more surprised when she found that she didn't avoid his touch. It felt like a comforting touch for once.

"Hey, sweetie," Colton said softly. Alexandria could barely hear him. "I'm gonna pick you up now and then take you to the car. And then drive like a maniac to the hospital for you."

Anna smiled, trying to contain the laughter.

"I'll meet you all at the hospital," Dr. Rizzoli said, opening the door for Colton.

Alexandria nearly burst into tears at the sight of Colton carrying Anna; she looked so fragile, so tiny in his muscle-filled arms. She held it in though and followed Colton out with Mark.

"Alexandria, I need you to get into the car first. I'm probably going to have to put her head on your lap," Colton said when they exited the house.

"All right," Alexandria said, jogging to the car and getting into the back seat and putting her seat belt on. When Colton started to get Anna into the car, Alexandria took her shoulders lightly and helped him get her into the car so that her head was on Alexandria's lap.

When Colton drove, Alexandria played with Anna's hair and sang softly to her. She was surprised when Anna began to speak when Colton took her out of the car. "Alexandria, you're gonna make a great mom one day."

"Thanks," Alexandria said.

She unbuckled her seat belt and followed the group into the hospital. Dr. Rizzoli immediately took Elizabeth, Duncan, and Anna with him. No one else was allowed even though they were all almost family.

Colton was pacing the hospital waiting room while Alexandria sat there, staring at her hands, and Mark was reading a magazine.

Alexandria kept looking at her tattoo: hope and faith. She kept repeating the words in her head. God would take care of Anna. He had let her live this long. He wouldn't end her life that easily, not when she still had so much to offer the world.

"Would you stop pacing, Colton? You're going to burn a hole in the floor," Mark stated. He was getting annoyed with the man that just kept walking past him. He knew that Colton was worried about Anna; they all were.

"It's the only thing that's relaxing me right now," Colton stated.

"Sit down," Alexandria said. "Please."

Colton reluctantly sat down beside her after meeting her eyes for a second. They were quiet for a minute until Alexandria spoke, "Are you two religious at all?"

"A little," Colton said.

"A little more than him," Mark said.

Alexandria put her hand out so that they could see the tattoos on her wrist. "I got this tattoo on my eighteenth birthday. I was going through a really tough time. I went to church and found God again a few months before. Elizabeth and Duncan had brought me up religiously, but my adoptive parents weren't religious. So after a short while, I got these tattoos together. I had to remind myself that God was there for me and that no matter what, I could get through it all. And so every time I need that reminder, I look at my wrist. I have them on the inside so that no one else can see them but me." She flipped her wrists over and held her hand out. "Do you two mind if we pray together?"

Mark immediately put his hand in her right hand, and Colton put his in her left hand a moment later. They all closed their eyes and Alexandria began to pray, "Lord, please be with Anna as you are there for us all. You are the Healer. You can make her feel better. Please protect and heal her. You have done amazing things in the past, and I know you will continue to do it. Thank you, amen."

They sat there for a moment, none of them letting go of one another. Alexandria finally looked up and saw Elizabeth and Duncan staring at them in shock.

"Is there any news?" Alexandria asked. The two men immediately looked up and let go of Alexandria's hands. Her left hand immediately felt awkward.

"There is nothing that they can really do. They think she has epilepsy," Elizabeth said.

"They're going to give her some medications that will help her," Duncan said.

Alexandria sighed. So they couldn't do surgery. But they could get Anna medications. That was better than nothing. Hopefully, it wouldn't take long for the medications to kick in.

"There is no surgery that would help her?" Mark questioned.

"It would be expensive and it would be dangerous. It would be brain surgery," Elizabeth said.

"So what? Don't you care about what happens to her?" Colton shouted.

"She's dying anyways, Colton," Alexandria stated. "The medication can help her."

"So she's going to just continue to deal with seizures?" Colton exclaimed. "Is that what you want for Anna?"

"If I could have what I want for Anna, then she would be perfectly healthy! But that isn't the case, Colton! The medications can help her with the seizures! This was one of the first times she had seizures anyways. They may never come back, especially with the medications," Alexandria said. Colton stared at her and then walked out of the hospital.

"I'll go after him," Mark said.

"No, let me go. I'm the one that got him angry," Alexandria said. She jogged out of the hospital and saw that it was pouring rain and that he was standing in the middle of it. "Colton!"

"What do you want?" Colton said, turning toward her.

"Get under here so that you don't catch a cold! We don't need two of us sick!" Alexandria said. She stood under the canopy in front of the hospital, and Colton stood in the middle of the sidewalk a few yards away.

"I'm perfectly fine here," Colton said.

"You are so infuriating to me, Colton!" Alexandria shouted, walking out to stand beside him in the rain.

"And the same to you," Colton said. "What do you want?"

"I wanted to apologize," Alexandria said. "I don't know Anna like the rest of you do. But I still care about her. I still love her as if she was my own sister. Anna reminds me a lot of myself when I was young—so full of life and of hope and dreams for a beautiful future. But Elizabeth is right. The surgery would be very risky. It's her *brain* that they would be working on. It isn't something to be taken lightly."

"She deserves to be given a chance at least, a chance to live longer," Colton debated.

"She probably won't die of the seizures, and she's going to die anyways," Alexandria said.

"You don't get it, do you?" Colton said, staring into Alexandria's eyes. She looked at him in confusion. "When I see Anna, I see my little sister, the sister that I couldn't save when I was sixteen, the sister that I would lay down my life for. I want Anna to live."

Alexandria raised her hand up and showed Colton her tattoo. "Hope. Faith. God will take care of Anna. She will live the life that God has planned for her, and when He calls her back, she will go and she will be with your family and with her own family. She will be in heaven, watching us all, hoping that we're doing all right without her."

"You really piss me off when you're right," Colton said after a moment. He ran a hand through his hair, frustrated that she was right.

"You better get ready to be angry most of the time," Alexandria said with a smirk.

Colton shook his head. "How about we tell everyone that we screamed at each other for a few minutes and are still angry when we get back in there?"

"All right," Alexandria said. They went back inside, growling at each other.

"Wow, you got him to come back inside," Mark said.

"I knew Anna would want him around here," Alexandria responded.

"So are you guys even considering the surgery?" Colton asked.

"We talked to Dr. Rizzoli, and he said that it normally would help, but we think the medications will do just as good, and with the lupus, it's just going to be easier to have her take the medications," Elizabeth answered.

"I don't have a choice. I'm not family," Colton muttered. "I just want her to come home."

"They're going to observe her overnight and then she'll come home. So we can all go home," Duncan said.

"Can we go and see her?" Colton asked.

"Unfortunately not," Elizabeth said, shaking her head. "They are being really careful about who sees her."

"I don't see why," Mark said. "Dr. Rizzoli knows we are all practically family."

"It's not Dr. Rizzoli. It's the security here," Duncan said.

"Still," Colton said. "We should be able to see her."

"Let's just go home. She'll be home before we know it," Alexandria said.

"Alexandria's right," Elizabeth said. "We really need to head back. There's nothing we can do here."

Colton just turned around and left the hospital. Mark looked toward him and sighed, "Sorry about his behavior Alexandria."

"I understand it," Alexandria said. "There's no reason to apologize on his behalf."

"Did he apologize already?" Mark asked.

"Not in so many words," Alexandria said. Mark and Colton were best friends. Clearly Colton wouldn't be too mad if she told Mark that single line.

"Just be happy with what you got from him. He doesn't tell people a lot about his life," Mark said.

"Again, I understand it. I don't usually tell people about my own life," Alexandria said. "Come on, let's just go home."

"We'll meet you guys there. We're going to pick up some groceries," Elizabeth said.

"All right," Alexandria said, and she and Mark went to the car, where Colton was in the passenger seat. "Wow, he's in the passenger seat."

"Yeah, the only time we really let him drive is when we need someone to drive like a maniac," Mark said. "Usually he just sits in the passenger seat, mumbling about how slow we drive and how he could have gotten us to our destination within half the time it was taking us."

"Sounds entertaining," Alexandria said.

"It is when it's not directed at the way I drive," Mark said with a smile.

"Good point," Alexandria said and got into the back seat.

Chapter Five

They were quiet the rest of the time that they drove home. They sat in the living room, watching television until Elizabeth came in and asked for their help in bringing the groceries in. Alexandria helped take care of the groceries, glad that most of the things hadn't moved since she was younger.

"Hey, Elizabeth," Alexandria said when she was putting the last of the groceries away.

"Yeah," Elizabeth said.

"Would it be okay if I were to use the ballroom to dance right now?" Alexandria asked.

"Of course," Elizabeth said. "This place is your home."

"All right," Alexandria said. "Thanks."

Alexandria went into her bedroom and was shocked to see Mark sitting on her vanity chair. "What are you doing in my room?"

She didn't like the fact that she didn't have any privacy around this house. She constantly had to be around people and had them getting into their things. She was used to being left alone and not having to deal with people.

"I was waiting for you," Mark said. "Sorry if I invaded your space."

"Apparently, there is no personal space here," Alexandria muttered.

"Nope," Mark said with a grin.

Alexandria shook her head. "So what's up?"

"I was just wondering if you wanted to go for a walk," Mark said.

"I was actually just about to go upstairs and dance," Alexandria stated. "I really need to relax right now."

"All right," Mark said.

"Maybe after I'm done dancing we can go for a walk though," Alexandria said. She felt bad for saying no to Mark since he seemed like a nice guy.

"Sounds good," Mark said. "I'll probably be in the gym downstairs if you want to come find me when you're done. If I'm not down there, I'll be in the library probably."

"All right, I'll find you," Alexandria said. "See you later."

"See you later," Mark said and left the room.

Alexandria quickly changed into a loose T-shirt and a pair of yoga pants and grabbed her speakers and headed upstairs to the ballroom. She was slightly surprised to see Carlee dancing. Alexandria could tell that Carlee had passion; she was a beautiful dancer.

"You're a beautiful dancer," Alexandria stated as Carlee stopped.

"Oh, you scared me," Carlee said, holding her chest.

"Sorry," Alexandria said. "I was actually just about to dance. Do you think it's big enough for us to share the space?"

"I was about to go anyways. I just needed to relax with all that's going on with Anna," Carlee said.

"That's exactly why I came up here," Alexandria said. "But Anna will be okay. God will watch over her."

"I'm sure He will," Carlee said. "I'm still scared about it all though."

"Yeah, I know," Alexandria said. "Me too. That's why I think I'm going to dance for a really long time right now."

"Yeah, I was up here since you guys went to the hospital. What is the news on Anna?" Carlee asked and took a drink of water.

"They think she may have epilepsy, but they're keeping her overnight to make sure," Alexandria said. "They aren't going to do surgery on her. Just give her some medications."

"How did Colton take that?" Carlee asked.

"Not that good," Alexandria said. "Screamed at me for a while and then cooled down, and I have no idea where he is right now."

"Probably in the gym," Carlee said. "I'm amazed he cooled down. He's extremely protective of Anna. Did Mark take it okay?"

"As far as I could tell," Alexandria said. "I've noticed that he doesn't let things get to him as much as Colton does. Or at least he doesn't show it as much."

"Yeah, that's for sure," Carlee said. "Colton is very hotheaded, but Mark is always levelheaded and doesn't let people see when things worry him. He really only lets people see his happy emotions and ones like that."

"Yeah, I've noticed that," Alexandria said. "But they seem to be good friends."

"Yeah, well, besides Collin, they're the only guys here, and I think they got here pretty close to each other," Carlee said.

"Actually, I think it was like five years apart. Mark said he came just a short while after I did, and Colton came when he was sixteen. So Mark came about ten years ago, and Colton came six years ago," Alexandria said. "But you're right about them being the only guys."

"When you were here, were there many people here?" Carlee asked.

"Yeah, there were. When I left, there were fifteen people total, counting me, Elizabeth, and Duncan. I think you and Collin actually came just a short while before I left," Alexandria said.

"Oh my gosh, yes! I remember you!" Carlee exclaimed. "I remember thinking that we could be friends because we were close to the same age! At least you were closest to my age from the people there! And then you left."

Alexandria smiled. "I was thinking the same thing. It was nice to actually have someone here that wasn't at least five years older than me!"

"Well, at least we can get to know each other now," Carlee said, smiling.

"Yeah, that is true," Alexandria said. "And we have something in common besides being here—dance."

"I love having it in common with people," Carlee said. "It's so relaxing."

"Yeah, it is," Alexandria said.

"All right, we leave around 7:00 p.m. for my dance class," Carlee said. "I'll see you at dinner."

"All right," Alexandria said. Carlee smiled at her and then left the ballroom. Alexandria started stretching and then turned her music on.

Alexandria was dancing for what felt like five hours, but had only been two in reality, when Colton began to watch her. He watched her complete her dance and then started clapping. Alexandria looked over at him and started blushing.

"How long were you standing there?" Alexandria said.

"Fifteen minutes, tops," Colton said. "It was a beautiful dance."

"Thanks," Alexandria said.

"Did you choreograph it yourself?" Colton asked.

"I improvised it," Alexandria said with a shrug. Colton handed her a bottle of water, and she immediately took a large drink of it. "Thanks."

"No problem," Colton said. "Dinner is almost ready. Elizabeth sent me over."

"Oh, okay," Alexandria said. "Do I have time to shower?"

"Did you find her, Colton?" Elizabeth shouted up the stairs. "Dinner is ready now!"

"Apparently not," Alexandria said and gave Colton a small smile. "Thanks for coming and getting me."

"No problem. We can't have you starving. You're skinny enough as it is," Colton stated as he headed down the hallway.

"Yeah, I know," Alexandria said.

She couldn't help but think that if her adoptive parents had fed her rather than doing drugs at dinnertime, she might be a little bigger. They were quiet as they walked downstairs to the dining room.

"Sorry about that, everyone. I got caught up in a dance."

"Do you choreograph your dances yourself, or do you go through previous dances that you've learned?" Mark asked as she sat down beside him and Elizabeth.

"I usually just do improvisation, but sometimes I take parts of old dances that I've learned," Alexandria said. "It usually depends on my mood. When I need to relax, I tend to do improvisation more than going through old routines. I don't have to think as much. I can just let my body move."

"I do the same thing," Carlee said. "When I really need to just unwind, like today, I just improve something. It really just depends on my mood."

"Yeah, same here," Alexandria said. She knew that she was letting her barriers down around these people. It seemed to just be part of this house. She had always been much more relaxed and carefree when she was here. She felt safe for once in her life.

They all just made small talk during dinner, and afterward, Carlee changed back into her dance clothes. Alexandria thought of changing into something different, but if the owner of the dance studio wanted her to show her what she did as a dancer, she needed to be comfortable.

"Do you mind if I walk with you two ladies to the dance studio?" Mark asked as Alexandria and Carlee were talking in the foyer.

"No, that would be fine," Carlee said with a smile.

"Sounds good, and then maybe after we drop her off and I talk with the owner, we can go for the walk I told you I would go on earlier?" Alexandria said.

"Sounds great," Mark said, smiling. "I just have to put my shoes on really quickly."

"All right," Alexandria said.

"He likes you," Carlee stated after Mark was out of earshot.

"Yeah, I know. He was flirting with me when we were out to lunch today, and Colton told him to just ask me out already. It was actually kinda cute. Mark got really red and then said that he had hoped to get to know me better, which is why I think he wanted to go on this walk with me earlier," Alexandria said.

"Probably. Mark does three things to relax: read, spar with Colton, and walk," Carlee said.

"Yeah, that would explain why he told me that when I was done dancing, he would either be in the gym or in the library," Alexandria said, nodding.

"Who is that?" Colton asked as he entered the area.

"Mark," Carlee said. "What do you want?"

"I was gonna see if you two needed someone to walk with," Colton suggested.

"Mark is walking with us," Alexandria stated, and Mark appeared behind Colton.

"All right," Colton said.

"See ya after, Colton," Mark said as he opened the door for the girls. "Do you want me to wait outside or go inside with you?"

"It will probably be best if you just wait outside," Alexandria said. "Especially since I will be applying while I'm in there."

"Yeah, probably a good idea," Mark said. "I may just walk around for a few minutes since you will probably be awhile. Do you have a cell phone with you?"

"Yeah," Alexandria said.

"I can give you my number and then when you get done, you can call me if I'm not right outside," Mark said.

"All right," Alexandria said and got her phone out of her purse. She got it to a new contact before handing it to him. "Here, add your number."

Mark added his number and then handed Alexandria her phone back. They were then in front of the dance studio, and Alexandria followed Carlee up the stairs. Before Carlee opened the door, Alexandria took a deep breath and looked behind her to see Mark smiling at her. For some reason, it made her relax a little more and smile.

"Hey, is Ms. Becky around?" Carlee asked, looking to the receptionist.

"She's stretching in your studio, Carlee," the receptionist said. "Who is this with you?"

"This is my friend, Alexandria. She was hoping for a job. I was going to introduce her to Ms. Becky so that she can talk directly to her," Carlee said.

"All right," the receptionist said, and the two girls walked down the hallway. Carlee took off her shoes before entering the dance studio, and Alexandria followed her lead.

"Ms. Becky," Carlee said.

"Hey, Carlee," Becky said. Becky was a forty-year-old woman with long, bright red hair and shining green eyes.

"This is my friend Alexandria, and she was looking for a job. She dances and was hoping to be able to get a job here," Carlee explained. "I figured it would be easiest if I just brought her here since you're my teacher."

"That would work," Becky said. She stood up and held her hand out. "Hello, Alexandria. I'm Becky White. I'm the owner of this dance studio."

"It's an honor to meet you," Alexandria said.

"So are you looking to be a teacher, a receptionist, or what?" Becky asked.

"I'm really looking for anything, but I would love to teach dance," Alexandria said. "I just want to be around dance again. I was only away from it for a couple of months now, and it's been driving me crazy. I've been dancing every chance I get in an extra room in the house I stay in."

"That shows real passion. Can you show me a quick routine right now?" Becky inquired.

"Of course, what do you want?" Alexandria said.

"Whatever you would like," Becky answered.

"All right," Alexandria said. She put her music player on the floor and put it as loud as it could get, knowing that the speakers weren't that great on it. She went to the middle of the dance floor and started to do a routine that she had choreographed a week before. It was only a minute long, and she hoped that that was enough for Becky. When she was done, she saw that more students had entered the dance studio.

"Wow," Becky said. "I don't have any immediate positions as teachers open, but I definitely need a fill in some nights if you would be available. Did you choreograph that piece yourself?"

"Yes," Alexandria said, grabbing her music player.

"Then if you'll take it, I have a position open for a choreographer," Becky said.

"I don't have any formal classes in choreography," Alexandria said, her eyes widening.

"That doesn't matter. Your talent just proved to me that you have what it takes," Becky said. "Let's go and talk to the receptionist and do a formal application, and then we'll work on hours and such."

"All right," Alexandria said. She followed Becky to the front desk area and began to fill out the application.

"I actually have to go and teach my class. If you want to drop that off with Angela here, I'll call you tomorrow and we can meet sometime to figure out your wages and everything," Becky said.

"That would be good," Alexandria said. "Thank you so much."

"Of course, Alexandria," Becky said and then walked down the hallway.

Chapter Six

Alexandria finished the application, gave it to the receptionist, Angela, and then went outside. She didn't see Mark anywhere around and pulled her phone out.

She smiled when she saw that it said, "Mark ;) Call anytime" on the contact list. She hit the call button, and he picked up after a second.

"Hey, Alexandria," Mark said.

"Hey, nice contact by the way," Alexandria said.

"I thought you might like that. I'll head back over. I'm at the park right down the street right now, so I'll only be a minute," Mark said.

"Do you just go straight one direction from the dance studio? I have no problem meeting you at the entrance of the park," Alexandria said.

"When you exit the dance studio, turn left and go to the corner, then turn left and go straight. I can meet you halfway if you want," Mark said.

"Sure," Alexandria said. "See you in a minute."

"See you in a minute," Mark said and hung up.

Alexandria walked quickly over toward the park. She saw Mark standing right next to the entrance, and she smiled when she saw him.

"Hey," Alexandria said.

"So how did it go? Do you have a job?" Mark asked.

"Yes, I do. She actually wants me as a choreographer," Alexandria said. "She asked me to show her a dance, and I did a dance that I choreographed just a few days ago, and she apparently loved it because she said that she didn't have any teaching positions open, but she had a choreographer position open. I told her I didn't have any formal training, and she said that it was fine and gave me the job. I just had to fill out an application, and then she's going to call me about wages and stuff."

"That's great, Alexandria," Mark said.

"Yeah, I am very happy," Alexandria said. "It's going to be so nice to be able to dance again."

"Yeah, I bet," Mark said.

"I am guessing you wanted to go for a walk to get to know each other," Alexandria said. Mark started blushing and Alexandria smiled. "I'm glad."

"I'm glad you came with me," Mark said. "I was kinda nervous about it at first."

"I've never been in a relationship before or even on an actual date," Alexandria said.

"Really?" Mark said. "I feel like guys would be all over you."

"Nope. They didn't really see me in high school. I tended to avoid people in high school," Alexandria said.

"Why?" Mark asked.

"I was scared. I had been good in the house here, but the real world is so different, and I wasn't sure what to do or anything. And when people found out that I was adopted, they thought it was strange and made fun of me for it, especially when I was older and they found out who I was adopted by," Alexandria said.

"What do you mean?" Mark said.

Alexandria bit her lip. She hadn't intended on telling him, but she apparently didn't really have a choice now.

"You have to promise me that you will not tell anyone what I'm going to tell you," Alexandria said. She really was not looking forward to having to explain all this to him. She still wasn't completely sure if she could trust him or not.

"I promise you, Alexandria," Mark said. He had always known something had gone wrong with the adoptive parents, but he wasn't sure what it had been.

"My adoptive parents used to do and deal drugs. They would abuse me and kept me shut up in a room in the basement and acted like they hated me when it was only us," Alexandria said.

"I am so sorry, Alexandria," Mark said. He had figured it was pretty bad, but not that bad. He wasn't sure he wanted to know what she meant by them abusing her—whether it was physical, mental, emotional, or what. He wanted to hug her, to hold her tightly but knew that she wouldn't want that.

"I've gotten through it. That was why when Colton degraded me, I flipped out. They would degrade me so much that I felt like I was nothing. I don't need people doing it now too," Alexandria said.

"I don't blame you. Colton comes off rather strong. He has a rough past too although not as bad as yours. So he has a pretty bad exterior. You and he are very similar, actually," Mark said. He knew the reason why Colton didn't tell anyone his real story of why he was there, but he wasn't going to tell Alexandria. That was Colton's job.

"I've realized that. I think that that is why we get on each other's nerves so easily," Alexandria said.

"Probably," Mark said, chuckling. "But Colton is a good guy. You just have to get past his cold exterior and get to really know him."

"Unfortunately, he's like me and doesn't let people in that easily," Alexandria said.

"You seem to let people in easily," Mark said.

"Only because Anna asked me," Alexandria said. "The day that I went in there when I first got here, she said that she wants me to bring everyone closer and to take care of Colton. And the only way that I can really bring people together at the house is to let my barriers down."

"Why did you promise that?" Mark asked.

"I wasn't about to tell Anna no," Alexandria said. "She reminds me too much of myself."

"I can see it," Mark said, nodding.

"So tell me about you," Alexandria said.

"Well, my family died in a car accident when I was twelve. I've been living with Elizabeth and Duncan ever since then, so ten years this year. I want to get my own place soon, but it's nice to be here to help Elizabeth and Duncan and to not have to pay for anything really. But I feel bad taking all their food and stuff, and so I usually give them some money every month. I was depressed when no one wanted to adopt me, but after a while, Colton came and I wasn't the only guy around my age. I got to school and became pretty popular because I was on the soccer team, and I met some good friends. I went to school for business, but I haven't been able to get a job yet in business. I have one at the grocery store, thankfully," Mark explained.

"That's too bad about not getting a job. But at least you have a job to tie you over until then," Alexandria said. "And I know what you mean about being depressed. I was abandoned when I was a baby. My parents only left me with this ring. I tried to find them when I was a teenager, but they said that they didn't want me. They had three kids after me though. It hurt. It still hurts. And it was made worse with the fact that my adoptive parents were abusing me."

"When did your adoptive parents start doing drugs?"

"They were doing them when they adopted me. They just stopped long enough to pass the drug tests. They usually did it after I fell asleep, at least, until I was old enough to know what was going on and to be staying up late at night. And they actually offered me some."

"Did you do any?"

"Nope, but that was what started the abuse. At first, they just would make small comments to me, grab my wrist just a little too tightly. And then after I told them that I wouldn't do the drugs with them, they began to make it worse. They started hitting me, degrading me at any moment they could. When I turned sixteen, he forced himself on me. They said I was either abused or I did the drugs or I died. The people at school thought I did the drugs. It was really rough."

"It sounds like it. Why didn't you go to the cops? You could have come back here."

"And seemed weak? I wasn't about to do that. And I thought that it was all because I wasn't good enough for the parents. I thought that it meant that I wasn't living up to Elizabeth's and Duncan's expectations of me. I thought I could live through it. And I wasn't sure if I would be able to come back here. I was scared. I still am scared."

"Well, they're gone and you're safe with Elizabeth and Duncan."

"That's the way I'm trying to think of it. Sometimes it works, and sometimes it doesn't."

"Hopefully it works more than it doesn't work."

"It's about even," Alexandria said, shrugging. They had looped around the entire park, and Alexandria looked at her phone to see that it was almost eight thirty at night already. Just as she was about to say something, Mark's cell phone went off.

"Hey, Carlee, what's up?" Mark said. Alexandria couldn't hear what Carlee was saying, but Mark looked at his watch and then his eyes widened. "Yeah, we're in the park right now. We'll head right over. Sorry about that." A second later, he hung up. "Uh, so we got lost in time. Carlee's done with her class."

"Sounds like we better head back over then," Alexandria said.

"Probably a good idea," Mark said with a smile.

Alexandria smiled. "Um, I feel like I don't have to say this, but I want to anyways, but will you please not tell anyone what I told you? I don't want everyone to know and feel bad for me. I don't like people feeling sorry for me."

"Completely understandable, and I promise, I won't tell anyone," Mark said. "Especially Colton."

"Yes, he is the last person I want to know all this about me," Alexandria said.

"I figured," Mark said. They made small talk as they walked back to the dance studio and saw Carlee standing outside.

"So how was class?" Alexandria asked.

"Good. Ms. Becky asked me about you," Carlee said. "I told her I didn't know too much about you but that you were a beautiful dancer."

"Thanks," Alexandria said.

"I can't believe she wants you to be a choreographer already. She's usually really picky about her choreographers. I've seen her turn down like twenty choreographers since I started dancing here,"

Carlee said. "But your dance was beautiful. I could tell that Ms. Becky really liked it."

"I'm glad that she liked it enough to hire me," Alexandria said. "I filled out the application and she's gonna call me later about meeting to figure out the wages and hours."

"Hopefully, she will give you a lot of hours," Carlee said.

"Yeah," Alexandria said.

*****

Everyone was hanging out in the living room, playing cards and watching television. The three of them entered the living room as well, and Carlee sat on the floor beside her brother, Mark sat on the recliner, and Alexandria sat on the couch between Colton and Elizabeth.

"So how did it go?" Elizabeth asked.

"Really good. I performed a dance that I choreographed last week, and she really liked it apparently. She wants to hire me as a choreographer. I filled out an application, and she's supposed to call me about meeting to figure out my wages and hours," Alexandria said.

"That's great!" Elizabeth said.

"And then hopefully, I can start giving you guys money to help pay for groceries and everything else," Alexandria said.

"Alexandria," Elizabeth said, "you know you don't have to do that."

"But I want to. You guys have taken me in for my entire life, except for eleven years," Alexandria said. "You didn't even question it when I asked if I could come back. You just welcomed me."

"That's what family does, Alexandria," Duncan said from another recliner. "You're family to us. That's all that matters."

"Still," Alexandria said.

"Enough, Alexandria. They're right," Colton said. "Stop trying to be such a good girl when we all know that you're not, and just take the free housing."

Alexandria stood up and glared at Colton. "You can stop trying to be such a tough guy. I'm tired of your attitude and the attitude of all guys that are like you. I'm sorry that Elizabeth and Duncan raised me to not take advantage of people like you obviously are."

"I'm not taking advantage of them!" Colton said, standing up as well.

"Can you two take this outside of the living room? I'm trying to watch television," Jessica said.

"And you can stop being such a bitch! I'm so tired of this place!" Colton said and stormed out. Mark and Alexandria followed him out and into the foyer. He started pacing, and Alexandria stood in front of him and he spoke, "You can leave me alone."

"No way," Alexandria said. She crossed her arms in front of her chest, glaring at him. "I'm not leaving until you pull up your big boy pants and stop being such an ass to everyone around you except Anna."

"You have no clue what I've been through," Colton said through gritted teeth.

"And you have no idea what I've been through either," Alexandria said. "So you can stop thinking that your story is the worst that there is. Some of us have pretty bad stories too."

"She's right, Colton. She told me her story, and it's pretty bad. It's worse than yours," Mark said. "She's right. You can stop thinking that the world is against you completely and that your story is the worst that there is. You know, it wouldn't be a bad idea if you both told each other your stories."

"Mark," Colton and Alexandria said. They both turned their glares from each other over to him in shock.

"I'm not telling him my story," Alexandria said, shaking her head.

"And I'm not telling her mine!" Colton said, pointing his finger at her.

"Tough shit," Mark said. "You're both about to tell each other the truth about your pasts. I'll be able to tell."

"Why should we do this?" Colton asked.

"Because you need to learn that your story isn't that bad, and it wouldn't be fair to have her tell you her story if you don't tell her yours," Mark said.

"I don't trust him," Alexandria said. "I'm not telling him my story."

"Yes, you are, Alexandria," Duncan said, appearing in the hallway.

"Duncan—" Alexandria began.

"Enough," Duncan said. "You both need to learn from each other. You're both caught up in your own worlds, thinking that your stories are the worst. And yes, both of your stories are pretty bad. But you both need to get past yourselves and learn that other people have a pretty bad life too."

Alexandria stared into Duncan's eyes and knew that she had lost. She wanted to just go up to her bedroom and cry and just be by herself. She sighed and ran a hand through her hair. "You know I can't say no to you, Duncan."

"And that is exactly why I came here, especially since we could hear you two screaming at each other in the living room," Duncan said. "I actually suggest going up to the ballroom so that only you guys hear the stories."

"Come on," Alexandria said, heading up the stairs. She looked at Duncan at the top of the stairs as he was at the bottom. She was hurt that he was taking everyone else's side, but she understood why he was doing it. "Duncan, I really want to be mad at you right now for this, but I can't be. And you know it all too well."

Duncan just laughed, and the three of them entered the ballroom while Duncan went back to the living room. When they entered the ballroom, Alexandria sat down on the floor and Colton started pacing.

"If you keep pacing, then I won't tell you my story," Alexandria said. "Come and sit down in front of me. Please."

Colton sighed and sat down in front of her. As Alexandria began to explain her story, she refused to look at him; she only looked at her hands as she twirled her ring. She didn't want to see his expressions and see what was in his eyes—the pity. She hated seeing the pity in people's eyes that she saw whenever she explained her story. Finally, she was done and looked in Colton's eyes. She saw everything but pity. She saw pain, worry, and care. She was amazed. She felt a tear roll down her cheek and was about to brush it away when he wiped it away. His hands were soft, but she could feel a slight callous starting on his thumb. It felt so much like Colton that she didn't know how else to explain it in her mind.

"My parents abandoned me when I was fifteen. They told me that I was going to be staying with family friends for a while. I waited for them to come get me for months. Finally, after a year, Elizabeth and Duncan told me that my parents weren't coming back and that I was going to live here until I was ready to leave. I tried to find my parents again and to go back to them, but then I discovered that they had died in a car accident a few months after they had left me with Elizabeth and Duncan. I never found out why they sent me here. And it's scared me. Because of it, I've always put people away from me. I don't let them near because I know they will abandon me again," Colton explained.

"Well, we have something in common at least," Alexandria said. "Although it's rather depressing, we were both abandoned by our parents."

"So are you both okay now and not going to kill each other?" Mark asked.

"I think we're both okay now," Alexandria said. She felt much better after having explained everything to Colton and felt better knowing that she wasn't the only one who had been abandoned by her parents. "I am at least."

"Me too," Colton said. "That calmed me down a lot actually."

"It always feels good to let things like that off your chest," Alexandria said.

"Now, hug each other," Mark said.

"No way," Colton said, shaking his head. He really didn't want to hug her; he wasn't sure if he would break himself if he did that.

"Hugging her isn't going to kill you, Colton," Mark said.

"It's fine. We're still going to piss each other off, whether we like it or not," Alexandria said. "We're too similar for our own good."

"That is for sure," Mark said with a smile. "All right, I guess I'll let it go."

"I'm going to the gym," Colton said.

"All right," Mark said.

Alexandria just sat there, and Mark went and sat down beside her. He wasn't sure what to say exactly or what to do. But he wanted to make sure that Alexandria knew that he was there for her at this moment.

"I'm sorry for making you tell him," Mark said.

"I understand why," Alexandria said. "It's strange. I'm not mad at you. I don't know why, but I'm not. I think it's because I know this is probably a good thing. Maybe I will be able to help Anna get what she wants after all."

"You would be amazed at the things you can do," Mark said.

"I have come to realize that," Alexandria said. She stood up and Mark stood up as well. "Mark?"

"Yes," Mark said. He looked in her eyes and could see the pain that she felt about her past and telling Colton about what had happened.

"Can I have a hug?" Alexandria asked. She just wanted to be held by someone who she knew cared about her. She just needed to have someone hold her and tell her that it was all right now and that she was safe.

Mark found this an odd request from her but wrapped his arms around her and pulled her to his chest tightly. He could feel her starting to sob against his chest. He wished he knew what to do to make her feel better, to stop her from crying.

"It's gonna be all right, Alexandria. You're safe here. Elizabeth and Duncan will take care of you and so will I if you'll let me," Mark said into her ear as he rubbed her back. "We won't let anyone hurt you like they did. I promise you."

The words had seemed to calm Alexandria down quite a bit, and after a few minutes, she was done crying. She leaned back and was about to brush her tears away when Mark had already reached up to do it. He surprised her by kissing her on the forehead.

"I'm sorry for all that, Mark," Alexandria said.

"Don't worry about it, Alexandria. I'm glad you feel comfortable enough around me to do that," Mark said.

"Yeah, I just … I really needed someone to just hold me and tell me exactly what you told me," Alexandria said. "I owe you something."

"You don't owe me anything, Alexandria," Mark said.

"I will still feel like I owe you," Alexandria said.

"Then how about you go out on a date with me? Since I know there is no way that I won't be able to make you stop feeling bad," Mark said.

Alexandria laughed. "That would work."

"All right. How about Saturday night we go out then?" Mark suggested.

"Sounds good," Alexandria said with a smile. "Thanks, Mark."

"Of course. Now come on, let's go downstairs before people wonder if you two have killed each other," Mark said.

"True," Alexandria said.

They headed back to the living room, and everyone was staring at Alexandria and Mark. "Don't worry, I didn't kill Colton. He's in the gym right now. I can't promise anything, but hopefully, we won't kill each other anytime soon."

"Good," Duncan said. "How are you doing?"

"Better," Alexandria said. "I don't feel like biting his head off now."

"That is good," Elizabeth said with a smile.

"I'm gonna go down to the gym," Mark said. Alexandria looked in his eyes and could see the worry in his eyes. She nodded, and he silently left.

"Had to attend to your girlfriend first?" Colton said as soon as Mark came into view. He was punching the punching bag with a force that Mark hadn't seen him use in a while.

"She's not my girlfriend," Mark said. "And I know how you are. You wanted to be alone for a while. I don't know the way that she is. And it's a good thing I stayed with her."

Colton was silent for a moment. The only sound in the gym was the sound of his fists coming into contact with the punching bag.

"Why did you make me tell her?" Colton said after a few minutes. "Everything was fine."

"It was not fine, Colton. You two were constantly at each other's throats. You two could barely stand to be in the same room together," Mark said. "And something had to be done. Ever since Anna has gotten sicker, you've gotten in a worse mood."

"Anna reminds me of my little sister," Colton said.

"I know that, Colton. You've told me that numerous times. But she's not your little sister. She's strong. God will take care of her," Mark said.

"What is with you and Alexandria and God? If He is so great, why isn't He saving her now? Why is He causing me so much pain? Why did He have my parents abandon me? Why did He put me in here with you all?" Colton said. He thought his voice was going to be getting louder with every word, but it got quiet. Mark had barely heard him but knew exactly what he was feeling.

"Because He has a greater plan in store for you. He wants you to learn from this," Mark said.

"What am I supposed to learn from being abandoned? That the world is a cruel place and that no one will ever truly care for me?" Colton said.

"That there *are* people in the world that care for you, that are willing to take you in at your worst and try to help you become a better person," Mark said.

"And who is that?" Colton said.

"Elizabeth. Duncan. Me. Alexandria."

"Alexandria hates me."

"She does not hate you. She understands you, and that's what you hate. You hate that she can see through you, just like I can. You hate that she reminds you of yourself and of your little sister also. You hate that she brings out this part of you that you're not used to. You hate that she's stirring up emotions in you that you haven't let yourself feel in years."

Colton was silent for a while. "How do you know this?"

"Because I know you, Colton. I can see it all in your eyes. You think that you can hide your emotions from everyone, but you cannot hide them from me at all. I could see when you two were up here yesterday, you were about to kiss her. For whatever reason, you don't want the rest of us to know that you care about her. And I understand. I don't want to take her from you, Colton, but it may be the only way to make you realize that you need to let her in. And I feel the same way, kind of. I am scared that she is bringing up these emotions in me that I'm not used to. I'm not used to caring for someone like I care about her already."

"Why did she have to come here? Things were going okay before she showed up."

"I don't know, Colton," Mark said, shaking his head. "I've been wondering the same thing myself."

"Mark," Colton said, looking at his best friend, who looked at him in confusion and worry, "we have to promise that we won't let her get in between us. We can't let her ruin our friendship."

"For sure," Mark said.

Chapter Seven

The rest of the night was quiet, with everyone staying away from one another and just going to bed early. The next day, Elizabeth and Duncan visited Anna in the hospital and were told that she wouldn't be able to leave until later in the day, so Duncan stayed at the hospital and Elizabeth went back to the house and picked up Alexandria, Carlee, and Jessica, and they went to the mall. The dinner party and dancing was semiformal, and Alexandria was partly grateful for it because she didn't like big ball gowns.

For Carlee, they found a short dress that was black and silver and had sparkling beadwork in black and silver on the strapless bodice. It fell about the middle of her thighs. For Jessica, they found a short dress that had spaghetti straps and had sequins on the bust as well and then flowed out to end about her knees. For Alexandria, they found a red sweetheart neckline floor-length dress that had beads along the bust and some near the hips.

It was Wednesday evening now, and everyone was just watching television when Alexandria's phone went off. She saw that it was an unfamiliar number and went into the hallway to answer it. "Hello, this is Alexandria."

"Hi, Alexandria. It's Becky from the dance studio. Would you be able to come in right now to sign some paperwork and talk about your wages and hours?" a voice asked.

"Sure, I will head right over now," Alexandria said, looking at the large grandfather clock that told her it was nearly 7:00 p.m.

"Thanks," Becky said and hung up.

"Hey, Mark, can you walk me to the dance studio? Becky just called me and asked me to come to sign some paperwork and talk about the wages and hours," Alexandria said, entering the living room again. "You can go to the park again like before. I just don't know how to get there and don't really feel like getting lost."

"Sure," Mark said smiling and stood up. "I just have to get my wallet."

"All right," Alexandria said.

"I'm so glad that you got the job, Alexandria," Carlee said happily.

"Yeah, that really is great," Elizabeth said, smiling. "Hey, what do you think of showing everyone a dance on Friday night for the fund-raiser?"

"Sure," Alexandria said. "I may end up just improvising if I can't figure something out by then, but either way, I'll do a dance."

"Great," Elizabeth said. "Will you be able to dance in the dress we got you?"

"Yeah," Alexandria said. "I once had to dance in a full ball gown, so this dress is nothing."

"Good," Elizabeth said.

"All right, I'm ready, Alexandria," Mark said.

"Great, thanks," Alexandria said. They made small talk as they walked to the dance studio, and Alexandria went inside the dance studio.

"Hi, Alexandria. Becky is in her office. It's right behind me," Angela, the receptionist, said as Alexandria entered the dance studio.

"Thanks, Angela," Alexandria said.

She knocked before entering the office. She sat down in one of the chairs and began talking with Becky. The meeting didn't last very long; they went over her job description as a dance choreographer and discussed how much she would make and how many hours she was expected to put in. Becky hoped that Alexandria would put in a full forty hours a week. She was expected to come up with five dances a week and then would teach them to the instructors every Saturday. She was going to be paid $18 per hour, which amazed Alexandria. They signed a contract, and Alexandria then took her paperwork and went back outside. She couldn't believe the amount of money she would make: $18 an hour, and if she were to put in forty hours a week, that was over $700 a week. She almost couldn't believe it. She was about to call Mark when a figure loomed in front of her.

"Hey there, cutie," a deep voice, belonging to a tall twenty-five-year-old man, said. Alexandria could smell the mix of alcohol and weed that she had gotten used to during college. "Why don't you come back to my place and show me some of your dance moves?"

"I'm sorry. My boyfriend is waiting for me," Alexandria lied. She wished that this man would leave her alone. She really didn't want to hurt him.

"He can wait a little while, don't you think?" the man said, putting his hand on hers.

"I'm sorry, he can't," Mark said. He appeared behind Alexandria and stepped in between the two, making the man drop Alexandria's hand. "And he'll hurt you if you even come near her ever again."

"Hey, sorry, guy, just trying to have a good time," the man said, holding his hands up.

"Well, go have it somewhere else," Mark said. The man nodded and immediately walked away. He turned to Alexandria and put a hand on her shoulder. "Are you all right?"

"Yeah," Alexandria said. She shook the memories of her adoptive father out of her mind. "Just distract me. Please."

"How did the meeting go?" Mark asked.

"Amazing. I'm getting $18 an hour, and she wants me to work forty hours a week. I make my own hours pretty much, but I'm supposed to work on Saturdays to teach the teachers my dances. I have to make up five dances a week," Alexandria said.

"That's a lot of dances," Mark said.

"Not really. Essentially whenever I improvise a dance, I'm making a dance. It's just perfecting it that is the issue," Alexandria said. "I just can't believe how much I will be making."

"Yeah, that's great," Mark said, smiling.

"Oh, thanks, by the way," Alexandria said.

"For what?" Mark questioned. He gave her a look of confusion as to why she was thanking him for anything.

"For walking me over here and then for also helping me with that guy. I could have handled it, but it was still nice to know that you were there," Alexandria said.

"I wasn't about to let some guy try hitting on you and who knows what else," Mark said. "Don't worry about it, Alexandria, all right?"

"All right," Alexandria said, smiling.

"You're a lot more open now," Mark stated. "Ever since Anna went to the hospital."

"Yeah, I know. I promised her that I was going to try to get everyone together, and the only way to do that is to be open with everyone," Alexandria said. "Which reminds me, you can call me Lexi if you want. I usually only let Duncan and Elizabeth call me it, but I wouldn't mind if you call me it too." She tried to keep her cheeks from turning pink at admitting this fact to him.

"Good, because it's been really weird saying Alexandria. I keep wanting to call you Lexi, but I wasn't sure how you felt about it," Mark said.

Alexandria giggled.

"I'm glad," Alexandria said. They made small talk as they headed back. Alexandria was confused when she saw that Duncan's car was missing. "I wonder what is going on."

"Duncan probably went to pick Anna up from the hospital," Mark explained.

"Oh yeah," Alexandria said. "I can't believe I forgot."

"You just got a job. I don't think we'll blame you," Mark said.

"You never know, I might," Colton said, appearing at the top of the steps toward the entrance to the house. "Duncan went to get Anna from the hospital."

"I'll be glad that she's home," Alexandria said.

"I think we all will be," Mark stated.

"For sure," Colton said. He turned to Alexandria. "We still got a deal going on?"

"Of course," Alexandria said. Mark looked at them in confusion. "We promised that we wouldn't kill each other around Anna."

"Good idea," Mark said. "Especially with how much you two like to go at each other's throats."

"We're too similar for our own good," Alexandria stated.

"Definitely," Mark said. "Come on, let's go inside."

They all were hanging out in the living room with everyone else when they heard the front door open. Immediately everyone got up and ran out to the foyer. They were all disappointed when it was only Duncan.

"I thought it was okay for Anna to come home," Elizabeth said.

"Just before I got there, she had another seizure," Duncan stated. There was a depressed tone in his voice, and it broke Alexandria's heart.

Alexandria's hand went to her mouth. She had a bad feeling about this for some reason. "It's not good, is it?"

"No," Duncan said. "They want to keep her for another week for observation. No one but Elizabeth and I can see her."

"We're her family!" Colton shouted.

Alexandria looked over to him and saw the pain in his eyes that she knew she was reflecting in her own. She could see how hard he was trying not to cry.

"Not legally, and that's the problem that the hospital has," Duncan said. "I tried to get them to let you all in, but they refused. They said that you all are not legally family and so, therefore, have no right to visit her."

"That is not fair!" Carlee protested.

Colton walked toward the door angrily. Duncan stood in front of him, stopping him. "Colton, you can't go there and cause a scene!"

"Well, obviously you and Elizabeth aren't trying hard enough," Colton spat.

"That is enough, Colton!" Elizabeth shouted. She was slightly appalled at his attitude. She knew that he was close to Anna, but she didn't understand why he was acting the way that he was.

"No! We should all be allowed to see Anna! She is our sister! You two took us all in as a family! So therefore, she is our sister!" Colton debated. "Someone has to go and make a scene since you two aren't trying hard enough to let us all see her!"

With that, he pushed past Duncan. Alexandria immediately started following him, not really sure what she was thinking but knowing that she had to go with him. She didn't hear any footsteps behind her, which surprised her. She expected Mark to be behind her and Colton.

"Colton!" Alexandria shouted, running after him.

"What? Are you here to stop me from helping Anna?" Colton said.

"No, I'm here to come with you. But you're letting me drive because you are way too bad of a driver to drive right now," Alexandria said.

Colton stared at her for a moment, not understanding the woman in front of him at all. "Why are you doing this?"

"I promised Anna that I would bring us all together. The one way to do that is to make sure that she can see us all," Alexandria said. "And I promised her I would take care of you, which includes not letting you to the hospital to yell at the nurses. At least not by yourself."

Colton just smiled at her. "I don't like the whole idea of you taking care of me, but it is a good thing someone is there to keep me from killing some of the nurses."

"Now hand me your keys," Alexandria said, holding her hand out. Colton shook his head and handed her the keys in his hand.

"I can't believe I'm actually letting you drive," Colton said.

"Yeah, well, it's better than you getting us killed on the way to see Anna," Alexandria said.

Alexandria looked back at the house and saw Mark looking out at them. She felt her phone go off a moment later. It was a text message form Mark: "Are you two gonna be okay without me?"

She smiled and replied, "Yeah, I think so. I got him calmed down a bit, so now he won't kill the nurses."

"Good. Just call if you need anything."

"Will do. Thanks, Mark :)."

Alexandria locked her phone and put it in her purse before finally starting the car.

"What was that about?" Colton asked.

"Mark making sure that you weren't gonna kill the nurses," Alexandria said.

"Of course," Colton said, chuckling. "He always has been over-protective of me."

"I can't say that I blame him," Alexandria said. "You can be a little … rash. You just do whatever you want and don't think about the way that it is to rest of us."

"I never said I didn't see what he was thinking," Colton said. "It's just slightly annoying when he asks me all the time where I'm going or what I'm doing."

"I can see how that would get annoying," Alexandria said. "I never had that issue with my adoptive parents when I was teen."

"I bet not," Colton said. "Did you really say no every time they offered?"

"I wasn't about to mess my life up the way that they messed their lives up and were attempting to mess mine up," Alexandria said. She turned and saw that no one was coming and got into the road.

"At least you're out of there now," Colton said.

"Yeah," Alexandria said.

The only sound in the car was Colton telling Alexandria which way to turn to get to the hospital. Alexandria took a deep breath before she and Colton got out of the car and headed over to the hospital.

"Can I help you?" a receptionist said.

"We're here to see Anna Blackwood," Colton said.

"Who are you?" the receptionist questioned, looking at them.

"We're her siblings," Alexandria said.

"Her records show that she has no siblings," the receptionist stated, looking up at the two.

"Look, her family is dead. She lives with Duncan and Elizabeth Rhodes. We both lost our families. We live with Duncan and Elizabeth also. We're the closest thing she has to family," Colton said.

"We cannot allow you to see her unless you are legally related to her," the receptionist said.

"We both live with Elizabeth and Duncan! We're under their legal protection," Colton said.

"Actually, you're not. You two are both over eighteen, so you actually have no right," the receptionist argued. "Now I suggest you two leave before I call security."

They were quiet for a moment, trying to figure out what to do and not to have security called, and Dr. Rizzoli turned the corner. Alexandria instantly got an idea in her head. "Dr. Rizzoli!"

"Oh well, hello, Alexandria. Are you here to see Anna?" Dr. Rizzoli said, smiling at Alexandria.

"Well, we would, but the nurses won't let us," Alexandria said.

"Why is that?" Dr. Rizzoli said, turning to the nurses and the receptionist.

"They say that we're not legally related to her," Colton said, glaring at the receptionist that had spoken before.

"If you stop glaring at the nurses and receptionist, I will give your entire group full permission to visit Anna," Dr. Rizzoli said.

Colton immediately stopped glaring and looked at Dr. Rizzoli in shock. Alexandria just smiled at the doctor.

"Thank you," Colton said.

"Of course," Dr. Rizzoli said and turned to the receptionist. "I have a list of names that I'm going to give you that have my full permission to go and see Anna Blackwood. These two—Colton Rogers and Alexandria Hawthorne—as well as Mark Weston, Jessica Woods, and Carlee and Collin Carter may see Anna."

"Understood," the receptionist said.

"I was just about to check up on her if you two want to come with me," Dr. Rizzoli said.

"That would be great," Alexandria said, smiling. Colton just stared at her. She could easily put on the charm and make any man do what she wanted them to do.

They were quiet as Alexandria and Colton followed Dr. Rizzoli down the hallway to one of the rooms, and Alexandria nearly wanted to break down when she saw the tubes and everything going around Anna. There were tubes and wires connected to something that was around her head, and Alexandria could see heart monitor pads on her chest, and there were tubes connected to her arms, keeping a clear fluid pumping into her blood system. Alexandria didn't like it at all and almost wanted to just turn around and break down.

"Alexandria ... Colton," Anna said softly.

"Hey, sweetheart," Alexandria said. She walked over and stood beside Anna. She smiled softly as she brushed a hair out of Anna's face and then kissed her forehead. "Call me Lexi, okay?"

"Okay, Lexi," Anna said smiling. "How is ... everyone?"

"Wishing you were home," Alexandria said.

Anna smiled and then looked to Dr. Rizzoli. "Hi, Dr. Rizzoli."

"Hey, Anna," Dr. Rizzoli said with a smile. "How are you feeling?"

"Better," Anna said. "I wanna go home."

"Soon," Dr. Rizzoli said. "We still have to keep you here for a while just to find out what's going on with these seizures."

"I guess I don't have a choice," Anna said sighing.

"Pretty soon we'll have you home though, Anna," Colton said and stood on the other side of Anna with a small smile. "And then we'll go and get ice cream together, okay?"

"That sounds great," Anna said.

Dr. Rizzoli just checked up on Anna and then left the room. When he left, Alexandria and Colton both pulled chairs up right beside her bed. "Why didn't anyone come yet?"

"The nurses refused to allow us to come and see you because we're apparently not legally siblings," Colton said.

"But I just talked to Dr. Rizzoli and he allowed us all to come and visit you from now on," Alexandria said with a smug grin.

"Yeah, how did you do that?" Colton said.

"He used to be the family doctor when I was really young. I ran into him a few times in high school, and we talked a lot," Alexandria said. "And he doesn't know me as the coldhearted girl that you do Colton. He thinks I'm a sweet innocent little girl."

Colton had to chuckle at that and Alexandria stuck her tongue at him. They all made small talk for a while until a nurse came in and said that visiting hours were over. Alexandria got into the car, and Colton got into the driver's side.

"I didn't get to thank you for getting us in to see Anna," Colton said.

"I wanted to see her just as badly as you did," Alexandria said. "And I knew Dr. Rizzoli wouldn't say no to me. And he knows us all. He knows that we're practically a family there."

"True," Colton said.

Chapter Eight

As soon as they entered the house after returning, everyone was in the living room.

"What happened?" Carlee asked.

"We're all allowed to go and see Anna now," Colton said.

"What? How did you manage that?" Elizabeth questioned. She had no idea how that had managed to happen for the two younger adults when she and Duncan had been fighting it since Anna first got into the hospital.

"We talked to Dr. Rizzoli," Alexandria said. "He asked if we were here to see Anna, and we said that we would if the nurses would let us in and he said that we could all go in and he listed us all by name."

"I didn't think he would be able to do that," Duncan said.

"I wasn't sure either, but I figured it was worth a shot at least," Alexandria said, shrugging.

"That is true," Elizabeth said, nodding.

"All right, I'm gonna go and get ready for bed. I'm supposed to start work tomorrow," Alexandria said.

"Oh yeah, how did that meeting go?" Elizabeth asked. She felt bad for having forgotten that Alexandria had just gotten a new job.

"Really well. I have to put in about forty hours a week and I have to work on Saturdays to teach the teachers what they will be teaching the students, and I have to make at least five dances a week. But she's giving me $18 an hour," Alexandria said.

"Holy crap," Jessica said, her eyes bulging.

"You won't have to stay here much longer at that price," Colton said.

"But she is more than welcome to stay as long as she wants," Elizabeth said, glaring at Colton for his remark.

"I know," Alexandria said, smiling. "But I'll see you all tomorrow sometime. Good night."

"Good night, Alexandria," they all said.

Alexandria went into her bedroom then, and she showered and then lay in bed for a while, just staring at the ceiling. She was surprised when there was a knock on her door later that night. She was even more surprised when she opened her door to see Colton standing there.

"What's up, Colton?" Alexandria said.

"May I come in?" Colton asked.

"Yeah, sure," Alexandria said and let Colton into her bedroom. He looked around and then sat down on the vanity chair. "So what's up, Colton?"

"Anna looked terrible. I don't like seeing her with all that crap connected to her," Colton said.

"Me neither. Anna looked so terrible, so frail," Alexandria said. She had been trying not to think about it since they returned, but it kept popping up in her head no matter what she did.

"So much like a little child," Colton said, shaking his head.

"She is one. She's only ten years old," Alexandria said, "But at least soon she'll be home and we'll know what is going on."

"Hopefully. They've been trying to find a cure for lupus her entire life, and they haven't gotten anywhere," Colton said. "I just don't have faith in the medical field anymore."

"I don't blame you," Alexandria said. "I just hope that they find a way to stop the seizures."

"But, of course, the one thing that they could do, Elizabeth and Duncan refuse to do," Colton said. "I don't see why they don't do it."

"It's expensive, and the insurance may not cover it," Alexandria said.

"So? If they really cared for Anna, they would spend all the money in the world on her," Colton said.

"But she's going to die anyways, Colton. We had this talk, remember?" Alexandria said, recalling when they started screaming at each other in the hospital. "It's a risky surgery, and there are med-ications that can help her."

"Why didn't the medicine work to stop this last seizure?" Colton asked.

"The meds probably didn't get into her system right away," Alexandria said. "But I don't know. I don't know, and it scares me."

"It scares me too," Colton said. He could hear Alexandria's voice waver when she had admitted that it scared her, but he didn't know what to do. He didn't even know why he was here. He just knew he had to talk to someone, and she had been the only other one to see Anna in that terrible condition as well.

"I just want her to be home," Alexandria said, and tears started to fall down her cheeks. She didn't want Colton to consider her to be weak, but she knew that she needed to finally let all this emotion out. She had been keeping it in ever since she found out about the seizures.

"Me too," Colton said. He wasn't really good at consoling women. That was what Mark was best at. But he couldn't just let Alexandria sit there, so he went and sat down beside her and put his arm over her shoulder, just like he had seen Mark do with many girls in the past.

Alexandria was surprised when Colton put his arm over her shoulder and was more surprised when she didn't fight it. She just let her head fall onto his shoulder and continued to cry. She needed to finally let everything out. She cried for a good five minutes before she finally stopped.

Alexandria was about to apologize for crying when she looked up and saw that Colton had a few tears rolling down his cheeks also.

"Don't tell anyone," Colton said as he brushed the tears away.

"I won't," Alexandria said. They just sat there for a while, Alexandria with her head on Colton's shoulder, and he was rubbing her upper arm. "When I was young, the doctors thought I had a serious heart condition. They were about to do surgery for me when the surgeon realized that the doctors had been wrong. I think that that may be the reason why Elizabeth and Duncan are afraid to do the surgery. They don't want the doctors to open Anna's head up and then discover that they were wrong, especially if they don't realize it until after they cut through her brain."

"That would explain it," Colton said. "They've always been hesitant about having them do surgery on any of us, especially Anna with all her health problems."

"I just wish there was a way to get rid of all these health issues," Alexandria said.

"There is a way, but none of us like it," Colton stated.

"Yeah, I'm trying to ignore that idea," Alexandria said, looking up and smiling slightly at him.

"Me too," Colton said. He stared into her eyes for a moment, and he hated the fact that he wanted to kiss her badly at that moment. Mark really seemed to like her, and he could never do that to his best friend. He then stood up and took a few steps away. "I should go to bed. Thanks for the talk, Alexandria."

"Anytime, Colton," Alexandria said, and Colton left the bedroom.

The next day, Alexandria started work. She went into the dance studio around eight and immediately began to compose new dances. She had two done when she left for the day around four. She got back to the house and was confused when she couldn't find anyone. She called Mark, who didn't answer his cell phone.

She was confused but quickly changed into a pair of jeans and a T-shirt and then went to the ballroom to see if that was where everyone was. Sure enough, everyone was in the room, starting to decorate. Mark and Colton were up on ladders, hanging streamers up. Carlee was bent over a large banner with a paint palette beside her. Collin and Jessica were blowing up balloons. Elizabeth and Duncan were bent over a table, discussing some papers in front of them. Alexandria immediately felt that Anna was missing in the distance of the group.

"Hey, there you are," Mark said with a smile. "I was wondering when you would get home."

"I tried calling your cell phone, but you didn't answer," Alexandria stated.

"Sorry, I left it in my room. I don't generally have it with me because people don't really try to get ahold of me," Mark said, rubbing the back of his neck.

"It's okay. I had a feeling that everyone was up here," Alexandria said.

"Do you mind painting the banner with Carlee?" Elizabeth asked.

"Nope," Alexandria said.

"So how was work?" Duncan asked.

"Good. I just danced the entire time," Alexandria said. "I composed two new dances."

"What style?" Carlee asked.

"One ballet and one jazz," Alexandria said. "Tomorrow, I think I'll finish up another two—one lyrical and one tap. Hopefully she won't mind that I only got four done this week."

"I'm sure she won't. She's pretty relaxed about a lot of things," Carlee said. "Especially since you started Thursday instead of Monday."

"Yeah, hopefully," Alexandria said. "Any news on Anna?"

"She's coming home tomorrow as long as she doesn't have any seizures in between now and then," Colton said. "She hasn't had any seizures today, and everything seems to be normal. They did an MRI, and it seems like normal. They still don't know why the seizures are happening, but they are using those medications to try to stop them. We went and saw her today, and she seemed a lot better than yesterday."

"Thank goodness," Alexandria said and looked up to Colton and met his eyes. She wanted to know if Anna had as many wires and tubes connected to her as yesterday, but she didn't want to ask in front of the others and worry them. She would just have to ask him later.

"Yeah, that's for sure," Mark said. "Hopefully then Colton will be in a better mood."

Colton just rolled his eyes and Alexandria smiled. As bad as all their pasts were, they all seemed to be coming together. Alexandria was grateful. Maybe she could bring the group together before Anna was gone.

"Do you think she will be well enough for the party?" Jessica asked.

"Probably not," Elizabeth said. "We may allow her to come down for a little bit of it, but probably not a lot. We don't want to wear her out."

"That is very true," Alexandria said.

"Have you thought about your dance at all?" Duncan asked.

"Yeah, I have it all in my head already," Alexandria said. "I've had it in my head for a while actually."

"Do we get any hints about your dance?" Mark asked.

"No," Alexandria said, shaking her head. She didn't want to give any hints about the dance. It was an extremely personal dance, and she almost couldn't believe she was going to dance it in front of all those people.

They all made small talk while they finished decorating the ballroom. The group started bringing and setting up chairs and tables and a portable stage after they got the streamers and the banner up that said the House of Hope. When they were done, they all started to watch television together.

Colton found himself standing in front of Alexandria's bedroom that night. He wasn't sure why he found himself unable to sleep lately and why he always seemed to want to talk to Alexandria. He stared at the door and finally decided to just go back to bed.

Chapter Nine

On Friday, Alexandria went to work from eight to four again and then ran home quickly, and she quickly found Carlee in the living room with Elizabeth and Jessica.

"Thank goodness it's just you three. I need some help with my hair. I don't know what way to wear it," Alexandria said.

"Your hair is usually really curly anyways, so I would say just do a half do. When you did it earlier this week, it looked really good," Carlee said. "And it would be simple, just blow-dry your hair, put some cream in it to keep it from getting too frizzy, and it should be okay. And then it won't take very long either."

"Thank you," Alexandria said. "All right, I'm going to shower and then do that. Where is everyone?"

"The boys all went to see Anna since they don't take as long to get ready," Jessica said. "And can you hurry up? I have to shower too."

"Yeah," Alexandria said and then ran up the stairs to her bedroom. She showered and then wrapped her robe around her tightly when she went back downstairs to the living room. She was slightly embarrassed when the men were back. "Uh, hi, boys."

"Well, that's a welcome home," Colton said. He looked her up and down and had to admit that it turned him on. Mark smacked the back of his head.

"Thank you, Mark," Alexandria said. "I didn't think you guys would be back so soon. I just came down to tell Jessica that she can shower. Is Anna home now?"

"Yeah, but she's sleeping right now," Duncan said. "She's going to join us at dinner and then probably come back upstairs and sleep."

"I'm just glad that she's home," Alexandria said with a smile. "All right. Now I'm going back upstairs since I have thoroughly embarrassed myself."

Everyone just laughed as Alexandria quickly ran out of the room. She headed upstairs and blow-dried her hair and put some frizz cream in. She pulled it into a half ponytail and saw that it was about five. She took a deep breath and put her dress on and was glad that she had ran the dance in a long skirt earlier that day a few times. She ran the dance in her head once before there was a knock on her door. She opened it to reveal Mark standing there in a black suit with a white dress shirt and a red tie.

"I have been asked to escort you to the doors. We personally greet everyone downstairs at the door," Mark said. "You look beautiful."

"Thank you," Alexandria said. "And thanks for getting me. When I was young, we never had fund-raisers."

"Yeah, Elizabeth realized that and was hoping that you were done getting ready," Mark said.

"She got lucky that I was," Alexandria said. "I was just running my dance through in my head one last time."

"Are you going to be able to dance in that?" Mark asked as they began to head down to the foyer together.

"Yeah, I practiced it today in a large skirt similar to this one," Alexandria said. "I would have practiced in this dress, but I lost track of time at work and didn't have the time because I had to shower."

"I see," Mark said, and they were down in the foyer.

"Thank goodness, you were ready!" Elizabeth said. "I am so sorry, Lexi. I forgot completely that we didn't do fund-raisers when you were young. You will stand beside Duncan, and we will personally introduce you to everyone that comes."

"Thank you," Alexandria said.

They made small talk as they waited for the people to arrive. Anna was still too tired to see anyone, which disappointed Alexandria, but she understood. When the people began to arrive, there were a couple that would look at Alexandria and say, "You're little Lexi?"

Alexandria felt bad not remembering some of the people, but some of them she did recall slightly. She was glad though when it was all over, and they went upstairs. She hadn't realized just how hungry she was.

"I'm starving," Alexandria muttered to Mark as they headed up the stairs.

"Me too," Mark said. "I always hate how long that takes."

Alexandria smiled, and they were at the ballroom. They were all going to be separated, and Alexandria was grateful that she was sitting at the same table as Dr. Rizzoli and his wife. During dinner, they all made small talk. After dinner was done and served, Colton, Mark, Collin, and Duncan removed some of the tables from the center of the room to make room for dancing. Elizabeth got onto the stage.

"Before we begin with our own dancing, Alexandria has a dance that she would like for us all to see," Elizabeth said. Alexandria went up onto the stage, and Elizabeth took the microphone with her when she left. The music started playing, a soft lull, and Alexandria began to dance. Her dance told the story of her life—from being a baby being dropped off at the doorstep, to being adopted by the family, to the abuse by the adoptive family, to the death (although she hid how they had really died) and finally to the return to the house and to the meeting of all the people around her.

Many people were crying by the end of the dance, and Alexandria could feel the tears starting to fall down her own face.

"That is my story. It is the story of my life. When I was lost, I found God, and I found Elizabeth and Duncan standing beside me, always supporting me. It is people like me who need your help, people who have no hope, who have had everything they know destroyed. It is people like the six other people that stay at this house, who don't know what they're going to be doing in the future but who know that they are always welcome in this house. Thank you," Alexandria said.

She immediately got off the stage and wiped her eyes carefully before going to where Elizabeth and Duncan stood with the other six of the house. The large group was silent while the orchestra got onto the stage, unsure of what to say to Alexandria and to the dance she had just done. Dr. Rizzoli walked over to the group.

"I will give the house $10,000 to help," Dr. Rizzoli stated.

Elizabeth and Duncan just stared at the doctor in amazement, not sure what else to say. They couldn't believe that he was going to donate that much money to the house.

"Thank you," Alexandria said. She stepped forward and held her hand out. Dr. Rizzoli shook it and then brought her into an embrace.

"I thought that you were being abused when I saw you when you were a teenager. But I had no way of knowing for sure. I'm sorry," Dr. Rizzoli said into her ear. He genuinely felt guilty for having not investigated it more or anything else.

"It's okay. I didn't want you to know," Alexandria said. "Thank you so much for the support."

"Of course," Dr. Rizzoli said, and they stepped away from each other. He looked to Elizabeth and Duncan. He reached into his pocket and got out his checkbook, quickly writing the check and handing it to Duncan.

"Thank you," Duncan said. Alexandria could see the tears threatening to fall in his eyes, and the tears that were falling from Elizabeth's.

While the orchestra got set up, a few more people came up to Elizabeth and Duncan and gave donations. They ranged from $100 to $5,000. When the orchestra started to play and people started to dance, Elizabeth and Duncan both hugged Alexandria tightly.

"Thank you so much. We never could have gotten as many donations if you hadn't danced," Elizabeth said.

"Anything I can do to help you guys," Alexandria said. "You guys saved me on more than one occasion. It was the least I could do."

"We love you, Lexi," Duncan said.

"I love you guys too," Alexandria said. "Now come on, enough tears. You two go out and dance together!"

Duncan and Elizabeth laughed and then went out onto the dance floor. Alexandria just stood there for a moment before Mark appeared in front of her.

"Dance with me?" Mark asked, holding his hand out.

"Sure," Alexandria said with a smile. They started to dance, and Alexandria was surprised to find herself remembering when she danced with Colton and found herself wanting to be with him instead. But she couldn't let Mark see that. The two were best friends, and it was obvious that Mark really liked her. She also knew how dangerous Colton seemed to be around her, and she didn't want to risk her heart anymore.

"That was a beautiful dance," Mark stated.

"Thank you," Alexandria said. "I can't believe I did that dance in front of everyone."

"It had a huge impact," Mark said. They were quiet for a moment until he spoke again. "So do you have anything you want to do tomorrow?"

"Not really. I'm okay with just about anything," Alexandria said.

"All right," Mark said. "I will have to think of something good then."

The song ended and everyone clapped for the orchestra, and then they started a new song. Both Mark and Alexandria were surprised when Colton appeared in front of them. Alexandria had to admit that he looked good even though he was in a simple black pair of pants, white shirt, and black dress jacket.

"May I dance with Alexandria?" Colton questioned.

Mark looked to Alexandria, who nodded, "Sure."

Colton didn't say anything. He just held his hand out, and Alexandria slipped hers in it, feeling the electricity course through her veins. She was glad that the song was more of an upbeat song so that they weren't staring at each other awkwardly, trying to figure out what to say.

"Do you want to show them what dancing really is like?" Colton inquired.

"What?" Alexandria said. She gave him a confused look, wondering what he was possibly talking about.

"Let's really dance," Colton said. "Give this a little more energy."

"Um, okay," Alexandria said. She wasn't entirely sure what she was getting herself into, but she knew that Colton wouldn't hurt her or embarrass her. At least she hoped he wouldn't.

Colton then twirled Alexandria around and then pushed her out and spun her into his arms. They were just having fun, and Alexandria didn't even notice it when people stepped out of the way and started watching them dancing in perfect harmony together. When the song ended, Colton dipped Alexandria and everyone started to clap as they stared into each other's eyes and were breathing heavily. It was then that Alexandria noticed that everyone was watching. She immediately started to blush as she bowed with Colton before the next song began to play, and Alexandria and Colton went over to the side of the room.

"That was awesome!" Carlee said, walking over. "You two were so together and so spot on! How did you manage it?" Carlee knew just how difficult it was to stay together with someone while dancing, and it was amazing how together they were.

"I have no idea. I just followed whatever Colton did," Alexandria said, shaking her head. "I need a drink after all that though. I'll—"

"Here, I got you a bottle of water," Colton said, appearing with two bottles of water. "I was really thirsty, and so I assumed you were too."

"Thanks," Alexandria said. She smiled at him as she took the water from him and immediately started gulping it down.

"That was amazing!" Elizabeth said, appearing with Duncan. "Colton, I never knew you could dance like that!"

"Me neither," Colton said, shrugging one of his shoulders.

Someone tapped Alexandria's shoulder, and she turned to see someone she had never expected to see again. She nearly dropped the water in her hand.

It was her father.

Chapter Ten

"What are you doing here?" she spat, albeit weakly.

"Alexandria, that is no way to talk to Mr. Herondale!" Elizabeth said, shocked.

"Don't you know who this is, Elizabeth?" Alexandria questioned. Elizabeth gave her a confused face, and Alexandria instantly knew that she really had no idea who was standing in front of them. "This is my father."

"What?" Everyone around Alexandria and her father said. They instantly looked between the two people, trying to find a resemblance so that they could put the two together.

"This is my father, Mr. James Herondale," Alexandria said. "He is the one who abandoned me when I was a baby."

Colton couldn't explain the urge to punch the man in front of him. He hoped that no one else noticed the tenseness that he felt in his entire body. He saw Mark's body tense and knew he was feeling the same thing.

"I did not want to give you up. It was your mother who did," James said. He felt the need to defend himself, hearing the way his biological daughter was speaking to him.

"I thought you didn't know who your parents were," Elizabeth said.

"I researched them when I was in high school, hoping that they would take me from my adoptive parents. They didn't want me although they had three other children," Alexandria said. She was seething at just seeing her father, and she wasn't sure she would be able to calm down.

"If I had known what had happened, I would have taken you in a moment no matter what Alice said," James said. "I cannot apologize enough to you, Alexandria."

"I don't want your apologies," Alexandria said. "I want to know why you abandoned me, and yet you had three more children!"

"Lexi, why don't we take this out of the ballroom?" Mark said, putting a hand on the small of her back.

"No, I want this entire room to know what this man did!" Alexandria said. She twisted her ring constantly, trying to keep herself from exploding even more.

"Alexandria," Colton said. "Take it outside. We can all go with you if you want."

"I want to speak to my daughter alone," James said. "I promise I won't do anything to you, Alexandria. I just want … I just want to explain everything to you."

"You can explain everything to me right here," Alexandria said.

"You are as stubborn as your mother," James said, shaking his head and then smiling at Alexandria. "Please let me explain this outside."

Alexandria stared at the man in front of her for a moment. "I want Mark to come with me." She had almost wanted to say Colton, but Mark was better at making her feel better. She knew that Mark would know better about what to do with her reactions.

Colton couldn't explain the pain and the jealousy that ran through him when she said Mark's name rather than his own. He really hated the way she was making him feel at that moment.

"Only he can come," James said after a moment.

"All right," Alexandria said and turned to Mark, who nodded and followed the two out to the hallway. "So what is it? Why did you abandon me when I was a newborn?"

"I had no choice," James said. "Your mother was sixteen. I was eighteen. We wouldn't be able to take proper care of you. Your mother refused to keep you. She is the one that abandoned you, not me. I have supported the House of Hope throughout the years because of you. I have come to all the fund-raisers since they started so that I can support you. I have always loved you, Alexandria. I cried for months after we dropped you off at the house. I wanted to meet Elizabeth and Duncan and know that you were going to be taken care of, but your mother refused. She didn't want anything to do with you anymore. I don't know why. I just know that she said that if I was to have any contact with you, she would leave me. I loved her. I couldn't lose her. I couldn't lose both you and her at the same time."

"You never say my mother's name. You refer to her as my mother. And you used the past tense. Why?" Alexandria wondered.

"I left your mother after you contacted us. I couldn't handle living with her. The thought of you haunted me for years. I tried to get information about the adoption from Elizabeth and Duncan, but they said it was confidential and no one else was to know about it. They didn't know I was your father. I didn't push the subject, thinking that you were being taken care of. I had no idea that they were abusing you. I would have killed them myself if the other people hadn't done it," James explained. "Alexandria, I know that I probably can't mend all that I have caused. But I want to be part of your life now. I want to see any grandchildren I may have one day because of you. I want my baby girl."

"You have two other baby girls," Alexandria retorted.

"No, they aren't my baby girls. They aren't my firstborn daughter. They aren't the girl that I held and loved immediately. They aren't the girl that I cried for months over," James said. "They aren't my Alexandria, my Lexi."

Alexandria was silent, and a tear rolled down her cheek. She didn't know what to do. She wanted to be so angry with the man in front of her, the man who abandoned her. But all that he was saying was making it nearly impossible. Alexandria was trying so hard to understand James and why he had done what he had done to her.

"Can we work on our relationship, Lexi? I'm not saying that we need to be the best father-daughter there is right now. I'm not saying we ever have to be the best. I just want to have a relationship with you," James said. "I want to try and make up for the last twenty-one years that I wasn't around for you."

Alexandria took a deep breath and looked in his eyes and saw her own eyes staring back at her. She saw the pain and love in his eyes; she saw that he meant what he was saying. She smiled at him as she spoke, "We can at least work on it."

James immediately wrapped his arms around her and held her tightly. "I always wanted to hold you. I wanted so badly to watch you graduate and be overprotective of your boyfriends. I wanted everything that I didn't have."

"Well, you didn't miss that really. I didn't have any boyfriends in high school or college. I'm going on my first date tomorrow," Alexandria said as they separated.

"Who will you be going out with?" James said. His eyes immediately went to Mark, who stood awkwardly to the side. "Is it Mark?"

"Yes, sir," Mark said, holding his hand out. "I would like to take your daughter out on a date tomorrow night."

"Did you know her past before tonight?" James asked. He gave Mark an examining look and shook his hand.

"Yes, I did," Mark said. "And I promise that I will take good care of your daughter and make sure that she is back here at a reasonable time."

"She's twenty-one, and I know a reasonable time is different now. And I'm not going to be here to make sure," James said with a shrug. "Just be careful."

"We will be," Alexandria said, rolling her eyes. "So should we go back inside?"

"Sure," James said smiling. The three entered the ballroom again, and Elizabeth and Duncan walked over to them.

"Is everything all right?" Elizabeth asked.

"Everything is perfect," James said with a smile. "We're going to work on our relationship. I don't plan on taking her from you all. I know that you can take care of her better than I can right now. I recently lost my job and am working on getting some financing to start my own company and do a few other things also."

"Oh, okay," Duncan said. He was grateful that he was not taking Alexandria from them. Alexandria was like a daughter to him.

"Now come on, let's dance!" Alexandria said. She grabbed Mark's hand and went onto the dance floor with a smile.

Alexandria watched the people as she and Mark danced and saw Colton dancing with another beautiful young woman. She felt a pang of jealousy but tried to ignore it. After that song was over, Alexandria went to get another drink, and Mark danced with a different woman. Colton appeared beside Alexandria as she grabbed a cookie.

"How did things go?" Colton asked.

"Will you come to my room tonight?" Alexandria asked. "I don't want to talk about it right now. I have to think things through."

"Yeah, the party will end about eleven. I'll be there around twelve thirty, okay?" Colton said.

"Okay," Alexandria said, nodding. "Thanks, Colton."

"No problem," Colton said, giving her a slight smile.

The rest of the night was spent with everyone dancing and having a good time. At the end of the night, the group had raised nearly $20,000. Elizabeth and Duncan had begun to cry when they realized how much money had been raised, and they hugged Alexandria tightly. After that, they finally started to file out to go to bed. Alexandria went up to her room and took a quick shower and changed into a pair of sweatpants and sweatshirt and had just put the sweatshirt on when there was a knock on the door. She looked at the clock and saw that it was twelve thirty. Colton was apparently good at being on time. She opened the door and let Colton in, and he sat down at the vanity while she sat down on her bed. She looked at her hands for a moment, which were sitting on her lap as she sat cross-legged.

"So what happened with your father?" Colton asked after a moment of silence.

"He told me that the reason why they abandoned me was because my mother was sixteen and he was only eighteen. My mother refused to keep me. He supported this house throughout the past years in my honor. He came to all the fund-raisers. He said that he cried for months after he dropped me off here, and he wanted to talk to Elizabeth and Duncan about me, but my mother refused. My mother apparently didn't want anything to do with me at all anymore. He said that she said that if he was to talk to me, she would leave him, and he couldn't handle to lose both me and her.

"He confused me because he never called her by name and used the past tense. He had left her after I contacted them as a teenager because he couldn't handle living with her and that the thought of me haunted him for years. He said that if he had known about the abuse, he would have killed my adoptive parents himself if the other people hadn't done it. He told me that he wanted his baby girl. I reminded him that he had two other baby girls. But he responded by saying that they aren't his baby girls. They aren't his firstborn daughter. They aren't the little girl that he held and loved immediately or cried for months over.

"He asked if we can at least work on our relationship. He told me he wanted to try and make up for the last twenty-one years that he wasn't around. I told him we can at least try."

Colton went and sat down beside Alexandria and put his arm over her shoulder. "At least you got to talk to him and are able to mend your relationship with him."

"Yeah, I know," Alexandria said, sighing. "I just … I don't know if what he's saying is the truth or not. And I don't know if I'm doing the right thing in starting a relationship with him."

Colton took her hand in his and flipped it over and pushed her sweatshirt up. She smiled when she saw the words on her wrist. He didn't say anything more. He just got up and headed toward the door. She was grateful for this simple gesture that he had done. It meant that he understood her thinking more than most people did.

"Thanks, Colton," Alexandria said.

"Just don't take advantage of it. I would kill to be able to have my family back, especially my little sister," Colton said and then left the room.

Alexandria knew that Colton wouldn't be lying to her about that. She wished that she had gotten the chance to ask him about what Mark would be like on the date, but she knew she would find out soon enough.

She lay down in her bed, staring at the ceiling, and she realized that that night she was going on an actual date with someone, someone who knew her past and still wanted to get to know her and possibly be in a relationship with her one day. Mark seemed like a great guy. She still had no idea why he would want to go out with her. He had a good body and was a great guy. He was the guy that every girl wanted. So why was he interested in her? She couldn't help but think about it and question herself and his motives.

She closed her eyes and could hear the shouts: "You little slut!" "Did you really think that he would like you?" "You're not good enough for even the dirtiest man!" "Who do you think you are?"

She peeled her eyes open, forcing the memories to escape her mind. But she knew then that she wouldn't be able to sleep, or at least not for a while. She could only think about how she wanted to be with Colton again. She wanted to talk to him, to have him distract her from everything around her. She didn't know what she was doing until she had begun to walk around the halls. She didn't know which room was Colton's or Mark's. She found herself standing in front of Anna's door. She opened it softly and was surprised to see Colton sitting in the chair.

"Couldn't sleep either?" Colton said quietly.

"Yeah," Alexandria whispered. "I had actually been looking for you. My feet took me here, and I was just going to check on Anna before trying to go back to sleep."

"My bedroom is to the right of Anna's," Colton stated. He gave her a look of confusion, wondering why she could possibly want to be looking for him. He could tell that something was bothering her, but he wasn't sure what was going on with her. "Why were you looking for me?"

"I needed a distraction," Alexandria said, wrapping her arms around herself.

"And so you were trying to find me?" Colton said. He didn't understand why she was looking for him in order to find a distraction.

"You get me so riled up sometimes that I figured it might work," Alexandria said with a slight smile. She knew it wasn't the truth, but she didn't want him to know that he gave her comfort, that he seemed to help her feel like it was going to be okay.

Colton shook his head. He had a feeling that wasn't the only reason why she was looking for him, but he wasn't about to challenge her. For some reason, she was looking for a distraction. And he would give it to her.

"Anna looks a lot better," Alexandria stated, sitting down on the chair beside him.

"At least she doesn't look as bad as you," Colton muttered. He hoped that she knew he was joking. In truth, she looked beautiful to him. Even with her hair being messed up from sleeping a little on it and her makeup was removed.

"Please don't," Alexandria said, shaking her head. "I don't need you degrading me."

"It was a joke. It was supposed to get you riled up," Colton said.

"This was a stupid idea," Alexandria said, getting up again. She couldn't believe she had been so stupid as to think that he would really be nice enough to soothe her.

Colton got up and followed her out of the bedroom. She was a fast walker, but he quickly caught up to her and came into step beside her.

"I'm sorry, Alexandria," Colton said. "I thought that was what you needed."

"It was the one thing I did not need at all," Alexandria said.

"I can't help you if you tell me that you needed a distraction and that I get you riled up and then tell me that getting you angry is the one thing that you don't need," Colton said.

"It's not getting me angry I don't need. It's degrading me," Alexandria said. "That was my problem. When I closed my eyes to go to sleep, I could just remember what people said to me in high school when I tried to ask a guy out."

"What did they say?" Colton asked.

"Called me a slut, said that I wasn't good enough for even the dirtiest man," Alexandria said, and a tear rolled down her cheek.

"Colton, what are you doing to Lexi?" Carlee inquired. She had heard people talking and stepped out just as the tear fell down Alexandria's chin and onto the floor.

"He didn't do anything, Carlee. Go back to sleep," Alexandria said. "Please."

"Lexi," Carlee said. She was concerned for the older woman in front of her. Alexandria seemed to rarely let people see her emotions.

"Go back to sleep," Alexandria said. This time, her voice held more force, and Carlee nodded before going back to the bedroom. Carlee knew not to get in the middle of whatever was going on with the tone in Alexandria's voice.

"Let's go into my room," Colton suggested. He turned to the door to the right of Anna's and opened it before holding the door open for Alexandria to enter.

Colton's room had a large double bed in the center with black and red sheets on it, and Alexandria was surprised to see that there weren't any pictures of half-naked women lining his walls. He had a bookcase full of books on one wall, a beanbag chair, and a dresser, and that was all that was in the bedroom. Alexandria sat down in the beanbag chair, albeit reluctantly.

"You can sit on my bed," Colton suggested. Alexandria was grateful. She never had really liked beanbag chairs in the first place. "The beanbag chair was Mark's idea. I never really did like it. I prefer regular chairs."

"Me too," Alexandria said and sat down on the bed beside him. "I'm sorry for confusing you. I should have been clearer."

"It's understandable," Colton said with a shrug. "So you were trying to get a guy to go out with you and the girls all called you these names?"

"After he said no, yeah, they did," Alexandria said. "I had known none of them liked me. I should have expected it, but ... I had hope at that point."

"Hope is a good thing," Colton said. "I had no hope for too many years. And now, you've brought it back."

Alexandria looked at him in confusion. "What do you mean?"

"I had lost hope that Anna would ever be able to be healthy again. I didn't think that she ever would be able to live a good life. But then you came in here and shocked me. You pissed me off, drove me crazy, and yet ... gave me hope. You gave me hope that even though she is sick, she can still have a good life," Colton said. He was avoiding her eyes, and she could see a faint blush on his cheeks. "Don't tell anyone what I've told you."

"I have no one to tell, Colton," Alexandria said. "And I don't see how I gave you hope. I have little hope myself."

"I don't know either," Colton said. "I just know that when you say that you think the doctors can help Anna, you mean it."

"True," Alexandria said.

"And what do you mean you have no one to tell? You've got Carlee, Elizabeth, Duncan, Anna, and Mark," Colton said.

"I wouldn't tell Mark because he's your friend. I'm not that close to Carlee. I really only talk to her about dance. Anna already knows that you're like a hard candy. Elizabeth and Duncan, I wouldn't tell my personal life to," Alexandria explained.

"I'm surprised at that," Colton said. "You seem really close to them."

"I was when I was ten. I don't trust people easily now because of what happened with Joseph and Marie and because of the girls at my high school," Alexandria said and shrugged.

"I don't blame you with what happened," Colton said. He was involuntarily rubbing her shoulder, and it felt nice to both of them. It felt comforting.

"Do you know what Mark is like on a date?" Alexandria asked after they were quiet for a moment.

"Mark actually asked you out?" Colton said, looking at her. She glared at him. "I meant it against him. Usually he's a chicken with asking girls out."

"Oh, okay," Alexandria said. She had almost thought Colton was saying something against her. She was glad he understood what her look meant. "Yeah, he asked me out after he made us tell each other about our pasts. He made me feel better, and I felt that I owed him, and he said I can repay him by going out on a date with him."

Colton recalled the conversation that the two men had had that very same night—that they both cared about Alexandria, that they wouldn't let her get in between them, and that there was something about Alexandria that made them feel something that they hadn't felt in years. *I don't want to take her from you, Colton, but it may be the only way to make you realize that you have to let her in.* The words rang in his head like church bells. Mark had been serious apparently.

"I think you should go, Alexandria," Colton said.

"What?" Alexandria questioned. She had thought that the two of them had been getting along for once since she had gotten there.

"I think you should go back to your own room. I need to sleep," Colton said. "And you probably should too."

"Oh, okay," Alexandria said. She stood up and headed toward the door. She paused at the door. "Thanks, Colton. You distracted me. Which room is Mark's?"

"He's directly across the hall from me. He may be asleep now though," Colton said.

"I was just wondering for the future," Alexandria said. "Thank you."

"Good night," Colton said, and Alexandria left the bedroom.

Colton lay in bed. He didn't know what to do. He didn't know what Alexandria was making him think. He knew that he wanted to protect Alexandria; he wanted to be there for her and to help her. He wanted to give her the hope that she was giving to him. He sat up and smacked his pillow. He couldn't feel this way. He refused to feel this way. He wasn't going to have children and hurt them the way that his parents hurt him. He wasn't going to put a new life through the torture of today's world. He couldn't love anyone. He couldn't trust anyone.

And yet he knew that he had already broken those ideas.

Chapter Eleven

Alexandria walked around for a little bit before finally going back to bed. She didn't know why Colton had suddenly wanted her out after she mentioned that she and Mark were going out, but she had to try to ignore it. She lay in bed for a while, trying not to think about it. She finally managed to get to sleep although it was far from restful.

She was surprised when there was a knock on the door. She opened it and saw Mark standing there.

"Hey," Alexandria said, rubbing her eyes.

"Hey," Mark said. "There is a problem."

A bad feeling went through her entire body. "Is Anna okay?"

"She's back in the hospital. She had seizures in the night. It's not looking good," Mark said. Alexandria could hear the pain in his voice as he explained this.

Alexandria's hand flew to her mouth. She had never felt her world crash down around her as badly as it did at that moment. And all she could think about was Colton. Was Colton okay? Did he know? "Are we able to go to the hospital?"

"Yes," Mark said. "Hurry up and change. I have to go tell Carlee, Collin, and Jessica."

"Did you tell Colton?" Alexandria asked.

"He was the first person I told. You were the second," Mark stated.

"Thanks," Alexandria said. She was glad that Mark had told her early and that he had told Colton already. She knew how close Colton was to Anna.

Mark surprised Alexandria by putting a hand on her shoulder. Alexandria smiled up at him and he spoke, "She's going to be okay.

You helped us raise nearly $20,000. That will be able to help to pay for surgery for her and for the rest of her health issues."

"Thank goodness," Alexandria said. "Thanks, Mark."

"Of course," Mark said. He kissed her forehead and then walked away.

Alexandria quickly changed into a pair of blue jeans and a purple T-shirt. She grabbed her high-heeled boots and her purse after throwing her hair in a half ponytail and then headed downstairs. Colton was the only one standing there.

"Everyone else is still getting ready," Colton said when Alexandria walked up to him.

"How are you holding up?" Alexandria asked.

Colton shrugged. "Mark reminded me that we raised a lot of money yesterday, so that helped a little."

"Same here," Alexandria said. "I had forgotten until he reminded me. Maybe now she can have the surgery."

"Hopefully," Colton said. Mark walked over to them in a pair of blue jeans and a black T-shirt that brought out his muscles and slightly pale skin.

"So depending on how this goes, Lexi, did you still want to go out tonight?" Mark asked.

"It depends on how things go today. If they go well, we can. And even if it doesn't, I may just need to get away for a while," Alexandria said.

"All right, we'll see how it goes," Mark said with a smile.

"Sounds good," Alexandria said, returning his smile. "Thanks, Mark."

"No problem," Mark said. He looked over to Colton and could tell that Colton wasn't happy. "Do you think you could go and find the others and see what's taking so long, Lexi?"

"Sure," Alexandria said. She had a feeling the two men wanted to talk without her around, so she headed out of the front room and walked slowly around.

"I didn't know you had actually asked her out," Colton stated. He wasn't sure why, but he didn't really want Mark to know that

Alexandria had told him the night before that they were going to be going out.

"Yeah, I asked her after you two told each other your pasts. She felt like she owed me, and I knew I wouldn't be able to convince her otherwise," Mark said and shrugged. "So I figured it would help us both."

"Whatever," Colton said. "Try not to get your heart broken."

Mark shook his head. "I doubt that will happen. But thanks."

"Yeah, yeah," Colton said. He had realized the night before that he needed to stop getting so close to Alexandria. He needed to let Mark have her. He deserved a good woman; he deserved to be happy.

"Anna's going to be fine," Mark reassured.

"So Jessica said that she's not going to come," Alexandria said. She walked over to the two with Collin and Carlee.

"Whatever. She never cared about Anna anyways," Colton said. "At least now we can all fit in one car."

"Are Elizabeth and Duncan already there?" Collin asked.

"Yeah, so let's go," Mark said. "I'm driving, Colton."

"Whatever," Colton said. Alexandria could tell that something was wrong with Colton, and it wasn't just the fact that Anna was not doing well. But she knew that there was no way he would tell her, especially not with the way that he was to her last night.

*****

Elizabeth and Duncan were waiting in the waiting room when the group arrived at the hospital. The two looked up when the five of them entered. Alexandria hated seeing how beat up the two adults looked, how dejected they seemed.

"What's going on?" Alexandria asked.

"They're prepping her for surgery right now. We've decided to go through with the brain surgery," Elizabeth said.

"It's so risky, though," Carlee said.

"It's the only way to stop the seizures," Duncan said. "And the doctors said today that if we don't do the surgery, she's more likely to die from the seizures than she is from lupus. So they have no choice really but to do the surgery."

"At least they can stop this," Mark said.

"They said that the surgery shouldn't take long since they did the MRI just recently. They didn't have the brain surgeon look at the shots of her brain before, but he looked at them today and could tell immediately what was going on," Elizabeth explained.

"Good," Alexandria said, releasing a breath she hadn't realized that she was holding. Her cell phone went off, and she realized it was Becky. "Hi, Becky."

"Where are you, Alexandria? We are all at the studio waiting for you to show us your dances," Becky said.

"I'm sorry, Becky, I can't do it today. A family emergency came up," Alexandria said.

"What kind of family emergency?" Becky questioned.

"My sister is having brain surgery," Alexandria said.

"Oh, okay. Do you think you would be able to record the dances tonight and e-mail them to me? I can give you Monday off too if you would like," Becky said.

"I will let you know if I need Monday off later. But I should be able to record them tonight and e-mail them to you," Alexandria said. "It depends on how the surgery goes."

"How about we just plan on next Saturday working overtime and we go through this week's dances and the ones you create next week?" Becky said.

"That would work out best, I believe," Alexandria said. "I have to go now though. Sorry about that, Becky."

"It's okay. I hope your sister gets better," Becky said.

"Thanks," Alexandria said, and they hung up.

"What was that about?" Carlee asked.

"Every Saturday, I have to teach the instructors the dances that I choreograph, and apparently, it's early on Saturdays. I forgot about it, and then we had this happening. She's going to let me just work overtime next week and teach it then," Alexandria said.

"That's good," Mark said.

"I may need you to record the dances tonight though. I need to start recording these dances anyways," Alexandria said.

"Sure," Mark said. "I have no problem watching you dance."

"Good," Alexandria said, smiling.

The door to the emergency room opened, and a doctor came out. "Hi, I'm Dr. Anderson. I'm the brain surgeon here. I'll be taking care of Anna. It's a delicate surgery, but it's a simple one. It shouldn't take me long. I should be done by ten, but I want to keep her here in the hospital until Wednesday probably just to monitor her and make sure everything is okay although it should be. Dr. Rizzoli has been notified of the surgery and her hospital stay. I have all your names down for visitation until she can leave. We're going to have to put her to sleep while I'm doing the surgery, and I'm not sure when she will wake up. I don't know if you will want to see her when she gets out because she will probably still be asleep."

"Thank you," Elizabeth said. "Thank you so much."

"Of course, Elizabeth," Dr. Anderson said with a smile. "I will let you all know as soon as I am done with the surgery."

"Thank you," Duncan said. Dr. Anderson nodded and walked away.

"I'm surprised the surgery won't take very long," Alexandria observed.

"He said it was a simple procedure," Elizabeth said. "I'm just glad that it's simple and probably won't affect her."

"I think we all are," Duncan said. "Why don't you guys just sit down?"

Everyone but Colton sat down. Alexandria sat down beside Mark, and she was surprised when she found herself wanting to be held in his arms or at least holding his hand. She put her wrist up so that she could see the tattoos.

Mark looked over at her wrist. They looked so frail, and yet he knew that they had to be strong due to her dancing. He reached over and took one of his own fingers and traced the words gently, slowly. Alexandria could feel goose bumps going through her body at his light touch.

"Hey, everyone," a deep voice said. They all looked up and Dr. Rizzoli stood there in a pair of jeans and a T-shirt. "I got the call and came here immediately."

"Thank you," Elizabeth said. "Do you think it will go well?"

"Dr. Anderson is the best surgeon in the area. I was the one that called him when Anna started having the seizures," Dr. Rizzoli said. "He is the only person I trust with Anna's brain."

"Then we trust him," Duncan said, nodding. "Thank you."

"Anything for your family," Dr. Rizzoli said. He turned to Alexandria. "Alexandria, may I speak with you privately please?"

"Sure," Alexandria said. She stood up and followed him to the hallway. "So what's up?"

"I was the one that delivered you," Dr. Rizzoli admitted. "I was your mother's doctor."

"I don't want to hear it," Alexandria said, shaking her head. "I talked to my father last night. I don't want to hear about my mother."

"You need to, Alexandria," Dr. Rizzoli said. "What did your father tell you?"

"That mother was the one who didn't want me. She was sixteen and didn't want to have to take care of me and refused to let him have any contact with me," Alexandria said.

Dr. Rizzoli sighed. "At least he didn't lie to you. But there was a reason why your mother didn't want to see you or anything. It hurt her to see you again. She had never wanted to really give you up, but she had no choice. She was only sixteen, and she wanted to give you a good home. She knew that Elizabeth and Duncan would take good care of you. Elizabeth and your mother had been good friends before Alice got pregnant with you. But Alice was just looking out for you. She wanted what was best for you."

"Then why didn't she take me back when I found them and said that I wanted to be with them?" Alexandria said.

"Because she thought that you were in a good home. No one knew about the abuse, Alexandria, no one," Dr. Rizzoli said. "You were good at hiding it."

"I wish I hadn't been," Alexandria said. "But why are you telling me all this?"

"Because your mother is having health issues, not terrible ones, but she's been having heart complications. I just thought that if she were to die soon, you should know that your mother did love you. It took all her energy to leave you at the doorstep. She came to me for a long time after she dropped you off and was often crying. She loved you more than anyone else—more than your father and more than she loved her own self," Dr. Rizzoli said. "I just thought you should know all this."

"Why didn't you tell me before?" Alexandria said.

"I didn't think you were going to be able to understand," Dr. Rizzoli said. "But after seeing your dance last night and all that you had been through, I knew you would understand."

"Thanks," Alexandria said. "I'm glad you told me."

"Let's go back to your family," Dr. Rizzoli said.

"Did Elizabeth know that my mother dropped me off?" Alexandria said. "Does she know who my mother is?"

"No," Dr. Rizzoli said. "She did not know who you were until you were adopted. She wasn't given your birth certificate until she came to the hospital to get it."

"Did you know when you would check on me as a child?" Alexandria asked.

"Yes, that was why I stayed with the family to make sure that you were taken care of. I would give your mother information about how you were doing, if you were healthy, how you seemed to be emotionally, anything she wanted to know," Dr. Rizzoli said.

"Thank you," Alexandria said, and they went to the waiting room. Alexandria sat down beside Mark and pulled her phone out and pulled up a blank text message: "He was the one who delivered me. He told me about my mother. She used to ask him how I was doing. She just wanted what was best for me."

Mark took her hand and gave it a squeeze. He wished he knew what to do to really help her but hoped that just being there was helping her. He didn't know what she was feeling; he hadn't been through the same things that she had been through. But he hoped that she knew that he was going to stand by her still no matter what.

"Lexi," Duncan said, walking over to them. Alexandria looked up at Duncan, who motioned for her to stand up. He hugged her tightly, and that was the first time Alexandria let herself break down in front of everyone. Within the last few days, she had been going all over the place with her emotions. She got a fantastic job, she saw her biological father, she revealed her past to an entire roomful of people, she found out her mother really had not wanted to give her up. She just needed to let it all out finally. She had been distracting herself every time that she felt she was getting close to a breaking point. She finally stopped crying after a moment and brushed the tears away.

"That felt good," Alexandria said with a smile.

"I had a feeling you needed that," Duncan said, smiling. "You've had a long week."

"Yeah, with my father showing up yesterday and then Dr. Rizzoli telling me about my mother," Alexandria said. "And showing everyone my dance."

"What happened with your father yesterday? You never told us," Duncan said.

"He told me that he never wanted to leave me and that he loved me," Alexandria said, shrugging. Colton and Mark looked at her in confusion. Both men knew it was a lot more than just that. "And Dr. Rizzoli just told me that he was keeping tabs on me for my mother."

Duncan shook his head. "You're stronger than I thought you were."

"It comes from years of practice and getting used to hiding everything from everyone," Alexandria said.

Alexandria sat down beside Mark again, and this time, she put her head on his shoulder. He was surprised but took her hand in his. He leaned over and kissed her head. "Tonight we can escape. I can take you anywhere you want."

Alexandria smiled. "Is it bad that I just want to go watch a movie and go to an okay restaurant? Nothing special and nothing really cheap either. And I really just want to curl up on a couch and watch television all day."

Mark laughed. "After we make sure that Anna is okay, we'll do that, okay?"

"Thanks, Mark," Alexandria said, looking up at Mark.

"Of course," Mark said and moved some hair out of her eyes.

Colton stared at the two of them. He knew then that he had no chance with Alexandria. Mark was making her happy, was making her smile after she had just broken down. He could only get her angry. She didn't want to go out on a date with him. She wanted to go out on a date with Mark. She wanted to be with Mark. And Colton had no idea why it hurt him so badly.

Mark looked over to Colton and could see the pain in his eyes even from across the room. But Mark was tired of Colton always getting the girls and using them. This time, it was Mark's turn to get the girl and to have a relationship that he was happy in.

Chapter Twelve

They all sat there for a while, just waiting to hear from the doctors about Anna's condition. It was nearly two hours later when Dr. Anderson came through the doors. Dr. Rizzoli stood in front of everyone else, knowing that they would be asking the other doctor many questions immediately.

"Let him just say her condition before you all bombard him with questions."

Elizabeth and Alexandria both smiled and blushed at the doctor, who knew them both all too well.

Dr. Anderson smiled at the family. "She's all right. The surgery went well. We think it was successful. She is breathing and her heart is beating fine. She is still asleep right now, and so we will have to wait until she is woken up to make sure that she is all right. I don't want too many of you in the room while she's asleep. Probably two or three of you at a time."

"All right, how about the twins go first then and then the three of you can go, and then you all can go home. We're going to stay here with her for a while," Elizabeth instructed.

"Okay," Carlee said. Carlee and Collin followed the doctor to the room and stayed there for a short while. When they got back, Alexandria, Mark, and Colton followed the doctor to the room. Colton and Mark each took a chair beside Anna, and Alexandria sat down on the bed.

"Hey, sweetheart," Alexandria said. "It's me and Colton and Mark. We all came by to say hi. You gotta stay strong for us, okay, sweetheart? I want you to be here to make sure that I keep my promise, okay?" She could hear her voice cracking, and she looked away from Anna, who had her head bandaged and wires around her body. She had thought she would strong enough to see this, but now, she knew that she wasn't.

Mark reached over and took Alexandria's hand, and Colton found himself wishing he would take her hand. But he didn't. He took Anna's instead. Colton kissed Anna's hand. "We're gonna be back really soon, okay? Don't be afraid if we're not here when you wake up. Just … wake up soon, okay? Please, Anna. I wanna be able to spoil you as much as possible."

Colton left the room then, and Alexandria got off the bed. "I'm going outside too."

Mark nodded, and Alexandria left the room. She saw Colton standing there. "Colton."

Colton slammed his fist against the wall. Alexandria flinched slightly but stepped closer to him. She could see the tear falling down his cheek. She put her hand against his arm. She knew that he was not only angry about all that was happening to Anna, but he was also upset that it all was happening.

"Why don't you go be with Mark?" Colton said. "I'm sure he needs you more than I do."

"I promised Anna I would take care of you," Alexandria said softly. "Not Mark."

"I don't need to be taken care of," Colton protested.

"We had this conversation already in this same hospital actually," Alexandria said. "You need to give up, Colton. I'm going to be around you whether you like it or not."

Colton looked over at her. He didn't want to tell her, but he wanted her around. He wanted to be able to tease her and see how cute she got when she was angry and hold her when she was upset. He closed his eyes and put his head against the wall. "I have noticed that."

"You two aren't going to kill each other, are you?" Mark said, walking over to them.

"No," Alexandria said. "Colton might destroy the wall, but not me."

"How do you know that?" Colton retorted, standing up straight.

"You could never hurt a woman," Alexandria said with a smile. "As much as you act all tough guy, you're a gentleman at heart and would never hurt a woman physically."

"Observant," Mark said with a nod.

"I've dealt with enough guys," Alexandria said, shrugging. "And I know he's not like my adoptive father."

"Did he really hit you that hard?" Mark asked.

"It always seemed ten times worse than it really was," Alexandria said. "But I got through it and that's all that matters."

"That is for sure," Mark said smiling. "So are you ready for an afternoon of just watching movies?"

"Actually, if you don't mind, I should probably go and put in some hours at work," Alexandria said. "At least if the instructors are still around."

"Are you sure?" Mark asked.

"Yeah, I want to dance and get some of this stress out," Alexandria said. "The crying helped a lot, but I want to dance also."

"All right," Mark said. "Did you still want to go out on a date tonight?"

"Wait, you two are going out on a date?" Carlee exclaimed. Everyone looked over at them. Alexandria hadn't realized that they were in the waiting room and that everyone cared about the fact that they were going on a date.

"It's one date," Alexandria said rolling her eyes.

"Can I do your hair?" Carlee asked. She looked up at Alexandria with excitement in her eyes, and Alexandria wasn't sure why she was so excited about this fact suddenly.

Alexandria looked at her in confusion and then smiled. "Sure. You can do my makeup too if you want."

"Yes!" Carlee said happily. "Are you going to the dance studio?"

"Yeah, I'm going for a while at least. I am going to call Becky and see if the instructors are there for me to show them some dances," Alexandria said.

"All right, just make sure that you're back early enough to shower and for me do your hair," Carlee said.

"So what time are we going to dinner and the movie?" Alexandria said, turning to Mark.

"Whenever you want to. We can catch a later movie if you want, and that gives you more time," Mark said.

"Sure. So dinner around seven, and then the movie at nine?" Alexandria said.

"Sounds good," Mark said, smiling.

"All right, so how long do you think it's going to take to do my hair?" Alexandria said.

"Have you straightened your hair before?" Carlee asked.

"Yeah, it just takes about an hour to do," Alexandria said.

"All right, so probably if you were back at the house by five, we should be okay. That will give you an hour to shower and then an hour to do your hair with my wet-dry straightener," Carlee said.

"Yeah, and that's all if it even takes that long to teach the dances to the instructors," Alexandria said with a shrug.

"Sounds good," Carlee said.

"We're going to see Anna, so we'll talk to you all later, okay?" Elizabeth said.

"Okay," everyone said. Elizabeth and Duncan went into the hallway that led to Anna's room, and everyone else went outside. Alexandria quickly dialed Becky's cell phone. "Hi, Alexandria. How is your sister?"

"She is doing well. She got out of surgery okay. We're mainly just waiting for her to wake up right now. But if the instructors are still there, I can come over and show you all some dances," Alexandria said.

"Are you sure? We don't want to take you from your family," Becky said.

"I need something to get my mind off it. I'll be there in about a half hour. I have to change my clothes," Alexandria said.

"All right. Thanks, Alexandria," Becky said.

"No problem," Alexandria said, and they hung up. "All right, I have to go back and change and then go to the dance studio."

"Let's get going then," Mark said. They all got into the car then and made small talk as they headed back to the house.

Alexandria quickly changed into a pair of yoga pants and a loose T-shirt before heading back downstairs where Mark was standing.

"Do you want me to walk with you?" Mark asked. Ever since that run-in with the guy trying to get with her, he had felt bad letting her walk to and from work alone.

"If you want to," Alexandria said with a shrug. "I should be fine, but I don't mind company on a walk either."

"Okay," Mark said. "I'll walk you there then. Do you think you'll be there for long?"

"Probably," Alexandria said. "I'm not sure how many times I'll have to run through each dance before they consider it good enough."

"Yeah, true," Mark said, and they headed out of the house. "Right now, I'm just glad that Anna is going to stop having seizures hopefully."

"Yeah, me too," Alexandria said. "I am glad that we raised enough money last night to pay for the surgery."

"Hey, it's all thanks to you. You showed what this house means—hope," Mark said. "And that dance really wowed people."

"I don't want to take all the credit," Alexandria said. "So please don't say it again."

"All right," Mark said. "You don't like praise much, do you?"

"When you've lived the last ten years being told that you're nothing more than trash, then it's difficult to think that you're anything more, especially when it was during your teenage years," Alexandria said.

"Yeah, I guess I didn't realize just how bad it was," Mark said.

"If I didn't have hope that as soon as I was twenty-one, I would move back here and be with Elizabeth and Duncan, I am pretty sure I would have killed myself. Oh, and if I didn't think that the drugs would kill my adoptive parents anyways," Alexandria said.

"That is one way to think about it," Mark said.

"It's the only thing that kept me going," Alexandria said.

*****

Alexandria took a deep breath before entering the studio. It was the first time that she had had to teach a dance to other fully trained dancers. Angela showed her which room it was going to be in, and she quickly grabbed her music player and picked a song.

"Sorry about everything today," Alexandria said as she entered the room. In the room were five other people besides Becky—four women and one man.

"You can't help it when your sister is ill. I'm just glad that you were able to get here for a little while," Becky said.

"Yeah, how many times do you want me to go through each dance? Each dance I have is about two minutes long, and I have four dances," Alexandria said.

"In two days, you have four dances already?" Becky questioned.

"I have a ton more in my head," Alexandria said. "And I'm good at improvising."

"You weren't kidding about this girl being good," one of the women said. She was tall and slender and had her black hair up in a tight bun. Alexandria immediately knew she was a ballerina.

"What styles do you have completed?" Becky asked.

"Ballet, jazz, lyrical, and tap," Alexandria said.

"You got lucky then. I teach lyrical along with Cassandra here," Becky pointed to an average-height woman with long brown hair pulled into a braid. "And then Maria is the ballet teacher. Michael there is the jazz teacher. And Rachel is the tap instructor."

"It's nice to meet you all," Alexandria said smiling.

"Do you mind starting with the ballet dance? I have to be somewhere soon," Maria said.

"That's fine," Alexandria agreed.

Chapter Thirteen

Alexandria left the studio at four and was exhausted. She had gotten to the studio at noon and hadn't stopped dancing at all. She pulled her cell phone out and dialed Mark's cell phone. "Hey, do you want me to come get you?"

"No, I'll be okay. I think at least. I'm exhausted right now," Alexandria said.

"Did you get a break at all?" Mark asked.

"Nope," Alexandria said. "And that is why I'm exhausted right now. It has been awhile since I danced for four hours straight without stopping for even a, like, five-minute break. But I'm heading home now."

"Did you still want to go out tonight? I understand if you're too tired," Mark said.

"No, I want to go out tonight. I just need some caffeine and a hot shower and I'll be fine," Alexandria said.

"All right," Mark said.

Alexandria continued to talk to Mark as she walked home. When she got home, somehow, she wasn't surprised when Mark was in the foyer with a can of soda. She laughed and opened the pop before taking a long swig of it. "Thanks, Mark."

"No problem," Mark said. "Carlee is waiting in your room for you. I hope you don't mind that I told her it was okay."

"No, it's fine," Alexandria said. "It works because I need help picking out an outfit."

"Okay," Mark said. "So did you still want to wait and go to the movie later, or do you think that you'll be ready before then?"

"Well, it's about four thirty right now. My shower will take about a half hour. Hair and makeup and that will take about an hour and a half, so I'll be done about six. So if we did dinner right after, we should be able to catch a movie at seven, but it also depends on the time for movies," Alexandria explained.

"Let me check right now," Mark said, grabbing his cell phone from his pocket. "Okay, all the movies are either at seven or seven thirty."

"It would be tight depending on where we go to dinner," Alexandria said. "Do you just want to make it a late movie, just to be on the safe side?"

"Yeah, I don't want you to feel like you're being rushed either," Mark said.

"Thanks," Alexandria said, smiling. "So original plan of dinner at seven and the movie afterward?"

"Sounds good," Mark said. "I'll meet you at your room at seven."

"All right," Alexandria said. She took another swig of her soda and headed upstairs. She smiled when she saw Carlee lying on her bed, sprawled out. "Hey you."

"Hey," Carlee said. "I hope you don't mind that I'm here. Mark said I could stay in here until you're back."

"Yeah, it's fine," Alexandria said. She was amazed at how comfortable she was with these people already, considering a week ago she hadn't wanted anyone else in her room. "I actually need your help in deciding what to wear tonight."

"All right!" Carlee said, jumping up from the bed. "What are you two doing?"

"Just dinner and a movie," Alexandria said. "So it doesn't have to be anything fancy."

"All right," Carlee said. "Do you prefer a dress or jeans?"

"Jeans," Alexandria said. "My jeans are in the top right drawer, and all my shirts are hanging up in my closet."

"Okay, I'll look at them now. Go and shower," Carlee said.

"Thanks, Carlee," Alexandria said. She smiled and then headed to the bathroom after grabbing her robe.

Alexandria took a shower and was done around five. She put her robe on and went back into her bedroom where Carlee was and had an outfit laid out on the bed. It was a pair of dark skinny jeans and a red T-shirt that had lace on the back and a small lace pocket on the breast.

"Good choice," Alexandria said, nodding. "I love this top. And the jeans look really good on me."

"I figured," Carlee said, nodding. "Do you want me to do your hair before or after you change?"

"Before," Alexandria said. "I don't want to get the shirt wet."

"Then get over here. I have a feeling it's going to take awhile for your hair to get straightened."

Alexandria laughed. "Yeah, it will. Usually not wet, it takes about an hour. I have a lot of hair, and it's really curly."

"But it's gorgeous. I just want to see what it will look like straight."

As Carlee straightened Alexandria's hair, they just made small talk. Carlee loved the way it looked straight, but Alexandria already missed her curly hair. It was about six thirty when Alexandria changed into her clothes after Carlee left the room and had done her makeup. She was surprised and confused when there was a knock on her door.

"Oh, hey, Colton," Alexandria said. She was surprised that Colton was standing there.

"Hey," Colton said, "look, don't break Mark's heart, okay?"

"I won't," Alexandria said, rolling her eyes. She looked at Colton and could tell that he was hiding something. "Come on in."

"Thanks," Colton said and went into her room.

"What's going on, Colton?" Alexandria asked. She closed the door behind him and leaned against the door, folding her arms across her chest. "You're hiding something from me."

"Mark's gonna kill me for telling you this. You're the first date he's been on in three years. He was in a relationship with a girl for about two years in high school and was about to propose to her when she broke up with him," Colton said. "So don't break his heart like she did, okay?"

"I'll try not to," Alexandria said. "It's my first date ever, so I think we're almost on the same page with that."

"Whatever," Colton said. "It took him a long time to even look at another girl. But I can tell that he really likes you. So just be careful."

"I will be," Alexandria said. She looked at Colton in confusion. He was still hiding something from her. "You're still hiding something from me."

Colton sighed, "I was just hoping to talk to you for a couple of minutes about Anna. I went and visited her again."

"Was she awake?" Alexandria wondered.

"No," Colton said. "I'm really worried. She hasn't woken up yet."

"It's only been a couple of hours. It could take awhile," Alexandria said.

"Aren't you worried about her?" Colton said.

"Of course I am, Colton! She's just like a sister to me too!" Alexandria said. "I'm tired of you accusing me of not caring about Anna! She's a sister to me too!"

Colton ran a hand through his hair. "I'm sorry, I just … I get really anxious about stuff with Anna."

"I understand that, but that doesn't mean you should jump down my throat every time," Alexandria said.

Colton stood up. "I don't mean to. I'm sorry. I gotta go. Have a good time with Mark."

"Thanks," Alexandria said. She could tell that something was bothering Colton. She let Colton out of the room and was surprised to see Mark standing there.

"You look great," Mark said with a smile. He handed her a bouquet of flowers. "These are for you. Do you have a vase or do we need to steal one from downstairs?"

"We need to take one from downstairs," Alexandria said. "Thanks."

"Of course," Mark said. Alexandria grabbed her purse and then shut her door behind her as they left. "So can I ask what Colton was doing in your room?"

"He just wanted to talk about Anna," Alexandria said. She wasn't going to tell him about what Colton had said about him not being on a date in a couple of years.

"That's surprising. He usually doesn't talk to people about that or anything really," Mark said. He was constantly amazed at how the woman beside him was getting everyone in the house to open up to her.

"Yeah, I don't really get it," Alexandria said, shrugging.

"You seem to relax us all, give us comfort," Mark said. "I think that's probably why. That's why I'm so drawn to you at least."

"I'm glad," Alexandria said, smiling at him. Mark smiled back at her. To anyone watching, they seemed like a great couple, smiling at each other, seeming happy. Alexandria wondered about this. Could they be happy? Could they be a good couple for each other?

"So how did the dance rehearsal go?" Mark asked as they entered the kitchen.

"Good. They all seemed to like my work," Alexandria said. "And they caught on to them quickly. The only thing I didn't like was the ballet instructor kept criticizing my technique. It was really irritating me, and I was glad when she had to leave early. I don't mind people criticizing me unless they take it to the extreme and pretty much say I can't do anything right, which was what she was doing. And she wasn't taking into consideration the fact that I haven't been dancing nearly as long as she has, especially because ballet is like my least favorite type of dance. I would much rather dance a jazz or lyrical routine."

"The dances I've seen you do have more energy than ballet does," Mark said.

"Yeah, I would much rather do upbeat dances for five minutes than a slow ballet number for five minutes," Alexandria said. She pulled a knife out of the cupboard and started to cut the end of the flowers while Mark got a vase out.

She got warm water ready and then put the water in the vase before putting the flowers in there. "Let's run these to my room and then we can head out."

"I should have just done that beforehand, huh?" Mark said, rubbing the back of his neck.

"It's okay," Alexandria said, smiling. "I didn't expect flowers."

"I figured your first date should be a little memorable," Mark said. "And I figured you might like being treated a little better."

"It is appreciated," Alexandria said. "I'm not used to being treated nicely."

Mark moved a hair out of her face behind her ear. "I understand. But you deserve to be treated like a princess. So tonight, that is how you're going to be treated."

Alexandria felt like crying. Why was Mark so nice? Why did she deserve to be treated that way? What had she done to deserve that?

"What have I done to deserve that?" Alexandria asked softly.

"A lot more than you think," Mark said. "You've given me hope. You've given *Colton* hope—of all people! You've given Anna hope. You've given us all hope. You've brought us all together. And you actually said no to your adoptive parents about the drugs. Most people would do anything to please their adoptive parents."

"There have only been three people I have ever worried about pleasing: God, Elizabeth, and Duncan," Alexandria said.

"But you really don't see the effect you have on us, do you?" Mark asked.

Alexandria shook her head, and Mark smiled. "I haven't seen Colton actually have hope since Anna came here, and we found out that she had lupus. Anna has lost hope lately, I know it. She will only tell Colton the way she feels about things usually, but lately her eyes have been shining brighter. Elizabeth and Duncan have so much more energy and happiness since you came back. It's something that you don't notice because you didn't know the way that they were before. But I did, and you've started to change us all already, Lexi."

"I hope it's a good thing," Alexandria said.

"It's a very good thing," Mark reassured. "Now come on, let's get going."

"All right," Alexandria said. They quickly ran up to her room and put the flowers on her bedside table before heading out of the house. They were surprised when Duncan and Elizabeth were in the foyer.

"Oh, hey, you two," Elizabeth said, smiling, "Are you about to head out?"

"Yeah, I decided to go and show the instructors my dances today," Alexandria said. "So we're going to be out a little later tonight."

"That's fine. You two are old enough," Duncan said. "Just make sure to have a good time."

"We will," Mark said, smiling.

Alexandria and Mark went out of the house and into his car. They made small talk as they drove to the restaurant, which was a nice little diner. Alexandria went in there and immediately recognized a man at the counter.

"Oh no," Alexandria said softly. Memories instantly began to hit her mind like a flood, but she tried to keep them at bay.

"What's up?" Mark said. He knew something wasn't good with her reaction.

"I just know someone here," Alexandria said.

"Do you want to go somewhere else?" Mark suggested.

"No, it's fine," Alexandria said, shaking her head. "I can handle it."

"Are you sure?" Mark asked. He didn't want her to feel like they had to eat there if someone was going to make her feel uncomfortable.

"Yeah," Alexandria said. She smiled at him, and they sat down in a booth.

"So who is it that you know?" Mark asked after they got their menus.

"He's at the counter eating right now. He … knew my adoptive parents, if you know what I mean," Alexandria said.

"Yeah, I get what you mean," Mark said. He could feel the anger coursing through his blood. It took all his willpower not to walk over and punch the man in the face.

"He … helped Joseph one day," Alexandria said. She shook her head, trying to stop the memories from coming. She looked over and saw Mark's hands suddenly in fists.

"In the way that I think he helped him?" Mark asked.

"Probably," Alexandria said.

"If he comes over here, I'm going to kill him," Mark said.

Alexandria smiled. "I doubt he will. Thanks, Mark."

Alexandria was wrong though. A second later, the man—a fifty-year-old man with short graying brown hair and green eyes—walked over and smiled a slimy smile at Alexandria.

"Hey, Alex."

"Hi, Carl," Alexandria said, giving him a slight smile.

"I'm so sorry for your loss," Carl said. "It must be devastating."

"I'm working on it," Alexandria said. "Thank you."

"Anything for you," Carl said with a wink. He then saw Mark. "And who is this?"

"I'm her boyfriend, Mark," Mark said.

"Oh, I didn't realize you were taken, Alex," Carl said. "How long? Joseph didn't say anything to me before he died."

"It was just recent," Alexandria said.

"Are you sure it's not just a rebound then?" Carl whispered.

Mark was up so fast that Alexandria didn't even see it happen. He had Carl by the collar and was puffing up his chest, showing his dominance to the older man, whose eyes were now wide-open and staring at Mark.

"What I am to her is none of your damn business. And if you were smart, you'd leave her alone," Mark said lowly.

"Mark, you're creating a scene. Let him go," Alexandria said, putting a hand on Mark's shoulder. "Please, honey."

Mark looked to Alexandria and saw the gratefulness and the worry in her eyes. He immediately let go of Carl, who walked away. Mark just stood there for a moment before sitting back down. Alexandria sat back down as well but could feel everyone's eyes on them.

"I'm sorry about that," Mark said. "I just … I can't stand people like that."

"Thank you," Alexandria said. "You're the first one who has actually stood up for me."

Mark just stared at her in shock for a moment. "That seems hard to believe."

"People aren't as kind as we would like to think," Alexandria said. The waitress handed her the chocolate milkshake she ordered and handed Mark a strawberry milkshake. Alexandria wrapped her hands around the milkshake and could suddenly imagine a younger her sitting in this booth with Duncan, doing the exact same thing. That day had been the day that Duncan told her she had someone that wanted to adopt her. "This was the same restaurant that Duncan brought me to when I was younger to tell me that they wanted to adopt me."

"Were you happy about being adopted?" Mark asked.

"Actually no. I didn't want to leave Elizabeth and Duncan. I liked it there. I didn't think that there was anything better," Alexandria said. "And I had a bad feeling about it, especially when I met the people. Just … something didn't strike me as right about them. But I didn't really say anything, knowing that I was too young to really know anything about people. And I didn't think that Elizabeth and Duncan would actually listen to me. Now I know I should have said something and that they would have listened to me."

"We learn from our mistakes," Mark said. "And it seems to have made you stronger."

"It has," Alexandria agreed. "I am just glad that I knew Elizabeth and Duncan would still be there for me after Joseph and Marie were gone."

"They are great like that," Mark said.

"So how often do you work?" Alexandria asked. "You haven't had to work the last few days, have you?"

"I've been working the same time you have actually. I work three days a week from nine until about four. I do pretty much every-thing—I stock items, help customers, cash out customers," Mark said.

"Do you enjoy it?" Alexandria asked.

"Yeah, it's okay," Mark said, shrugging. "I would rather be doing something else, but I'm working on getting a better job."

"Hey, at least you have a job," Alexandria said.

"You can't talk," Mark said, grinning. "Are you planning on staying there or looking for a job in accounting?"

"I'm not sure. It depends on how well this one goes. I mean, it's good and I love to dance. But I don't know what is going to happen if I lose my creative energy. I tend to go in spurts. I'll have a couple of months where I can create hundreds of dances, but then I'll go for a couple of months where I create maybe three. It's difficult. And I'm nervous that I'll lose my creativity and not be able to work very much."

"Yeah, I bet. That would be difficult."

"I'm thinking about still applying for the accounting places around here just to keep my options open and just in case my creativity stops."

"That's probably a good idea. It's always a good thing to have options, especially with jobs nowadays, what with the economy and everything."

"Yeah, that's for sure. So did you and Colton always get along as well as you do now?"

"Nope. There was actually one point in which we were at each other's throats. We really hated each other for the first year about. I guess it was probably a dominance thing. But there was one day that we actually got into a fistfight down in the gym, and then after we both beat the crap out of each other, we realized that we're actually a lot alike and have been best friends ever since then."

"Oh wow. With the way that you two are, it doesn't seem like you two could ever be at each other's throats."

"Most people say that whenever I explain that to them." He smiled at Alexandria, and their food was in front of them.

Chapter Fourteen

Colton sat beside Anna's bed. It was nearing the end of visiting hours, but he didn't want to leave her side. He didn't want to go back to the house where none of the people he cared about were. He kept having the urge to talk to Alexandria just to hear her voice. But he knew that Mark had claimed her now. They were on a date at that very moment. He wondered if Mark was playing on his nice-guy act or trying to seem tougher than he actually was.

He shook his head. He couldn't think about the two of them. He couldn't think about what the two may be doing later that night. He stood up, kissed Anna's forehead, and left the hospital room. He really needed a job, something to keep his mind off everything at least.

*****

Alexandria woke up a little late the next morning after her date with Mark but quickly changed into a pair of blue jeans and a T-shirt before going down to breakfast where everyone was. It was odd to her to actually be able to eat a meal besides dinner with them. She didn't really like not eating with everyone.

"Has there been any news on Anna?" she asked as she sat down.

"No," Duncan replied sadly. "Elizabeth and I need to do paper-work today, so we won't be seeing her until later if you want to visit her then."

"Oh," Alexandria said. She had hoped to go and see Anna earlier, but she would do it whenever there was a car available.

"I'm going right after breakfast if you want to come," Colton suggested.

"Only if I get to drive," Alexandria said. Colton glared at her, and she smirked.

"I would say no, but I know Anna wants to see you. And maybe if you're around, she'll wake up," Colton said. "So whatever. Just make sure you're ready as soon as we're done here."

"I am ready," Alexandria said.

"Oh, all right," Colton said. "Then we will head out when we get done with breakfast."

"Did you want to go, Mark?" Alexandria asked.

"I have to go to work. I got called in for a while today," Mark said. "Just try not to kill each other while I'm gone, okay?"

"I can't guarantee anything," Alexandria said. She had a twinkle in her eyes, and Mark hoped it just meant that she was joking.

"Please don't kill each other. We already have Anna in the hospital. We don't need you two in the hospital or in jail," Elizabeth said.

"I suppose then," Alexandria said. "I think I could take him though."

"I don't know. He's pretty strong," Mark said.

"I'm pretty strong," Alexandria said.

"We will have to see one day," Colton said.

"We will," Alexandria said with a smile. Colton shook his head.

In just a few minutes, Alexandria and Colton were done with breakfast. Everyone else had things to do at that moment, and so it was just Alexandria and Colton in the car.

"I'm not sure if I'm quite ready to see the shape that Anna is in," Alexandria said. "It was tough enough yesterday when she first came out of surgery."

"Then are you sure you want to do this? It didn't get any better," Colton said.

"I want to. I miss her," Alexandria said.

"And who knows, maybe the two of us actually being nice to each other will wake her up," Colton said.

"People do seem to believe that that is a rarity," Alexandria said. "If only they knew that we could actually have a civilized conversation sometimes."

"Only sometimes," Colton said.

"Very true," Alexandria said.

Colton smiled slightly at Alexandria and they were quiet for a short while. "So how did the date go last night with Mark?"

"Good. It was nice. It was my first date, so I can't really compare it to anything. We're going out again on Friday," Alexandria said.

"I hope you have fun," Colton said.

"Thanks," Alexandria said.

They were quiet the rest of the ride to the hospital. When they got there, the nurses just pressed the button and let them in. Alexandria smiled at them and couldn't help but be slightly surprised that they had done that without thinking about it.

"I was in here a lot of the day yesterday," Colton said when he saw Alexandria's confused expression. "So they know that it's clear for me to come in."

"Oh, okay," Alexandria said.

They went into Anna's room, and Alexandria turned around almost immediately upon seeing Anna. She had tried to brace herself for Anna's condition but knew that she hadn't braced herself enough. The wires and tubes connected to Anna were terrible, and her head was still bandaged. Alexandria turned around and was surprised when Colton simply put his hand around her waist, stopping her from leaving. He knew the pain that she was feeling. He felt it every time he came into the room. But he had slowly gotten used to it and was trying to fight it when Alexandria buried her head into his shoulder. He knew then that he would not be able to stop the single tear that was at the edge of his left eye.

"Come on, Anna, wake up please," he said softly. He saw the heart monitor start to bleep as Anna's heart rate quickened and saw Anna's hand twitch. "Alexandria, come on, turn around. It's all right. I promise."

Alexandria looked up at him and then looked to Anna. She saw the hand twitch and the heart monitor bleep. She started smiling.

She started walking over to Anna's bedside, and then the heart monitor started beeping at a slower pace and her hand stopped twitching. Alexandria took Anna's hand in her own two hands and brought them up and put her head on them. She said a silent prayer, and Colton surprised her by putting his hands on her shoulders and then praying aloud, "God, please help Anna. And help us all get through this difficult time. Please either heal Anna or put her out of her misery for good. Either bring her back to us at home or bring her up to sit beside you. Thank you, Lord. Amen."

"Amen," Alexandria said. She looked down to her wrist and smiled. "Thanks, Colton."

"Yeah, yeah," Colton said. He went around to the other side and took Anna's hand in his own.

"Oh, hi, Colton," a nurse said, walking in the room. "I didn't realize you would be here."

"Hey, Lindsey," Colton said. "Yeah, Anna is a close friend of mine."

"I see," Lindsey, the nurse, said. She looked at Alexandria and glared at her. "Who is this?"

"I'm Alexandria," Alexandria said.

"She's my girlfriend," Colton lied. Alexandria was going to give him a strange look but figured he would explain it later. She simply smiled up at Colton.

"Yeah, he's a pretty good guy," Alexandria said.

"When did you two start going out?" Lindsey asked. She was checking Anna's vitals, and Alexandria couldn't help but wonder what was going on in both Colton's mind and Lindsey's mind. What had happened between the two of them?

"We've been on a few dates, but he finally asked me to be his girlfriend last night," Alexandria lied. Colton had better have a good reason as to why she was lying to this complete stranger about this.

"I didn't know you actually went with one girl, Colton," Lindsey said, giving Colton a questioning look.

"This stuff with Anna has made me realize some things," Colton said. "And I'm happy with Alexandria. Happier than I was with you at least."

Alexandria glared at Colton, not believing what he had just said to Lindsey. "You could be a little nicer, Colton."

"You know me, Alexandria," Colton said, rolling his eyes.

"Good point. No matter how hard you try to train him, he just won't budge," Alexandria said, rolling her eyes and then smiling up at Lindsey. "I guess you know a little about that, don't you?"

Lindsey glared at Alexandria, and Colton smirked. Apparently Alexandria really could be a little rough sometimes even though she was starting to calm down a little now.

"The doctor is going to come to check on her pretty soon, just to warn you," Lindsey said and walked out of the room.

"You really can be a bitch sometimes," Colton observed to Alexandria once Lindsey left. He was impressed by her responses.

"Hey, I was on your side there," Alexandria said. "You just got lucky I went along with it and didn't give you a weird look or anything that would have given it away."

"Yeah, thanks," Colton said.

"Will you explain the situation later?" Alexandria said.

"Yeah, I will on the way home," Colton said. "Not right now though with her around."

"All right," Alexandria said.

They just sat there in silence for a while then until the doctor came in. It was a doctor that neither one of them knew named Dr. Reinhold. He was nice enough for Alexandria. The doctor said that there was nothing that they could do really for Anna until she woke up. Alexandria was nearly in tears and wished that Mark was there to make her feel better or that Colton was nice enough to make her feel better. She really just wished that Anna would wake up already.

"I'm going to get something to eat," Alexandria said. "Do you want something? I'm just going to the café."

"I'll come with you," Colton said. They both let go of Anna's hands and left the room. Alexandria held herself tightly as she walked down the hallway with Colton as they headed to the café. She was confused when Colton put his arm around her shoulders until she realized that Lindsey was walking around them. She leaned her head on his shoulder and couldn't help but realize that it felt natural and comfortable.

"Thanks," Colton whispered in her ear as they entered the café, and he dropped his arm from her shoulder.

"You owe me for all this," Alexandria said.

"How about I pay for any food we get today?" Colton suggested.

"That will cover part of it," Alexandria said with a smirk.

Colton shook his head with a small smile, and they got some food and then sat down in the café. Alexandria was surprised when her phone went off. It was a text message from Mark: "You and Colton haven't killed each other, right?"

"Not yet at least. I am just trying to somewhat ignore him right now. I'm worried about Anna."

"So she isn't awake yet?"

"Not yet. Her heart was starting to beat a little faster when we were talking and her hand twitched. But other than that, there hasn't been any change. I'm scared."

Alexandria brushed the tear away from her face as she sent the message to Mark.

"Is that Mark?" Colton asked.

"Yeah," Alexandria said. "He was making sure we hadn't killed each other and checking on Anna. I didn't tell him what you made me do though."

"Good," Colton said. "He really likes you."

"I've realized that," Alexandria said, blushing. Her phone went off again: "Movie date tonight after I'm done at work and you're done visiting Anna?"

"Sounds great. Thanks, Mark."

Alexandria smiled as she sent the text message to Mark.

"How do you feel about him?" Colton asked.

"I like him. I'm not really used to people actually liking and trusting me, so it's all new to me," Alexandria said. "And it helps that he's such a great guy. I'm not used to it at all though."

"I bet," Colton said.

"Did he tell you at all about last night?" Alexandria asked.

"I didn't see him until this morning at breakfast, and I didn't think he wanted to talk about it that much. Guys aren't like girls and don't tell everyone everything about a single date."

She glared at Colton and was about to make a smart remark when her phone went off: "Do you like popcorn? I can pick us up some."

"Yeah! Extra butter. Thanks!"

"No problem. We can go and pick out some movies from the house later, and there is also a movie rental place just down the street."

"Thanks, Mark."

Alexandria turned back to Colton. "Last night, a guy that once helped my adoptive father showed up at the restaurant we went to. I swear Mark was about to punch the daylights out of him when he came over to us."

"He cares a lot about you," Colton said, shrugging. "He will do anything for the people he cares the most about."

"I've noticed that," Alexandria said. Her phone went off yet again: "Thanks. I gotta get back to work though. I'll call you when I'm done on my shift, okay?"

"Sounds good. Thanks, Mark!"

"No problem." Alexandria finally put her phone back in her purse and finished eating her food in silence with Colton. When they were done, they went back up to Anna's room.

Alexandria sat down again and took Anna's hand in hers. "I'm so scared. Anna, you have to wake up soon. Please. I want to spend more time with you. I want to get to know you more. Everyone misses you so badly. I think Colton does especially. He's been here more often than any of us."

"Do you have to make it sound so sensitive?" Colton said.

"You are in her eyes anyways," Alexandria said.

Colton was silent in response. Alexandria then began to tell Anna about the past week—how she got a job at the dance studio, how she had danced at the fund-raiser, how they raised the money for her surgery, and about the date the night before. She didn't know if Anna could hear her, but she hoped that she could.

Colton was quiet. He wanted to talk to Anna, but somehow, it always turned into him solving his own problems and understanding if he was being an idiot. He didn't want to go through it when Alexandria was around, partly because it involved Alexandria.

Alexandria stopped talking and looked over to Colton, tears shining in her eyes. "I have to go, Colton."

"All right," Colton said. Alexandria leaned down and kissed Anna's cheek, and Colton did the same before they left. Alexandria swallowed and tried to act strong as they headed out of the hospital. She had to be strong for Anna. She had to be strong for herself and for everyone else at the house. She couldn't let herself break down quite yet.

"Lindsey and I went on quite a few dates a couple of months ago. She wanted a relationship and I didn't. I still don't. She said it was either we became a couple or she was out. I told her I wasn't going to be in a relationship with anyone anytime soon. I also had had sex with another girl at the same time I was with her. She also was a bitch most of the time and was very controlling. I was really just dating her for the sex," Colton explained after a while.

"That really just confirms the fact that I think you're an asshole," Alexandria stated. "But whatever. Why did you make her think that I was your girlfriend then, or did you do it just to rub it in her face?"

"When we broke up, she screamed at me that I would never be able to love someone and that I would never be able to stay with one girl. I just wanted to make her think that she was wrong," Colton said. "And she did the same thing to me before. She brought over a guy that I know was not her boyfriend to me in a restaurant and was making it obvious that she was trying to make me think that he was ten times better than me."

"Again, confirming the fact that you're an asshole," Alexandria said.

"Do you really think that I care about what you think about me? I know I'm an asshole. I have my reasons for it. You heard them," Colton said. His hands were tightening around the steering wheel.

"Just because your parents abandoned you doesn't mean you need to be like that," Alexandria said.

"I'm not going to have children though and hurt them the way that my parents hurt me. I'm not going to put another human through that."

"You don't have to. Just because you have children doesn't mean that you have to give them up."

"The world is a cruel world. I'm not going to put another life on this world just so that it can be put through hell and back before it's even dead."

"Life isn't just about the bad though. It's about being able to see through those bad times and realize that life is great. Life is about realizing that there is good in this world and that even though the world is cruel, there are good things and good people in this world."

"How can you have such an optimistic attitude when you have been tortured for eleven years?"

"In the beginning of my life, I had ten years of optimism. Elizabeth and Duncan taught me that there is good in this world even though we had all been through bad times. I've never forgotten that. It was the one thing keeping me alive in the last few years of my life."

"I'm not about to put another human life through that though."

"It's your own choice."

They were quiet when they got back to the house, and Alexandria's cell phone went off. It was Mark.

"Hey, Mark."

"Hey, Lexi, I'm on my way back to the house. Dinner should be ready soon, so we can start our movie date after dinner if you want," Mark said.

"Sounds great," Alexandria said.

"All right, I'll be home in a few minutes. You are home, right?" Mark asked.

"Yeah, Colton and I just got home," Alexandria said.

"And you both are still alive, right?" Mark inquired.

"Yeah," Alexandria said, smiling. She almost considered making a joke but decided against it.

"Good. I'll see you soon," Mark said.

"See you soon," Alexandria said, and they hung up. Alexandria ran up the front stairs and saw Colton heading up the stairs going toward the second floor. "Hey, Colton!"

"What?" Colton said, turning to face her. No one else seemed to be around, and Alexandria ran up the stairs to meet him.

"Thanks for the argument. It got my mind off Anna," Alexandria said. "Not sure if that's exactly what you had planned, but it worked."

"It was not what I had planned at all," Colton said. "And it did the same for me, so I guess we know what to do from now on."

"I guess so," Alexandria said smiling.

"Is that Lexi actually smiling to Colton?" Carlee said from the top of the stairs.

"I know. It's a miracle, isn't it?" Alexandria said, laughing. "Colton was actually being nice for once."

"Hey, it's not always me! You start it half the time!" Colton said.

"What? I don't know what you're talking about!" Alexandria said. Her eyes were shifting, and Colton knew that she was joking. He just shook his head and went up the remaining stairs. He didn't want anyone to know what her jokes were doing to him in reality.

"So how is Anna?" Carlee asked as Alexandria walked up to her.

"Okay, I guess. She's still not awake," Alexandria said, shrugging. "It's difficult to see her."

"That's why I don't want to go there. I know I won't be able to handle seeing her," Carlee said.

"I wasn't," Alexandria said, shaking her head. "I nearly broke down when I saw her today, and yesterday when I saw her, I almost broke down also. If Mark hadn't been around me, I probably would have yesterday."

"Yeah, Mark tends to calm girls down," Carlee said. "He's a great guy."

"Yeah, he is," Alexandria said.

"How did the date go? I never got to find out," Carlee said.

"It was good. We went to a little diner, where we ran into someone who knew my adoptive father, and then we just went to see a movie," Alexandria said. "It was nice."

"That's good," Carlee said. "What do you have going on tonight?"

"Mark and I are going to watch a movie after dinner," Alexandria said. "I don't know what else though or even where we're going to watch a movie."

"He has a TV and that is in his bedroom," Carlee said. "He used to have us kids come in sometimes whenever something was going on, especially with Anna. He's always known how to distract people when something has happened with her."

"Yeah, he's really good at that," Alexandria said. The front door opened, and she smiled when Mark entered the foyer. "Hey, Mark!"

"Hey, Lexi, hey, Carlee," Mark said, smiling up at them as he took his shoes off. "I got popcorn with extra butter, and if you want, we can melt some butter too. And I got some soda for you because I saw we were getting low."

"Thanks," Alexandria said. She gave him a soft smile and knew that she was already starting to like him a lot. He was sweet and caring. She was starting to like everything about him—the way that he smiled at her, the way that he was so caring for the rest of the people at the house, the way that he cocked his head slightly to the right when looking at her. Just everything was starting to make her heart flutter.

"I'll be right up there in a minute. I'm just going to put these in the kitchen, okay?" Mark said before the girls nodded and he walked away.

"You like him," Carlee said quietly, nudging Alexandria.

"This is all new to me. I'm not used to people actually being nice to me and caring about me," Alexandria said, trying to stop the blush she felt creeping on her cheeks. "But I'm trying."

"And that's all that matters," Carlee said. "Just try not to break Mark's heart. He's been hurt a lot because girls tend to like Colton more than him."

"I'll try," Alexandria said. She could see why girls would be more likely to go for Colton than Mark, but she needed someone who wasn't going to make fun of her all the time and be like her adoptive father was to her.

Mark skipped stairs as he headed up to the two ladies. "Hey, ladies."

"Hey," Carlee and Alexandria said.

"I'm gonna go see if Elizabeth needs any help in the kitchen," Carlee said and then went down to the kitchen.

Alexandria smiled up at Mark, who wrapped his arms around her. She was surprised but put her arms around him as well. She smiled as she leaned her head against his chest. They just stood there for a minute, and Alexandria couldn't help but feel safe and warm in his arms. Mark smiled as he laid his head against hers. It felt so good to hold her in his arms. She was all he could think about while he was at work. He couldn't wait to get out of work and be with her. He was glad that she accepted his idea of a movie date.

"Hey, you two, it's dinnertime! Can you go tell Colton?" Carlee shouted from downstairs.

"Yeah," Mark said, releasing Alexandria. "If you want to head right down to dinner, Lexi, I'll go and get Colton."

"Probably a good idea," Alexandria said. Mark smiled and kissed her cheek before she went downstairs and he went to Colton's room. He knocked on the door, and Colton opened it a second later.

"Dinner's ready," Mark said.

"All right," Colton said and left the room.

"I see you and Lexi didn't kill each other," Mark said.

"Yeah, she helped me out. Lindsey is a nurse there," Colton said. "And Alexandria helped me out with her by saying that she was my girlfriend."

"You really can be an asshole," Mark said, shaking his head. He knew the story of Lindsey and couldn't help but feel bad for the woman.

"Yeah, Alexandria called me an asshole after I told her why I did it," Colton said. "And then we started arguing."

"Of course you two did," Mark said, chuckling. "Can you two ever get along?"

"Probably not," Colton said. "Just be glad that we're not killing each other or fighting with our fists. It's only words."

"Yeah, but you would never hurt a girl anyways," Mark said. "But whatever. I'm going to be watching some movies with her after dinner."

"Yeah, she told me," Colton said.

"Okay," Mark said. They were then in the dining room where everyone else was.

"How is Anna doing?" Elizabeth asked.

"She's still asleep," Alexandria replied. "We still don't know when she's going to wake up."

"Hopefully soon," Duncan said.

"Hopefully," Alexandria said, nodding.

Chapter Fifteen

They all made small talk about anything but Anna while they ate their dinner. When they were done, everyone went to the living room.

"So where are the movies we can pick from?" Alexandria said, turning to Mark.

"There is the bookcase there that has some, and I have some in my room also," Mark said, pointing to a large bookcase that was in the corner.

"Are you two going to watch a movie upstairs?" Elizabeth asked.

"Yeah," Alexandria said. "I just need to relax before I start a hectic week at work."

"Probably a good idea," Duncan said.

Alexandria picked out a couple of movies, and then Mark and Alexandria went upstairs to his bedroom. It was a simple bedroom with a few pictures on the walls of his family and the people here at the house and blue sheets and comforter on the bed. On the dresser across from the bed was a large TV with a media player connected to it.

"You can sit on my bed if you want," Mark said.

"Thanks, Mark," Alexandria said. She sat down on his bed, not really sure what to do while Mark got the movie ready.

"If you wanna wait a second, I can make the bed more comfortable for us to lay on," Mark said.

"Sounds good," Alexandria said. Mark put the movie in the player and then went to the bed. He pushed the pillows up and brought the covers back a little.

"Oh, I forgot the popcorn. Do you want to come with me or do you want to stay here?" Mark said.

"I'll come down with you," Alexandria said. They just talked as they went down and started the popcorn. Mark told her about work and about his day while they waited for the popcorn to be finished popping.

They went back upstairs, and both lay in the bed under the covers with the popcorn in between them. They watched the movie, and halfway through, they were already done with the popcorn. Mark put the popcorn dish on the floor on his side of the bed and then moved a little closer to Alexandria. He put his arm behind Alexandria, slightly nervous. Alexandria's heart was racing. She had never been alone with a man in a romantic sense, so she didn't really know what to do.

Suddenly, a memory came in her head, something similar to this with her adoptive father. She had been watching a movie in her bedroom, and Joseph joined her. He started doing the same thing that Mark was doing, and before she knew it then, her pants were off and Joseph was on top of her.

Alexandria shot up in the bed, sweat lining her brows. Mark looked at her in worry and confusion. "What's going on, Lexi?"

Alexandria was brought back from the memory then and shook her head. "I ... I'm sorry. I was just ... remembering one of the times with Joseph. I was in my bedroom watching a movie when he came in, and he started to put his arm around me and stuff and the next thing I knew, he was already on top of me and raping me."

"I'm sorry. I didn't realize that this would trigger memories," Mark said. "I'm sorry."

"Mark, it's not your fault," Alexandria said, turning to Mark. "Don't think that way. It's really not your fault. You're trying to help me with this. I didn't even think that this would trigger a memory. And if it's anyone's fault, it's Joseph's."

"I still feel bad though that I caused the memory," Mark said.

"Stop it, Mark. Please," Alexandria said. Mark was quiet. "I'm sorry. I just ... I am really sensitive about this. I'm not used to people actually feeling bad about hearing my story."

"I don't blame you," Mark said. "But now, you're surrounded by people who care about you—me, Carlee, Elizabeth, Duncan, Anna, and Colton even though he won't admit it. We all care about you and want to help you. We want to help you get through all this."

"Thanks," Alexandria said, smiling. "When I came back, I thought I was going to act like a tough girl who didn't need anyone's help. It was the way I had been living the last few years. And then I met Anna while she was sick, and it all crumbled. I knew I couldn't be strong for very long. And you were so nice and sweet and just a great guy. You were someone whom I didn't think existed anymore. You helped me realize that I can't be strong all the time and that I have people here to help me. I owe you for that, Mark."

Mark brushed the hair out of her eyes and pushed it behind her ear. "Hey, you don't owe me anything, Lexi. I didn't tell you about my relationship's past. I haven't been on a date in three years. I was in love with this girl that I had been with in high school, and the day that I was going to propose, she broke up with me. Within a week, she was with another guy. I discovered a while later that she had been cheating on me for about six months. I thought that women were mainly out to use men and take advantage of them. Finally, I started to get out of that, but then every time I tried to get with a girl, they asked if I could introduce them to Colton. After being turned down enough times, especially for your best friend, your self-esteem goes down the drain.

"And then you showed up. With the way that you were fighting with Colton, I thought maybe I could finally have a girl that didn't want Colton more. And not only that, you were like a beacon of light for all of us. You finally helped us believe that Anna may live longer than we always thought. You made us believe that we could actually be a real family and belong together. You gave us the hope that we really needed. So you don't owe us anything. You gave us the one thing we needed the most: hope."

Alexandria smiled at Mark. She didn't really think she had done that for all the people in the house, but she was going to let Mark think whatever he wanted to. She didn't know what to say to Mark. Instead, she put her hand on his and kissed his cheek.

"I'm lucky to have you around, Mark," Alexandria said. "You really are a great guy."

"Thanks," Mark said. "So did that make you feel better?"

"Yeah, it did," Alexandria said. "Thanks, Mark."

"Of course," Mark said. "Now, do you want to continue to watch the movie?"

"Yeah," Alexandria said.

The two of them both lay back down, and Mark didn't put his arm around her until she leaned her head against his shoulder, and he was glad when she didn't bolt upright or anything. They made small talk during the movies that they watched until there was a knock on the door around ten. Mark got out of bed and was surprised to see Colton there.

"What's going on?" Mark questioned. Alexandria suddenly had a bad feeling in her stomach.

"Elizabeth and Duncan just got back from the hospital. They're calling a family meeting right now in the living room," Colton said.

"I don't like the sound of that," Alexandria said as she got out of the bed.

"Me neither," Mark said. Colton just shrugged. They started to follow Colton down to the living room, and Alexandria was glad when Mark took her hand.

"All right, now we have everyone here," Elizabeth said as the three entered the room. Everyone was in the living room, and the only spots available were two recliners. Colton immediately took one, and Mark let Alexandria take the other one and stood behind the recliner.

"We have some big news for everyone," Duncan said.

"Before you go any further, is it about Anna?" Alexandria asked. She needed to brace herself if this was bad news about her condition.

"No," Elizabeth said. Alexandria visibly relaxed and so did everyone else in the room. "Sorry about worrying you all. This is not bad news. It's good news."

"We have been throwing this idea around for a while now. But these health issues with Anna have made us realize just how much all of you mean to us. Each one of you is practically our children anyways. You've all been here for years. We've seen you grow up and become wonderful people. We finally realized that there's no point in not doing it. We've decided that we're going to adopt each one of you," Duncan announced.

"What about the fact that the three of us are twenty-one or twenty-two?" Mark asked.

"We can still adopt you," Elizabeth said. "We were actually filling out the paperwork today for all the adoptions. We are all already your legal guardians, so there really wasn't much else for us to do."

No one could really believe what the two older adults were saying. They were all officially going to be a family—not a broken-up, waiting-to-be-adopted family. To Alexandria, this was a great thing. She could finally have a real family. And then she realized that it would be twisted if she were to end up eventually marrying Mark. It would be too confusing and hard to explain to people. She wouldn't be able to do it.

Mark put his hand on her shoulder. He was staring at Colton at that moment. Both of them knew what they were thinking. They both cared for Alexandria, and by being adopted, they wouldn't be able to be with her.

"I can't," Mark said. Everyone stared at him in confusion. Alexandria looked up at him.

"What do you mean, Mark?" Elizabeth questioned.

"I can't be adopted. If I'm adopted, it means that I can't be with Lexi. And I'm not saying that we're definitely going to get married someday or anything, but I can't do that. I can't take the risk of possibly not being able to be with her because we're siblings," Mark said.

Alexandria relaxed slightly. She couldn't believe he was doing that for her. He had been waiting for years to be adopted, and now he was ruining the chance of it.

"Mark, I can't let you do that," Alexandria said. "If anyone in this place shouldn't be adopted, it's me. I'm the only one here who knows what it's like to be adopted. To think that you've finally gotten your break, you're finally going to get out of this place and be with people who care about you."

"But your dream was crushed with Joseph and Marie," Mark said. "I was with a family that loved me. And I never really cared about being adopted. I just cared about being with people who loved me."

Colton couldn't help but want to smack Mark. If Mark let Alexandria not be adopted, neither one of them had to worry. And then he wanted to hurt himself. What was he thinking? He wasn't going to take Alexandria away from Mark. He wasn't going to have anything to do with Alexandria in a romantic sense.

"Mark, please. Just … let them adopt you. I've felt their love enough to know that a piece of paper doesn't change that," Alexandria said.

"Lexi," Duncan said.

"Duncan, no matter what a piece of paper says, you've always been the closest thing to a father that I've had. And the same with you, Elizabeth. You two are the closest things I have ever had to parents. When I graduated high school, I didn't want my adoptive parents there. I wanted you two there. I wanted to send you invitations to the graduation ceremony, but Joseph and Marie wouldn't let me," Alexandria explained. "I have always felt your love even when I was with Joseph and Marie. When I was being abused, I just wanted to be with you guys. I couldn't wait until I was twenty-one so that I could get away from them and be with you guys."

"Are you sure, Lexi?" Elizabeth inquired.

"A piece of paper makes no difference to me for you guys. You all have done plenty for me," Alexandria said with a smile. "It's time for everyone else here to realize your love for us."

"All right, so if you all want to be adopted, then come into the library," Duncan said.

Colton hesitated at the door to the living room when he saw Alexandria sitting in the recliner, staring at the wall. Everyone was a good ways ahead of him. "Alexandria." She looked up at him in confusion. "Eleven thirty."

It took a moment for her to process what he was talking about, but she nodded and he went to the library. They all went to the library and filled out the paperwork for the adoption. Mark came back in the living room while everyone else went to bed. "Do you want to finish watching the movie, Lexi?"

"I think I'm going to bed if you don't mind," Alexandria said. She saw it was already nearly eleven, and she had to do some things before Colton came to her room.

"That's fine," Mark said. "I know you have work tomorrow."

"Yeah, hopefully, I can create a dance," Alexandria said. "I can feel my imagination going down already."

"I am sure it will be fine," Mark reassured. "And thanks for that, Lexi. I don't know how to repay you. I know how much it would mean for you to have their last name."

"A last name is just a last name. It makes no difference," Alexandria said and sat up. "Good night, Mark."

"Good night, Lexi," Mark said. He knew that Alexandria was upset but that there was nothing that he could do about it. He tried to stop her from doing it, but she wouldn't let him.

Alexandria sulked up to her bedroom and changed into a pair of sweatpants and a tank top before lying down on her bed. She had dreamt all her life of being adopted by Elizabeth and Duncan—of being their daughter legally. And she had just thrown that all away. She wanted to smack herself. What was she thinking? The one thing in the world that would make her happy, being adopted by Duncan and Elizabeth, and she threw it all away. She felt a tear roll down her cheek. She just wanted to go back in time and take it back. She didn't care if it meant that she couldn't be with Mark. She wanted to be part of that family.

There was a knock on her door, and a second later, Colton walked in. Alexandria's heart raced. That was another reason. She couldn't be with Colton either. She couldn't have these late-night talks with him. It would have changed everything. She wasn't willing to give up these conversations with Colton or the conversations and movies with Mark. She felt a peace wash through her. She had been right when she was talking. It didn't matter if she was their legal daughter or not. She was still their daughter to them. They were still more of parents than her adoptive or her birth parents.

"I have to admit, I'm surprised you didn't let Mark not be adopted," Colton said. "You are really attached to him, aren't you?"

"Yeah," Alexandria said. "I just didn't realize how much it actually hurt turning them down. All my life I have wanted to be a Rhodes, wanted to be their daughter. And now, I just blew any chance I could possibly have."

"You can go and sign the papers right now," Colton said.

"Not if I want to be with Mark at all," Alexandria said. "I don't know how the law works with adoptive siblings."

"So you're going to just give everything up for him?" Colton asked.

"For you too," Alexandria said softly. Colton stared at her in shock. "It would be strange for us to have these late-night conversations. I realized as soon as you came in that things would have to change if I were adopted as well. I am not going to give up these conversations with you or movies with Mark. I'm still a daughter to them, whether it's legal or not. I'm not willing to give up what I have with you and Mark."

"We don't have anything, Alexandria. You're dating Mark."

"I'm not saying we have anything romantic, Colton! I'm saying we're friends, aren't we? You come into my room late at night whenever either one of us has had a rough day. When we went to the hospital, you comforted me, and I hope that I comforted you. You can't say that we're not friends."

"We argue all the time."

"Friends do that. Siblings do that. No one can have a perfect relationship where you don't fight once in a while."

"All the time though?"

"We don't fight all the time."

"Practically."

"Am I not a friend to you, Colton? Do you not want to be my friend?"

Colton was quiet. "I guess so. But Mark can't know about these meetings. No one can know about these meetings."

"I'm not planning on telling anyone," Alexandria said, shaking her head. She was slightly confused about how Colton was reacting to her saying that they were friends and him saying that they couldn't tell anyone what they were doing.

"I've taken enough girls from Mark. I don't need to take you from him too."

"He told me about that today. Thanks for everything at the hospital, Colton. I wouldn't have been able to deal with that alone."

Alexandria brought her knees up to her chest and wrapped her arms around them. She really just wanted to wake up and have this all be a dream—that Elizabeth and Duncan had only wanted to adopt her. But obviously, that was not going to happen. She was stuck as the only one in that house that was not a Rhodes. She didn't realize how much it was all going to hurt.

"When I first met you, Colton, I thought you were a complete and total asshole. Anything you said annoyed me and drove me crazy. And then I fell down those stairs and you caught me. I felt something change in my point of view at that point. And then it changed again when you told me about your past. I like our late-night conversations. I like feeling that I can tell you things and you'll understand what I'm talking about. I like understanding you and finally feeling like I'm understood by someone."

Colton was quiet, not really sure what to say. He wasn't used to being told that he was actually helping someone. "I thought you were a bitch when we first met. I thought that you thought you were better than the rest of us. And then you told me about your past, and I saw how much Anna trusted you. I knew when I saw how much Anna trusted you and how much Mark seemed to like you that I had to learn to trust you. And then we started talking late at night like this, and I have to admit, they're better than some of the conversations I've had with Mark or Duncan or Elizabeth. You've given me hope, along with everyone else."

Alexandria smiled at Colton. "I enjoy these talks, Colton. I feel like you're the one that understands me the best here."

"Probably because I was the only one actually abandoned by their family. Everyone else had their parents die and their family unable to take them. You and I are the only ones who actually had their families abandon them. And no one else will ever be able to understand that pain."

"That is very true. Not to say that it's a good thing that your family abandoned you, but I am partly glad for it so that I have someone who understands me."

"Same here." Colton gave Alexandria a small smile.

They just sat there in silence for a short while, enjoying each other's company, until Alexandria spoke, "I should probably go to sleep since I have to work tomorrow. Thanks for everything, Colton."

"No problem," Colton said. He stood up and walked out of the room, pausing at the door. "Thanks for everything too, Alexandria."

"If you want, you can call me Lexi," Alexandria said.

"Only when we're alone," Colton said. He then left and walked down the hallway to his bedroom. He was shocked when Jessica appeared beside his doorway.

"You aren't going to hurt Mark by stealing her from him, are you?" Jessica said.

"What are you talking about, Jessica?" Colton questioned. He had thought no one knew of their secret meetings.

"I know that you've been sneaking into Alexandria's room at night. You need to stop. You can't hurt Mark like that. You've hurt him enough times by stealing the other girls. It's time he finally got one," Jessica said.

"I know," Colton said. "Alexandria and I are just friends. We're nothing more."

"Just be careful," Jessica said.

"Don't tell anyone, all right?" Colton said.

"I won't until something serious happens. And if at that point you don't tell Mark, I will," Jessica said.

"Thanks," Colton said. Jessica walked away, and Colton went back into his room.

Chapter Sixteen

Alexandria woke up and felt exhausted. She didn't know what to do. She knew that she had to stop dancing soon. As much as she loved it, she was not going to be able to be creative all the time, and she wouldn't be able to deal with the emotional roller coaster she was going through. She was surprised when she had a text message from Mark: "Good morning, beautiful. I'm off to work early but had to say good morning to you. Hope work goes well today."

Alexandria replied, "Thanks, Mark. I really needed this this morning. I will call you on my lunch break. I hope your day at work goes well also."

Alexandria changed and packed her bag for work and headed to the dance studio, putting her music on. But when she listened to the music, nothing came into her head. She knew she was in trouble. She was glad that she remembered past dances that she had created so that she could use those for this week. But she knew that she could only go so far with those dances.

"Good morning, Alexandria," Angela said as Alexandria entered the dance studio.

"Morning," Alexandria said with a small smile. Angela knew something was wrong immediately. Alexandria had been so bright and happy the week before.

"Alexandria," Angela said, and she turned around. "What's up? Is something wrong?"

"I'm fine. Thanks though, Angela," Alexandria said, smiling a little brighter. She then realized that her facade was fading. She had to act like she always had acted—strong and happy. It was the only way to fool people into thinking she was okay. When she got into her dance room, she locked the door. She didn't want anyone disturbing her today. She checked her phone one last time and was shocked to see a text message from an unknown number: "Hey, it's Colton. I stole your number from Mark's phone. How ya doing?"

She quickly replied, "Attempting to dance, so I'll text you later."

She didn't really want to deal with Colton. As good of talks as they could have sometimes, she could get too infuriated with him sometimes to really make it worth it. She didn't feel like getting angry with him at the moment. She needed to dance and get at least a couple of hours in.

She danced for about three hours before taking her first break, just running through some old dances, hoping that it would trigger her creativity. She was surprised when there was a knock on her door. She went and unlocked it and saw Becky standing there.

"Hey, Becky," Alexandria said with a smile.

"Hey, how's it going?" Becky asked.

"Okay," Alexandria said, shrugging. "I'm working on some dances right now."

"Do you mind showing me?" Becky wondered.

"Not at all," Alexandria said. She started the music and began a dance she had created in the last year when she was having a difficult time with classes. When she was done, Becky looked at her.

"Something's wrong," Becky said. "Not with the dance—with you."

"Nothing's wrong," Alexandria said.

"You just went through the motions. You didn't dance with the passion that you had last week. That was why I hired you, the passion that you poured out in your dance routine," Becky said. "So you better get that passion back this week or you won't be back. I'm not going to have a choreographer who has no passion."

"Yes, ma'am," Alexandria said. "Do you mind if I take the rest of the day off then? So that I can try to think of other things. I'm sure that's all I need."

"Fine," Becky said. "Just make sure you can show me that same dance tomorrow with ten times more passion than you just showed me."

"Of course," Alexandria said. Becky walked away then and Alexandria took a deep breath before collecting her dance bag. She checked her phone and saw that Mark had called her. She checked the voice mail and saw it was just him saying to call him back. She waited until she was outside and started to walk around the park while she called him.

"Hey, Lexi, how's it going?" Mark asked.

"Not too good," Alexandria admitted. "I've already lost my creativity quite a bit and, apparently, am not as passionate as I was last week. Becky said that either I get my passion back this week or I won't be back."

"I'm so sorry, Lexi. Do you think you'll have it back by the end of this week?" Mark wondered.

"I don't know, and frankly I don't care. I see it kind of as if I can't have a bad day at all. And I think that's what upsets me about this. I got the rest of the day off though," Alexandria said.

"Do you think this is because of last night?" Mark asked.

"I don't know. I'm just … emotionally not doing well right now, Mark," Alexandria said.

"Just remember that you can talk to me. I have to go back to work now though. I'll talk to you later, okay, Lexi?" Mark said. He felt guilty for not being able to talk to her more and to comfort her while she was going through such a difficult time right then.

"Okay," Alexandria said and hung up. She was shocked when an unknown number called her a second later. "Hello, this is Alexandria."

"Hi, Alexandria, my name is Carol Lockwood, and I'm from Lockwood Accounting," a soft voice said. Alexandria recognized the name as one of the accounting firms she had given her résumé to the previous week.

"Hi, Carol," Alexandria said, trying to sound a little more upbeat than she actually felt.

"I was just looking over your résumé here, and we have an accounting position that we're doing interviews for at the moment. Would you be willing to come in for an interview later today?" Carol said.

"I would love to. What time do you want me there?" Alexandria asked, looking at her watch. It was already eleven thirty.

"Would you be able to come in at two?" Carol asked.

"Yes, I would," Alexandria said, smiling.

"Fantastic. I'll see you at two then, Alexandria," Carol said.

"See you then," Alexandria said and hung up. She immediately dialed Mark's number, wanting to tell him. She got his voice mail. "I know you're at work, but I just wanted to let you know that at two this afternoon I have an interview with an accounting firm. Hope you're having fun at work!"

She started running back to the house then, too excited to only walk. She also knew she had to eat lunch and shower and pick out nice clothes for her interview.

"You're home really early," Colton stated from the bottom of the stairs as soon as she entered the foyer.

"I have an interview with an accounting firm at two," Alexandria said.

"I thought you liked your job at the dance studio," Colton said, looking at her in confusion.

"I do, but Becky just told me that either I get my passion back this week or I'm fired. And I can have months and months of creativity and then suddenly be out for months," Alexandria said. "And when I lose that creativity, I lose the passion. Becky said she hired me for the passion I had in my dances. I lose that passion, I lose my job. Although I love dancing, I would rather only do it as a hobby."

"I see what you mean," Colton said. "Good luck at the interview. Are you coming to lunch?"

"Yeah, I'm just going to put my bag upstairs and then I'll be there," Alexandria said, smiling.

"All right, I'll let everyone know," Colton said.

"Thanks," Alexandria said and jumped up the stairs. She quickly threw her bag in the bedroom and then ran downstairs to the dining room. "Hey, everyone."

"Well, this is different," Elizabeth said, smiling. "What happened at work?"

"Um, well, I've lost part of my creativity and my passion just because I'm having a bad day today. And Becky told me either I get that back this week, or I'm gone. But I did end up getting a call to come in for an interview with an accounting firm at two," Alexandria said.

"So you won't be working at the dance studio anymore?" Carlee said.

"Probably not. Dance is a huge commitment of both time and energy, and it takes a lot of passion. And Becky also put a lot of pressure on me. I can't work in a place where I can't have a bad day," Alexandria said. "Today was just a bad day, and Becky seemed to think it was the worst thing that could happen."

"So which accounting firm do you have the interview for?" Duncan asked.

"Lockwood Accounting," Alexandria said.

"Oh, they're a great family! They always come to our fund-raisers and try to help out. They actually do our taxes and everything for us," Elizabeth said.

"Yeah, you'll do great with them," Duncan said.

"Yeah, I'm not guaranteed a job or anything yet. I just have the interview today," Alexandria said.

"Well, good luck," Elizabeth said.

"Thanks," Alexandria said.

When they were done eating lunch, Alexandria went upstairs and took a shower and changed into a pair of black pants and a blue dress shirt. She was surprised when she was brushing her hair and there was a knock on the door; she was even more surprised when it was Colton there.

"Hey," Alexandria said. She opened the door more and Colton came in, and she closed the door behind him. "What's up?"

"Jessica knows that I've been sneaking in here at night," Colton said.

"So? It's not like anything happens," Alexandria said.

"But to Mark, it may seem like I'm trying to take you from him," Colton said.

Alexandria bit her lip. "She wasn't going to tell him, was she?"

"Not unless something serious happens. And then she'll tell if we don't tell Mark," Colton said. "Personally, I think she has a crush on him."

"Probably," Alexandria said. "But it doesn't matter. Mark, hopefully, will understand that we're just friends. It's my first chance at an actual relationship—I'm not about to ruin it by being with some other guy."

"The only problem is that Mark doesn't know you that well. Hell, none of us know you that well. You're still a mystery to us. And Mark knows that I don't stick to one girl for very long. And most of the time, the girls want me, not him. It's going to be a huge blow to him if he finds out," Colton said.

"Are you saying that we need to stop?" Alexandria said. Her heart sank at the thought of no longer having late night conversations with Colton.

"No, just make them later. Or meet somewhere other than our bedrooms. That makes it ten times worse as it is," Colton said.

"And we've got each other's numbers now, so if anything, we can text if we need to talk to meet somewhere," Alexandria said.

"Yeah," Colton said. "I hate to go behind Mark's back like this, but I don't want to make him think that I'm taking you from him. He really likes you."

"And I really like him," Alexandria said. "I'm not used to the feelings that he gives me, but I know that I'm really starting to like him."

"You can tell when you see the two of you together," Colton said. "You both seem happier since you've been spending time together."

"He makes me happy," Alexandria said. A blush was over her cheeks, and she was avoiding Colton's eyes. She looked at the clock and saw it was one thirty. "I gotta go. Thanks for the talk, Colton. I'll talk to you at dinner."

"See you," Colton said. They both walked out of her room, and she started running down the hallway. He shook his head when she turned back around, realizing she had forgotten her purse. She could be an airhead sometimes, but she was a sweet girl.

*****

Mark was finally done with his shift. He was glad that he had taken up the extra shifts lately. He had wanted to get something for Alexandria but was also trying to pay bills and help Elizabeth and Duncan. He looked at his phone and saw he had a voice mail. Usually people didn't leave voice mails on his phone. Then again, usually only Colton or Elizabeth called him. And even that was rare. He started grinning when he realized that it was Alexandria, who was calling him about an interview.

"I knew she could do it," Mark said. He looked at the time and saw that it was close to three. He didn't want to take the chance of her being in the interview still. He would just wait until they were both home to ask her about it.

He walked slowly back to the house, enjoying watching people. He was surprised when he was walking and heard a familiar voice shouting his name. He turned and saw Alexandria jogging toward him.

"Did you just get out your interview?" Mark asked as she fell into step beside him.

"Yeah," Alexandria said. "I think it went really well. Did you just get out of work?"

"Yeah," Mark said. "It was an easy day. I just cashed people out, sometimes helped elderly take their bags to their cars. I had lots of old ladies compliment me on my strength though."

Alexandria laughed. "You do seem pretty strong. I haven't seen it in full force yet though."

Mark shocked Alexandria, though, by picking her up and twirling her. She laughed and held on to him tightly. He put her down on the ground gently, and she was grinning.

"Did that prove my strength?" Mark asked.

"Yes, it did," Alexandria said. "My day is much better now."

"I'm glad," Mark said. "Do you think you have your passion back?"

"Not for dance," Alexandria said, shaking her head. "Becky just really annoyed me with that. It just feels like she's telling me I have to be perfect, and I can't handle perfection."

"Yeah, no one is perfect," Mark said. "But at least you may have another job already."

"Yeah, I'm very grateful for that," Alexandria said. "I'm just glad that Becky gave me the day off so that I had the real option of doing all this."

"Yeah, that's for sure," Mark said. "So are you heading back to the house?"

"Yeah," Alexandria said. "I was surprised to see you though. I didn't think you would be close to being done at work."

"Well, I took on an extra shift today so I got out earlier than usual," Mark said.

"Oh, that must be nice," Alexandria said.

"Yeah, I didn't do too much, but I get paid enough money to help pay for the things I need to pay for," Mark said, shrugging. "And it works as a job until I get a business position."

"That is very true."

"Did you tell Carlee yet that you might not be working at the dance studio?"

"Yeah, she seemed to take it well. She didn't seem to say much to me about it."

"I'm sure she understands the pressure that Becky puts on you and her dancers."

"Well, she has Becky as an instructor."

"Then she definitely understands."

Alexandria just smiled at Mark and was slightly surprised when he entwined their fingers together. She squeezed his hand, reassuring him that it was all right. They made small talk as they walked back to the house, hand in hand still. They didn't let go until Mark opened the door for Alexandria. They both went to their bedrooms to change and then met everyone downstairs in the living room.

"We have to go to child services and make sure that all the paperwork is complete and correct. Dinner is just going to be a fix-your-own type deal. You guys can all do whatever you want to do tonight. I'm not sure when we're going to be done because we're going to visit Anna too," Elizabeth said.

"All right," they all said.

Chapter Seventeen

They just sat and watched television. Elizabeth and Duncan left a short while later, and then Collin said he had soccer practice, Carlee had dance class, and then Jessica had cheerleading practice. It was nearing dinnertime, and Alexandria's stomach growled, causing both men to actually smile at her.

"Do you guys want to go out to dinner?" Mark suggested.

"We better go before we can't hear the television over her stomach," Colton said.

Alexandria rolled her eyes. "Where do you guys want to go?"

"Lady's choice is what I say," Mark said, shrugging.

"Depends on what she chooses," Colton said.

"Can we go back to that diner, Mark?" Alexandria offered.

"As long as none of Joseph's friends are gonna be there," Mark said. "Did I tell you what happened, Colton?"

"No," Colton said. He didn't add that Alexandria had already told him.

"When we went on our date, we went to a little diner around here, and one of Joseph's friends, who actually helped him one night, showed up. I nearly punched him. He made some comment to Lexi, and I shot right up and grabbed his shirt. I think the entire restaurant went silent," Mark explained.

"Yeah, I bet that would get to you with how much you care about her," Colton said, "Come on, let's go there before I starve to death."

"Just let me grab my purse," Alexandria said.

"It's my treat tonight, Lexi," Mark said.

"Mark, you don't have to," Alexandria said.

"I want to though," Mark said, smiling.

"Thanks," Alexandria said. She didn't really want to argue with him after she may be out of a job this week, and she wasn't sure if she had another one lined up yet or not.

"Of course," Mark said.

They headed to the restaurant and made small talk most of the time. Alexandria wanted to ask Colton how Anna had been but didn't dare. She partly didn't want to know the truth as to how Anna was doing.

They were disrupted from talking as Colton's cell phone went off. He checked the number and didn't recognize it but answered anyways, having an odd feeling. Alexandria had a weird feeling in her gut when Colton answered. "Hello, this is Colton."

"Hi, Colton. It's Sarah from the St. Joseph's Hospital." Alexandria saw Colton tense and immediately knew it was something with Anna. She put her hand on Mark's, hoping it would comfort her. "I've tried calling various numbers that were left with us, but no one's answering."

"Well, we're all out of the house and Elizabeth and Duncan had to go somewhere," Colton said. "Will you tell me what's going on?"

"Anna is awake," Sarah said. Colton visibly relaxed, and the two looked at him in confusion.

"You're not kidding, right?" Colton said.

"Not at all, Colton. She keeps asking for you and a Lexi girl," Sarah said.

"We'll be right over," Colton said and then hung up. "We have to go to the hospital."

"What's going on, Colton?" Alexandria asked.

"She's awake," Colton said, smiling at the pair.

Mark grabbed his wallet and put down enough money for the food and everything, and the three were out of the door. Mark handed Colton the keys, not even thinking about it. While Colton drove, Mark tried to get ahold of Elizabeth and Duncan, but neither answered their phones, and so he left a message on their answering machines.

When they got to the hospital, Colton was practically running down the hallway.

"Colton, stop running! You're gonna get kicked out!" Alexandria shouted.

"Not when Anna's asking for me!" Colton called back.

Alexandria just shook her head. She was glad that Colton seemed happier now that she was awake. Alexandria took Mark's hand before she entered the room, not sure if she would be able to handle it.

But the wires were all disconnected from Anna. She looked healthy finally; her skin was no longer sickly pale, her eyes were shining brightly, and she had a smile on her face. The only thing that was throwing Alexandria off was the bandage on her head.

"Hey, you guys," Anna said.

Colton immediately leaned down and hugged her tightly. Mark was next, and then Alexandria held her tightly and sat down on the bed while the men sat down in the chairs.

"How are you feeling?" Alexandria asked.

"Better than I have in a long time," Anna said. "I actually was able to get up and move around by myself although the nurses kept watching me. And I have been able to keep down foods and stuff so far."

"That's great," Colton said.

"It's so good to see you up again, Anna," Mark said.

"You didn't visit me that much, Mark," Anna commented.

"Honestly, I knew if I came in here I wouldn't be able to handle it," Mark said. "I couldn't handle seeing you with all the wires and stuff. And I had to work a lot."

"It's okay," Anna said, smiling. "You're here now, and that's what matters."

"Did you hear everything that was said?" Colton said. He had revealed secrets to Anna about Alexandria and his past because he didn't think that she could hear him. He wasn't sure how he would handle it if Anna had actually heard everything that he had told her.

"Yeah, but I don't remember everything right now," Anna said. "So, Lexi, are you and Mark together?"

"Just dating right now," Alexandria said.

"Okay," Anna said. "Where are Elizabeth and Duncan?"

"They're running some errands. We called them and the hospital called. They should be here soon," Mark said. He wasn't sure if Anna knew about the adoptions and if it included her.

"Oh, hello, everyone," Dr. Reinhold said as he entered the room. He seemed shocked to see the three of them there. "Are Elizabeth and Duncan on their way?"

"We don't know. They were running some errands and didn't answer their phones. The nurses have tried them, and I've tried them as well," Mark said. Alexandria couldn't help but notice the business style in his tone and knew he would be a good business person.

"Okay, do you think they should be here soon?" Dr. Reinhold questioned.

"Yes, they said after they were running their errands, they would be visiting," Mark said.

"Well, it seems they may just get a surprise then," Dr. Reinhold said with a smile. "Everything went well. She's up and moving and doing everything by herself although we would prefer for her to have the nurses help her." Anna started grinning at this statement. "And she's holding down her food so far, which we're happy about. The surgery seems to have gone perfectly. We'd like to keep her overnight though, just to make sure."

"Understandable," Alexandria said. "Although we would all love to have her back at the house instead."

"I don't blame you. She's a wonderful girl," Dr. Reinhold said. Anna seemed closed in as Alexandria watched her as he said that.

"What have you done to her?" Alexandria said, glaring at the man.

"Only what doctors are supposed to do, ma'am," Dr. Reinhold said. Alexandria looked over to Anna, who shook her head.

"Anna, do you know what my adoptive parents did to me?" Alexandria asked. Anna shook her head. "They used to abuse me terribly. Joseph used to do really bad things to me. And if this doctor did really bad things to you, then you can tell me, okay? It's safe."

"He tried to," Anna said softly. Colton and Mark were both up so fast Alexandria and Anna didn't know what was going on.

"I suggest you leave her alone from now on, Dr. Reinhold," Colton said coldly. "I will not have a problem punching you."

"And neither will I," Mark said.

"Boys, enough," Alexandria said, stepping in between the two and the doctor. "We'll get kicked out if you guys do that. If it turns out to be correct, then we're going to sue him and take away his medical license. If not, then his reputation will be damaged enough to make him at least lose his job here."

"What is going on here?" Elizabeth said, walking over with Duncan.

"We'll explain later," Colton said. "I just want this doctor away from Anna right now."

"I just need to explain what is going on to Elizabeth and Duncan," Dr. Reinhold said.

"As long as you weren't withholding any information from us, we can tell them what happened," Mark said.

"I will leave then," Dr. Reinhold said. He shut the hospital door behind him.

Alexandria clenched her fists tightly. She wished that she had been able to know that he was going to do that to Anna. She wished that she had had friends like Colton and Mark before that could stop Joseph from doing it to her. She felt memories of not being strong enough to fight for her own self coming into her head. She felt a tear roll down her face and Mark wrapped his arms around her tightly.

"She's okay," Mark whispered in her ear.

"What happened?" Elizabeth asked.

"Well, Anna's awake!" Alexandria said with a smile, pushing the pain and the memories away. "Dr. Reinhold said that the surgery seemed to have gone perfectly. She's been up and moving around and doing everything by herself and she's keeping her food down. They want to keep her overnight though, just to make sure."

"What happened with Dr. Reinhold? Why did the three of you look like you were going to kill him?" Duncan said.

"He had tried to abuse her the same way I had been abused," Alexandria said.

"I'm not letting that happen to another one of my baby girls," Duncan said.

Alexandria smiled.

"That's why the two boys threatened to punch him, and I said that we can just sue him and threaten to take away his medical license," Alexandria said.

Elizabeth laughed. "We will talk to Dr. Rizzoli and to the lawyer tomorrow."

"I'm going to the nurse's station and request that there always be a nurse in with the doctor at all times," Mark said. He released Alexandria and then left the room.

"So how are you feeling, sweetheart?" Elizabeth asked.

"I feel great," Anna said, grinning. "I just want to go home right now."

"And we want you home," Duncan said. "But we have to make sure that everything is okay. We'll be sure to get you home early tomorrow. And we have some big news for you."

"What's that?" Anna asked.

"We're adopting everyone in the house," Elizabeth said.

"So Lexi is gonna be my sister then? And Colton will be my brother?" Anna inquired.

"Well, Lexi isn't going to be adopted," Duncan said. Alexandria couldn't help but feel slightly guilty when she heard the disappointment in his voice.

"Why not? Don't you love her too?" Anna asked.

"We do. We have always loved her. But she doesn't want to be adopted," Elizabeth said.

"It's not that I don't want to be adopted. It's just … It's complicated," Alexandria said.

"I can try to understand," Anna said. Alexandria smiled at Anna. The younger girl seemed so much older in just those few words.

"See, a sister and a brother can't love each other in any way other than family and get married and have a family together. And I really, really like Mark. I don't want to take the chance of not being able to be with Mark because I was adopted," Alexandria said. She heard Mark open the door at the beginning and knew she was beet red. She had just admitted her feelings about him to the entire room.

"That must have hurt a lot," Anna said.

Alexandria nodded. "It does."

Mark put a hand on her shoulder. "But you're always a Rhodes at heart."

"Very true," Duncan said.

Alexandria smiled. "Yes, I know."

"And who knows, if you two do marry, you'll be a Rhodes," Elizabeth said.

"Oh, you're changing your last name, Mark?" Alexandria said.

"We all are," Mark said. "It makes it less confusing, and none of us really wanted to keep our last names anyways."

"I had no reason," Colton said. "My family abandoned me. I didn't want that last name anymore anyways."

Anna yawned and Elizabeth smiled. "We should probably let you rest. We'll see you tomorrow though, okay, sweetie?"

"Okay," Anna said. Everyone hugged her tightly before leaving the hospital.

*****

"Is Anna really awake?" Carlee asked. She and Collin were waiting in the foyer when they all entered the house.

"Yeah, she's hopefully coming home tomorrow," Elizabeth said. "I have to go and call Dr. Rizzoli though."

"Why? Did something bad happen?" Collin asked.

"The doctor tried abusing her like I was abused," Alexandria stated.

"The nurses said they will make sure that he isn't in the room alone with Anna," Mark said. "The nurse I spoke to said that she had had a bad feeling the one day that it happened and came in when he had his hand a little too high for her liking. She tries to make sure the doctor is never alone with a woman."

"Thank goodness," Alexandria said. She felt a shiver run down her spine at the memory of what had happened to her as a teenager.

Mark put his arm around her, having a feeling about the movement she made. Alexandria smiled at him and put her arm around him. "We won't let that happen to her," he said.

"I know," Alexandria said. She was surprised when her cell phone went off and was even more shocked when it was the number from Lockwood Accounting.

"Hello, this is Alexandria."

"Hi, Alexandria. This is Carol from Lockwood Accounting again," the voice said.

"Hi, Carol," Alexandria said. She grabbed onto Mark's hand, hoping that it meant that she had gotten the job.

"Would you be available to come in tomorrow in order to fill out some paperwork? You got the job," Carol said.

Alexandria started grinning. "Yeah, I would love to! When do you want me to come in?"

"Would two be okay?" Carol suggested.

"Sure," Alexandria said. "I have to go right now though, but I definitely will see you at two tomorrow. Thanks so much!"

"No problem, Alexandria. See you at two," Carol said, and they hung up.

Alexandria squealed and jumped up and hugged Mark tightly. "I got the job!"

"That's fantastic!" Mark said happily.

"That's great, Lexi!" Duncan said. Alexandria went around and hugged everyone.

"So you really won't be working at the dance studio, huh?" Carlee said.

"No," Alexandria said. "But I may take classes there. I'm not sure though. It depends on how difficult this job is and how the pay is and everything. I am going there in the morning and tell her that I'm not going to be able to work for her any longer."

"Yeah, I don't blame you. She's really hard on her people," Carlee said.

"I have to get new clothes," Alexandria realized. "I have, like, no dress pants. I have plenty of dress shirts that work with jeans, but I only have like one or two pairs of dress pants."

"We'll go tomorrow after you talk to Becky," Elizabeth said.

"All right, thanks," Alexandria said.

"Of course," Elizabeth said, smiling.

"Come on, let's go watch some television," Duncan suggested.

They all nodded and headed into the living room.

Chapter Eighteen

Alexandria woke up the next morning and changed into a pair of yoga pants and a loose T-shirt. She grabbed her dance bag and headed to the studio, not really wanting to arouse suspicion from anyone that normally saw her.

"Hi, Alexandria," Angela said.

"Hi, Angela. Is Becky in her office?" Alexandria inquired.

"Yes, you can go right in," Angela said.

"Thanks," Alexandria said. She knocked on the door before entering the room. "Hi, Becky."

"Hi, Alexandria. So did you get your passion back?" Becky said.

"Well, I needed to talk to you about that. I don't think that this job is fit for me. I just cannot handle all of it, honestly," Alexandria said.

"What can't you handle? You seemed to be fine last week," Becky said.

"I have a lot of emotional problems due to my past, and so there are days where I lose my passion a lot," Alexandria said. "And sometimes they happen frequently, and sometimes they only happen every few months. But usually, they last longer than a week."

"I understand," Becky said. "It was nice to know you though. I'll definitely put in a recommendation for you when you look for another job. I will give Carlee your paycheck on Thursday when we have class."

"All right, thank you," Alexandria said. She smiled at Becky and then left. She saw Angela give her a strange look, but she ignored it. She just wanted to be able to relax for once. Her entire life she had felt like she was running around, always looking for a job and always doing something. She just wanted to relax. These last couple of days off had been really nice. She pulled her phone out as she was walking home and texted Colton: "Can we talk tonight?"

She took a long walk, just wandering around. She was grateful that no one talked to her or anything. She was enjoying her time relaxing. She got a text from Colton later on: "Yeah, I'll text you around midnight to make sure you're still awake."

"Hopefully, I will be. I'm exhausted. Physically and mentally."

"Yeah, I know what you mean."

She didn't bother replying as she was almost at the house. She didn't bother eating and just went right up into her room. Now that she realized that she wouldn't be able to relax for a long time, she was back to being depressed. And the fact that she had just given up a great job helped also.

Alexandria was just lying on her bed when there was a small knock on her bedroom door that was opened. She looked up and saw Mark standing there in the doorway. "Hey, Mark."

"Hey, Lexi," Mark said. "Is it okay if I come in?"

"Yeah," Alexandria said. She closed her laptop and moved over. He sat down on the bed beside her. "What's up?"

"Nothing really. I was just wondering how you were doing," Mark said.

"I'm doing okay," Alexandria said, shrugging. "I don't know. It's just that the depression has started to get ahold of me a lot lately. It just feels like no matter what I do, it's not going away."

"I'm sorry," Mark said. "I would suggest dancing, but obviously that isn't working for you since you quit your job. Is there anything that I can do to help you?"

"No, I think a lot of it is that I need to actually go and see a therapist about all this," Alexandria said. "But I don't really want to because then I have to explain all that happened in my past and everything. I really have no idea what to do about it either. We will just have to see how long this lasts."

"Well, no matter what happens, we're all right behind you. We all care and love you," Mark said. He then started blushing.

Alexandria paused. "Mark, I'm still working on things. I really like you, I do. I'm just not ready to say that I love you."

"I understand. You've had a rough life," Mark said. "I didn't even necessarily mean to say that, but it just came out."

"I understand," Alexandria said, smiling. "Is Anna home yet?"

"She's supposed to be coming home soon," Mark said. "Elizabeth and Duncan just left to go to the hospital."

"All right," Alexandria said. "I'm so glad that she's coming home."

"Me too," Mark agreed.

They were quiet for a moment, and then Alexandria heard the front door open. She jumped up and smiled at Mark. "I just heard the front door open. Let's go see if Anna is home!"

"All right," Mark said. He was glad that Alexandria always seemed happier when Anna was around. He knew that although Anna thought that Alexandria could help them, it was mainly Anna that had helped all of them.

Mark took Alexandria's hand as they headed out of the room, and Alexandria smiled at him. Colton came out of his room and nodded to the two.

"Do you think she's home?" Alexandria asked, looking to Colton.

"I think so. Elizabeth called me to tell me that they were on their way home," Colton said.

"Oh, okay," Alexandria said.

"Oh, you are home. I wasn't sure if you were going to be home or not," Elizabeth said when Alexandria entered the foyer with the rest of them. "Duncan is helping Anna out of the car now."

"Does he need help?" Colton asked.

"I've got her," Duncan said, entering the foyer with Anna, who was walking slowly with Duncan's arms around her.

"Hey, sweetheart," Alexandria said with a smile. She knelt and hugged Anna tightly. "It's so good to have you home."

"It's good to be home finally. I hate hospitals," Anna said.

"Me too," Alexandria said. She released the younger woman and stood back. Although Anna looked much better, Alexandria's heart always broke when she saw her struggling. She almost couldn't stand the slow walk that Anna now had. When she first met her, she had been so strong, so lively. And now, it felt like she was nothing almost.

"I have to go," Alexandria said and started out the door. Mark and Colton looked to each other and then to Elizabeth and Duncan.

"Are any one of you going after her?" Anna said, looking at the adults as they just stood there. "I would, but I'm a little weak right now."

"I'll go," Mark said, starting toward the door.

"Mark, do you mind if I do actually? I promise, I'm not going to get her too annoyed," Colton offered. Mark looked at him and nodded. Elizabeth and Duncan looked at the two in confusion, surprised at this suggestion and the acceptance by Mark.

"Hey, Lexi!" Colton called. He had looked either way and saw Alexandria walking quickly through the crowd. Alexandria didn't stop moving swiftly. He sighed and started maneuvering through the crowds as well. "Lexi!" He was shouting as he continued to push his way through the unusual high crowd.

Finally, he caught up to her at the corner and grabbed her hand gently. "Hey, come on, let's go to the park," he said into her ear. He didn't release her hand.

Alexandria shook her head though and started leading him toward the opposite direction of the park. He was confused but followed her nonetheless, still holding on to her hand as they walked. They were silent the entire time until they arrived at an abandoned house that had a huge tree in the backyard. She went around the back and opened the back door, which squeaked in protest.

"What are you doing, Lexi?" Colton said. He was enjoying calling her Lexi rather than Alexandria. It felt nice on his lips.

"I used to come here when I was younger. No one knew about this place. It is said to be haunted," Alexandria said. "I discovered this place when I was about eight, when I was running around with some of the older children from the house. And then I was able to find my way after I was adopted. I used to come here a lot. I'm surprised that it's you and not Mark."

"He was going to come, but I asked if I could come instead," Colton said. "I wanted to talk to you anyways."

"About what?" Alexandria said.

Colton shook his head. He wanted to worry about Alexandria before admitting his own problems. "You're the one that ran off from us all."

"I just wish that Anna could be healed," Alexandria said. "I hate that she has to go through so much suffering. I wish I knew why she has to go through it."

"I was thinking about that and praying actually," Colton admitted after a moment. "I think that God has put her through this to make all of us realize just how much she means to us and how important life is. I don't think she's going through it for her to realize something. I think she's going through it for all of us to realize things."

"You're probably right. I've realized now just how much Elizabeth and Duncan mean to me. And how important life and family are," Alexandria said. "I just wish that she wasn't the one that had to go through it. She's so young."

"I know. I think the same thing every day," Colton said. "But we just go through it and deal with it. It's hard, yes, but we're all dealing with it together."

"Yeah, I know," Alexandria said. She led him through the abandoned house, which had dust covering everything. There was a small table in the living room. It was the only thing left in the entire house. Alexandria sat down on the floor and ran her hand across the wooden table, moving the dust around. "This table is where I used to write down my dances when I was younger. It's the only thing left in this entire house that's not connected to something."

"That's kind of strange that they would leave just a table," Colton said.

"There was a family murder in this house. The coffee table was where the family was sitting when they were killed," Alexandria said. "The rest of the family didn't want to take anything else, but they didn't want to sell it either because it was haunted. It's been abandoned ever since."

"That's really creepy," Colton said.

"I know. It used to freak me out. When I first heard the story, I was really freaked out and didn't come here for a long time. And then I returned and I had a calming feeling wash over me. I knew God was watching over me and wouldn't let anything harm me."

"You seem to feel that a lot, don't you?"

Alexandria nodded. "God has always watched over me, whether I realized it or not."

"That is a good thing though."

"So what was it you wanted to tell me, Colton?"

Colton took the envelope that was in his back pocket out and handed it to Alexandria. "I got this in the mail today."

The envelope had no return address, and the writing that said Colton's name was very neat. She opened it after looking at him for approval:

Dear Colton,

I have sat down and written this letter for years and years. I have never found the right words to explain to you what we did, why we did it. I wish I could hold you and tell you that there was a good reason why we left you. But there is never a good explanation for why you give up your child.

I was so proud of you. You were my baby boy, my firstborn child. It hurt so much to let you go. Every day, I regret that decision. We had to do it for your own protection though.

Your father had gotten mixed into some bad things. They said that they would come after you if they found you. We were put into protective custody and given new identities. They said that the entire family had died so that the gang would stop coming after you. There were always cops around you, just to make sure. The gang was a pretty bad gang. I have never forgiven your father for getting us mixed up in this. I have always wanted a divorce, but I have stayed with him for your sister.

You're wondering why you're getting this letter. It's because it's finally over. As I write this, I don't know if that means that the gang is gone or if that means that we're gone. But either way, remember that we always have loved you. We gave you to Elizabeth and Duncan to protect you. I hope that they have continued to raise you well, and that you have found happiness in this world after what we have done to you.

We're not asking for your forgiveness. We're just asking for your understanding. We had to do it to protect you.

I love you Colton, and I think of you every moment of every day.

Mama

Alexandria looked up to Colton. "Wow."

"I know," Colton said. "I don't know what to do or what to think."

"I don't know either," Alexandria said. "Have you told anyone else about this?"

"No, and please don't tell them. I usually check the mail, so no one would wonder what it was," Colton said. They were quiet for a second. "For the last few years, I have grown to hate my family. I thought that they were terrible people for abandoning me and leaving me with these people. I have hated them ever since they dropped me off. And now … I find out that they were doing it to protect me … I don't know what to think anymore."

"I don't know either," Alexandria said. "I can only tell you that it's probably a good thing that they left you. And it's like your mom said, you don't have to forgive them. You just have to understand what they're going through. What would you have done if you were the one in their situation? If you had a child that was possibly going to be taken hostage, would you leave it in order to protect it?"

"Not if I was going to be put into protection services! If I was, then I would take them with me! I wouldn't leave them to fend for themselves!" Colton exclaimed.

"You don't know that they knew that they were going there! They could have found out right after they left you. And who knows, maybe protective services thought that it was best for you to be left at the house," Alexandria said. "They said that there were cops watching you. You're safe, Colton, and that's all that matters to them and all that should matter to you!"

"Essentially your parents did the same to you! How can you forgive them?"

"I have never said that I forgive them. I am working on getting to the point that I can forgive them for that. Right now, I'm only working on my relationship with my father, who hasn't contacted me since the party. And I'm not really trying to forgive them. I'm trying to understand them. Understanding and forgiving are two completely different things."

"I don't understand the difference, I guess."

"Understanding why they did it means that you would do something similar or that you comprehend the reasons for why they did it. Forgiving means that you understand it and that you still love or care for them. It means that you still want to be around them."

"I don't know if I can do either one for my parents."

"I'm not going to say that you have to, but you should. If you ever want to try and have a family and have people around you that care about you, then you should."

"I don't want children, remember?"

"Don't you one day want to come home to a woman who doesn't care about anything other than you? Don't you want to know what being loved truly means?"

"Not really."

"I guess it's another one of those things that we will never understand about each other. I want one day to be able to put my past behind me and love someone unconditionally. I want to be able to call a place my home and to have my children grow up in it. I want to take the opportunities that my biological parents never did. I want to see my children graduate, to go to prom, and to get married. I don't want to lose those memories. I want my children to have a better life than I did."

"Then go talk to Mark about that. Mark will do anything to please you."

"I know. But you understand me better than he does. You understand the pain that I feel every time I see a happy family together."

Colton was quiet for a moment. He had lied to Alexandria. He did want to come home one day to a woman who loved him and wanted to make him happy. He wanted that person to be her. He wanted to smack himself after that thought. Alexandria was Mark's, not his. He couldn't take this girl from Mark. He needed to distance himself from Alexandria, but he didn't want to. He didn't want to lose the one person in the house that actually fully understood him.

"We should probably go," Colton said. "Mark was worried about you. And you have to get ready for your conversation with Lockwood Accounting."

"Yeah, I know," Alexandria said, sighing. She closed her eyes and then touched the table one more time. She felt a calming sensation going through her entire body and then she left with Colton.

Chapter Nineteen

When they got back to the house, everyone was gone. Alexandria walked to the living room but saw no one there. She wrapped her arms around herself and then headed upstairs. The house suddenly seemed so quiet, so lonely. She didn't like it. She longed for the noise, the happiness that was there when she was young, and she could hear it now in the evenings.

"Mark's in the library if you're looking for him," Carlee said, appearing in the hallway. "Are you okay, Lexi?"

"I'll be fine," Alexandria said, smiling. "Thanks, Carlee."

"No problem," Carlee said. "And my door is open if you ever want to talk. Or dance together."

"Thanks," Alexandria said. She stared at the ground, and her body just automatically took her to the library. She saw Mark sitting at one of the desks facing the window, staring outside, completely ignoring the book in front of him. She sat down beside him silently.

"I'm scared," she stated after a moment. "And ... I'm losing my faith."

"Do you want to go to church on Sunday together?" Mark asked.

"I would like that," Alexandria said. "Do you mind if we go to the church I usually go to?"

"Not at all," Mark said. "I've been looking for a good church to go to."

"Thanks," Alexandria said.

"What are you scared of?" Mark asked.

"It's kind of hard to explain. I'm scared for Anna. I'm scared about losing my faith. My faith and the thought that one day I could live with Elizabeth and Duncan again were all that have kept me alive. I'm afraid that because I'm losing my faith, I'm going back to the way I was before. I'm afraid that I'm going to do the one thing that I've always been afraid of."

"What have you always been afraid of?"

"Taking my own life. For years, the thought of suicide has haunted me. For years, I have wondered if anyone would notice if I was gone. I always have known that no one would notice. But I knew that Elizabeth and Duncan would be ashamed of me for giving up. And so I kept going. I kept dealing with the pain, dealing with the torture. I never could do it. I'm afraid that I'm going to be so depressed that I'm going to forget all that since I lost my faith. I'm scared that I'm going to get so depressed that I don't know who I am anymore."

Mark wrapped his arms around her, and she started crying. "I'm not going to let that happen, Lexi. I'm not going to. I'm going to stand beside you no matter what. As long as you want me to stand beside you, I'm going to be there. I'm not going to leave you."

That statement made Alexandria cry even more. She had never had someone who was so willing to stand beside her. She had never been so cared for and so loved by anyone.

"Why, Mark? Why do you want to stand beside me?" Alexandria asked when she was finally done crying.

"Because I see the pain that you're feeling and because I love you. I'm not saying that you have to love me back or anything, but I do love you, Lexi. I want you to be happy, and that's all that matters to me. I would do anything to make you happy. That's really all that matters to me. I hate seeing you cry. I hate seeing you so broken up over anything. I just want to see that smile that I saw when you were dancing the first day you were here. I want to see you always smiling and always happy," Mark said as he brushed the tears off her face. "I love you, Lexi."

"I'm still trying to learn how to love, Mark," Alexandria said.

"I know," Mark said. "And even if one day you discover that you don't love me either, that's okay. But it's the only way that I can explain how I feel and why I want to be beside you all the time. I love you."

Alexandria smiled. "I've never had someone care about me so much as to always be beside me. I've never actually felt the love that you're showing me."

"That smile is what I want to see," Mark said. "That smile that you just gave me is all that I care about. That's what I want to see every day."

Alexandria smiled again, and the library door opened, and Elizabeth walked over to them. "Lexi, can I talk to you privately?"

"Sure," Alexandria said. She was slightly confused but followed Elizabeth nonetheless to the drawing room. "What's up, Elizabeth?"

"So Anna needs new guardians because of the adoption, someone that can take care of her if something happens to Duncan and me. We figured that you're the one that makes the most sense because you know her and she seems to love you more than anyone. Her other guardian is going to be Colton," Elizabeth said. "And we also have done our wills. We want to let you know what we have done."

"I would love to be the guardian to Anna," Alexandria said, happy about this fact. She was okay with the fact that it was Colton that was going to be the other guardian. It didn't mean that much if they were her guardians, besides the fact that one of them would have to take care of her if something happened. "What did you put in your will?"

"We put everything in your name," Elizabeth said. Alexandria fell into the chair.

"What?" Alexandria said. She was shocked and confused at this fact. Why would they leave everything to *her*?

"We put everything—this house, the things in this house—in your name," Elizabeth said.

"What about everyone else?" Alexandria said. "They make more sense."

"They're getting some of the money. The money is going to be split seven ways, but everything else is going to be completely in your name. You will be in charge of this house and in charge of the people in it," Elizabeth said.

Alexandria couldn't believe it. It felt like a huge weight was lifted from her shoulders and yet was put on her shoulders at the same time. She had to make sure that this was still the House of Hope after Elizabeth and Duncan died. She didn't know if she could do it.

"I don't know if I can keep this house as the House of Hope," Alexandria said.

"We know that you can. Did you see the hope that you brought to everyone? You have no idea how much you have helped us all," Elizabeth said. "And we know that we gave you the right foundations. From now on, you will be helping us with finances and things, when you have the time of course."

"I can't believe this," Alexandria said. "I mean, I will try my best. Thank you."

"Of course, Lexi," Elizabeth said, "You're our daughter, whether it's legal or not."

"Thank you," Alexandria said. She went and hugged Elizabeth tightly.

"We love you, Lexi," Elizabeth said.

"I love you two too," Alexandria said with a smile. "Is it okay if I tell people?"

"Everyone here already knows. We told them at breakfast when you were at the dance studio last week," Elizabeth said.

"Oh, okay," Alexandria said.

"How are things with Mark and Colton?" Elizabeth asked.

"Things with Mark are going well. He told me today that he loves me, but I'm not sure because I've never felt this way before. And Colton and I haven't killed each other, so that's always a good thing," Alexandria said.

"Yes, that is," Elizabeth said, laughing. "All right, you can go with Mark if you want."

"Thanks, Elizabeth," Alexandria said.

"Of course," Elizabeth said, and Alexandria went back to the library.

"May I ask what that was about?" Mark asked as Alexandria took her seat beside him.

"They told me about the will and being Anna's guardian," Alexandria said.

"It took them long enough to make those two final with you," Mark said. "They told us like last Wednesday. I've been dying to tell you, hoping it would make you happy."

"It does, but it scares me also," Alexandria admitted. "I have a huge fear of not living up to people's expectations. With being given the house and all these other responsibilities, I feel like I have also been given a lot of expectations. And I hate not living up to expectations, especially when it is Elizabeth and Duncan. They're the two people that I have always tried to please and tried to live up to their expectations."

"I am sure that you will be able to meet their expectations," Mark said. "You're a better person than you think you are."

"I feel like arguing with you would be pointless," Alexandria said, smiling at Mark.

"Because it is," Mark said, returning her smile. "So are you feeling better now?"

"Yeah, thanks, Mark," Alexandria said. "What were you doing here in the library, not even paying attention to your book?"

"I was thinking," Mark said.

"Do you want to share?" Alexandria said.

"I was thinking about you and Anna. I was trying to find a way to help you get through this time. And I was trying to find something to do for Anna to make her feel better possibly," Mark said. "And I've been trying to get out of the grocery store or at least become a manager, and so I've been trying to find places to apply to."

Alexandria kissed Mark's forehead. "Thanks for caring about me so much. You're very sweet, Mark."

"And then Colton's been gone all day. We were supposed to spar earlier, but he disappeared before you got back," Mark said.

"I have no idea," Alexandria lied. She knew that Colton had disappeared because of the letter from his mother, but he couldn't tell Mark that. It was Colton's problem, not hers.

"Where did you run off to, anyways?" Mark asked.

"An old abandoned house I used to go to a lot when I was younger. It was the one place I found a safe place at," Alexandria said. "It's got a creepy past to it, but somehow it soothes me."

"At least you have one place that soothes you," Mark said.

"Very true," Alexandria said, smiling. "If you wanted to spar with Colton, I'm pretty sure he's probably in his room right now. That's where he said he was going at least."

"He's probably either there or in the gym. I haven't heard a car leave, and he hates to walk anywhere," Mark said. Alexandria laughed.

"Do you mind if I watch you two spar?" Alexandria asked.

"Not at all," Mark said. They stood up and walked out of the library and saw Colton standing in the hallway. "Oh hey, I was just gonna look for you."

"Are you ready to spar?" Colton questioned.

"Do you mind if Lexi watches us?" Mark asked.

Colton looked at Alexandria for a moment, trying to decide if he wanted to have her watch them or not. "I guess not."

"I won't watch if you don't want me to," Alexandria said.

"It's fine," Colton said. "I have to go change though. You probably should too, Mark."

"All right, we can all just meet at the gym," Mark said.

"Sounds good," Alexandria said. She looked at the clock. She decided to do her makeup while the men were changing. It was already eleven thirty in the morning when she was done. She went down to the gym and saw Colton watching her as she came down the stairs. She started blushing and went down the stairs slowly.

"You didn't fall this time," Colton observed with a smirk.

"Shut up," Alexandria said, glaring at him.

"Do I want to know?" Mark asked as he entered the gym.

"Well, when I was younger, I fell down the stairs here. And then when Colton had to show me around when I first got here, I came down here where he was and then I fell down the last couple of stairs," Alexandria said.

Mark smiled. "I used to fall down these when they were doing construction."

"Let's just spar," Colton said.

The two men started at each other. Alexandria was transfixed by it. It made her think of a dance. A dance of a man and a woman fighting, and she instantly wanted to start dancing.

"You two guys are the best! I just got a great idea!" Alexandria said. The two boys froze and stared at her in confusion. "I just thought of a dance, a duet."

"Okay?" the two men said in confusion.

"Can I have one of you two dance with me? I need a guy to dance this with me," Alexandria said.

"I'm terrible at dancing, if you didn't notice on Friday," Mark said.

"Do you mind, Colton?" Alexandria said.

"As long as no one else finds this out," Colton said. "And you're going to have to deal with the fact that I haven't had formal training."

"That's fine," Alexandria said.

She instantly began creating a dance that involved Colton and Alexandria swinging at each other, fake fighting. It went into a dance about love and about overcoming differences. Mark was staring at them in shock. They had worked perfectly together. Colton had never missed a beat of what Alexandria told him. Mark was in shock of their togetherness.

"Wow," Mark said, "that was beautiful."

"Thanks," Alexandria said. "I definitely had not expected that to come in my head all of a sudden. I have to go and write it down now."

"All right," Colton said. Alexandria smiled and then ran up the stairs. The two boys heard a thud and looked up to see Alexandria sprawled on the top of the stairs. She started laughing and looked down at the two boys.

"You jinxed me, Colton!" Alexandria shouted through laughter.

Both boys started laughing. Alexandria stood up, gave them a thumbs-up, and walked back up the stairs.

"She's a character, that's for sure," Colton said, shaking his head. "So do you want to spar some more?"

"Sure," Mark said. They started sparring, and Mark couldn't help but talk. "You and Lexi dance really well together. You were perfect together."

"She's an excellent dancer," Colton said.

"You seem really tense right now," Mark stated.

"I got a letter today," Colton said. Mark looked at him in confusion, wondering why he would mention this fact so randomly. "It was from my mother."

"What?" Mark said, frozen.

Colton put his arms to his side and stared at the wall behind Mark. "My mother had written a letter to me. It wasn't dated. She said that she regretted leaving me all the time. She told me what had happened. She said that my father had gotten into some bad stuff and that the people he got mixed up with would come after me if they found me. I was taken here, and they were put into protective custody and were given completely new identities. They lied about my family dying so that the gang wouldn't come after me. Apparently, cops were always around me. She said that I was finally getting the letter because apparently, it was over. She didn't know whether that meant that the gang is gone or if they're gone. They did it to protect me. She said they don't want my forgiveness. They want my understanding."

"Wow," Mark said, his eyes widening. "Are you okay?"

"I'm doing better now," Colton said.

"That's good. What made you do better? I figured you would be screaming or something," Mark said.

"I talked to Alexandria when she ran off," Colton admitted. He knew he couldn't hide this from his best friend, and he didn't really want to.

"I didn't know you two were close," Mark said.

"We're not. She just is the only one who understands what it's like to be abandoned. Everyone else here has only lost their family due to death, not because they physically gave us up," Colton said. "I knew she would be able to help me work through some things in my head because of the abandonment."

"Yeah, that's true," Mark said. He was honestly partly hurt that Colton was trusting Alexandria more than Colton was trusting him, but he understood what he meant. Colton needed to talk to someone about things like that.

Colton knew that Mark was slightly hurt because of him going to Alexandria instead of him first. But Mark could never understand the pain of being abandoned.

"Colton," Mark said. He was tired of losing any girl that he wanted to Colton. He hadn't felt this way about another girl since his ex-girlfriend who cheated on him. Colton looked at Mark. "Please don't take her from me. I love her."

"I know. I can see it in your eyes. I don't want to take her from you," Colton said. "Remember, she's not supposed to get in between us and our friendship."

"I know," Mark said. "Are we done sparring now?"

"Yeah," Colton said. The two went upstairs and Colton text Alexandria: "We need to talk later. Let's meet at the library at midnight."

Chapter Twenty

Alexandria was surprised when her phone went off. It was the text from Colton. She simply replied okay, and then Mark appeared in her doorway. "Hey, Mark."

"Hey, Lexi," Mark said, smiling. He sat down on her bed, and she suddenly got a bad feeling about him being there. "Why didn't you tell me Colton had talked to you about the letter from his mother that he just got?"

"I didn't tell you because it's not my problem to tell. It's Colton's problem, and it's so personal I didn't think he would want me to tell anyone. And I told him I wouldn't anyways," Alexandria explained.

"Do you two talk like that often?" Mark asked.

"Kind of. We've found that although we annoy each other to no end, we also understand each other better than most people do," Alexandria said. She was choosing her words carefully and hoping she didn't upset Mark. She didn't want to lose him and the relationship that they had at the moment. "We've only had a couple conversations like that."

Mark was quiet, and Alexandria feared that she had upset him or made him angry. She couldn't really read what it was his eyes were telling her. Sometimes, it really bothered her that she couldn't read him and what his emotions were about things.

"You're the first girl in three years that I have felt this way for and actually thought I had a chance with. As much as Colton has been a brother to me, he has hurt me a lot. It hurts to really like a girl and then discover that she's really only interested in your best friend. I'm tired of it. I'm so tired of it, Lexi."

"I'm not interested in Colton as anything more than friends, Mark. He doesn't make me happy like you do. He annoys me to no end. You know what to do to make me smile when I'm in a bad mood. You just ... You make me happy. Colton doesn't do that to me. And for once in my life, I want to be happy."

Mark stared at her for a moment and then stood up and walked over to her. He looked in her eyes and then hugged her tightly. "I'll try to make you happy."

"And so will I," Alexandria said. They stood there for a moment until Alexandria got out of his hold. "So what should I wear to this meeting?"

"The Lockwoods are pretty laid-back, but it doesn't hurt to dress up and give a good impression," Mark said. "I'm terrible at picking out clothes though."

Alexandria laughed. "Thanks. I'm thinking a pair of black pants and a light blue dress shirt."

"That would look good," Mark said.

"All right, I'm going to change quickly," Alexandria said. She grabbed her clothes and then went to the bathroom quickly.

*****

Alexandria was nearly falling asleep at midnight, but she woke up a little more when Colton texted her that he was in the library. She went to the bathroom and then to the library where she found Colton in the same spot Mark had been in earlier that day.

"Hey," Alexandria said, sitting beside him. "I told Mark about us having talks like this."

"Why?" Colton questioned. He was amazed that Alexandria had said something. They had said that they were never going to tell anyone else.

"He asked. I couldn't lie to him. He's scared, Colton." Alexandria's eyes drifted to the window. In the night, the lights around the city were lit up, and it amazed Alexandria how big the city really was that they were in.

"Yeah, he told me," Colton said.

"He told me everything. He was so shaken up." Alexandria hugged herself and looked at the desk. "I felt so terrible when he was telling me everything."

"What else did you tell him?" Colton asked.

"He asked me if we talked like this often, and I told him that we kind of do and that even though we drive each other crazy, we understand each other," she said.

"Why did you feel so terrible then?" Colton wondered.

"He told me that I was the first girl in three years that he thought he had a chance with. He told me that he's tired of you taking girls from him," Alexandria said.

"Then why do you feel bad?" Colton asked. He could never fully understand the woman in front of him and her constant changing. When she had first arrived, she had seemed so cold and distant, and yet here she was, feeling guilty about something she had done and pouring her heart out to him.

"Because I'm making him not trust me," Alexandria said.

"Because of me, not you," Colton said, running a hand through his black hair.

"Look, things are fine, so it doesn't matter," Alexandria said, not wanting to argue with him over her feelings. "How are you doing with your parents?"

"I'm working on it. I wish there was a way to tell if it's true or not," Colton said.

"Yeah," Alexandria said. "Maybe you could do some research and find some things out."

"I don't know if I really want to know," Colton said. "Part of me wants to leave it and forget I even got that letter."

"But you may never move on. You may never be able to get closure if you don't do that," Alexandria said.

"Yeah, that's what I'm debating. I don't want this over my head. I want to be able to actually have a good life," Colton said.

"Then I would say research the accident first and then talk to the detective on the case and go from there," Alexandria said.

"Yeah," Colton said. "So how are you holding up?"

"I'm doing okay, especially now that I've got the job with the Lockwoods. But I'm scared too," Alexandria said.

"Why?"

"Elizabeth and Duncan gave me everything in the house. And so I feel like I have a lot of new expectations. I'm grateful that they did it, but it still makes me feel this way. And I'm scared since they made us Anna's guardians."

"Yeah, that freaks me out too. I would be a terrible father to her. I have no idea how to take care of her. I'm not worried about you. I'm positive you would make a great mother to her. But I'm not going to be able to take care of her."

"I actually think you would be a great father to her. You take good care of her now."

"Well, hopefully, we won't have to worry about it for a very long time."

"Hopefully," Alexandria yawned. "I need to go sleep. Thanks for the talk, Colton."

"Thanks, Lexi," Colton said. Alexandria smiled at him and then left the room.

Colton stayed in the library. He felt so guilty. Alexandria felt terrible for something that was his fault; he was the one that always took the girls from Mark and made him question all girls. He sighed; there was nothing they could do about it now.

*****

Alexandria was surprised when there was a knock on her door the next morning. She looked at her clock and saw it was eight. If she hadn't wanted to wake up early, she would have been mad at the person at waking her up early.

She was happy, though, when she opened the door and it was Mark. "Hey, Mark."

"Hey, did I wake you?" Mark asked.

"It's okay. I wanted to wake up early anyways," Alexandria said.

"Oh, sorry," Mark said.

"Don't worry about it, Mark. So what's up?" Alexandria asked.

"I just wanted to say that I'm sorry for last night and that I didn't mean to upset you," Mark said.

"It's fine, Mark. Don't worry about it. I don't blame you for being upset and everything about it all," Alexandria said.

"I have something for you," Mark said, pulling a small box out of his pocket. "This was my mother's. She used to wear it every day. My father gave it to her on their twenty-fifth wedding anniversary."

He handed the small box to Alexandria, and she opened it and was amazed at the beauty. It was a gold chain with a small garnet pendant with small diamonds around it. "It's beautiful. Are you sure, though, that you want me to have it?"

"Yeah, you really do mean a lot to me, and I want you to have it," Mark said. "I know if my family was still here, they would have loved you."

"I'm glad. Will you help me put this on?" Alexandria asked, taking the necklace out of the box.

"Sure," Mark said. He took the necklace from her and put it around her neck. She smiled and turned around to face him.

"Thanks, Mark," Alexandria said. She leaned up and kissed Mark's cheek.

Mark smiled at her. "I have to go to work, but I wanted to give you that before I left."

"All right, thanks," Alexandria said. "I'll see you later."

"See you later," Mark said. He kissed her cheek and then left. She stayed in her doorway for a moment before going into her room fully. She changed into a pair of blue jeans and a V-neck T-shirt, which showed off the new necklace.

"That's a nice necklace," Anna said when everyone was at breakfast. She was sitting right beside Alexandria since Mark was gone to work.

"Thanks. Mark gave it to me," Alexandria said. She involuntarily touched the necklace.

"Wait, what?" Colton said. He had been in the middle of eating a forkful of scrambled eggs, and the fork was currently frozen in front of his mouth as he stared at the necklace Alexandria had around her neck.

"Mark gave me this. It was his mother's," Alexandria stated. "Why?"

"Did he tell you anything else about that?" Colton asked.

"Just that his father gave it to her on their twenty-fifth anniversary," Alexandria answered. She was confused by what he had said.

"That necklace is the only thing he has left of his mother, besides her engagement ring and wedding band," Colton stated.

"I … I didn't realize," Alexandria said. The necklace suddenly gave much more meaning to her and felt like a weight around her neck.

"He probably didn't want you to know," Colton said. "So don't tell him I said anything unless he asks."

"All right," Alexandria said.

"You two just had a conversation without arguing," Jessica observed, her eyes wide.

"Mark your calendar," Colton said. "It's probably the only time it will ever happen."

Carlee looked at the two. She knew they didn't always fight, but she knew there had to be a reason why they wanted people to think they hated each other. She wouldn't question it though. It was their decision to fool everyone.

Alexandria's phone went off. It was a text message from Mark: "Did Colton tell you about the necklace? My ears were ringing lol."

Alexandria looked up at Colton. "Mark just text me and asked if you told me about the necklace because his ears were ringing."

Colton laughed. "Of course. Tell him I did. There's no point in lying to him." He was tired of hiding things from his best friend about the woman in front of him.

"All right," Alexandria said. She pulled open a reply: "Yeah, he did. Can we talk about it later?"

"If you want, I still want you to have it."

Alexandria smiled at his answer and replied: "I'm glad :) I just want to hear it from you instead of Colton."

"All right. I will come find you after I'm done at work."

"Sounds good :)."

Alexandria wasn't surprised that he didn't reply. They all made small talk as they finished eating breakfast.

Chapter Twenty-One

Alexandria had been in the ballroom, dancing, when Mark got home from work. He stood in the doorway, just watching her dance, until she was done with the dance, and he stepped onto the dance floor.

"That was beautiful," Mark complimented.

"Thanks," Alexandria said smiling. She paused her music and walked over to him. "I would hug you, but I'm pretty sweaty right now from that dance."

"That's fine. I'm sweaty from work too," Mark said. He still leaned down and kissed her cheek. "It felt too weird to not do something."

"That's okay. I like it when you do that," Alexandria said.

"I'm glad," Mark said. They were quiet for a moment. "I had wondered if Colton would tell you after I gave it to you. But I still want you to have it."

"I promise I will take good care of it," Alexandria said. "Will you tell me what happened and about your family?"

"I had a pretty normal family life. I had two younger siblings—one brother and one sister. My brother was three years younger than me, and my sister was five years younger. I had been spending the night at my friend's house. They were on their way to pick me up. There was a drunk driver. He ran the red light and hit the passenger's side, and it pushed them into a telephone pole on the driver's side and they were sent into a ditch. They were all already dead when the ambulance and cops got there."

Alexandria took his hand in hers. She could see the pain in his eyes at the memory of his family. Mark squeezed her hand and smiled at her slightly. "I didn't see the accident, but sometimes I feel like I

190

did. The image will get into my head, and it's so vivid that I feel like it's the same day. I have nightmares about it sometimes."

"I'm so sorry," Alexandria said.

"Thanks. I've gotten over it for the most part. I just try to make them proud now," Mark said.

"I'm sure you do," Alexandria said.

"Thanks," Mark said. "But other than the accident, I've had a pretty normal life."

"That can be good though," Alexandria said.

"Yeah," Mark said, smiling.

"I'm going to shower if you don't mind," Alexandria said after a moment of silence.

"Yeah, I have to go shower too," Mark said.

"All right," Alexandria said.

Alexandria went to bed early that night, knowing she was going to work at eight that morning. She put her hair into a half ponytail and then changed into a tight black skirt and a pink dress shirt. She was doing her makeup when there was a knock on her door. She quickly opened her door and smiled when she saw Mark. "Good morning, Mark."

"Good morning," Mark said. He was blushing as he held up a brown paper bag. "Um, I made you lunch. I wasn't sure how long of a lunch break you would get, so I made it simple. I hope you'll like it."

"Aw, thanks, Mark," Alexandria said. She leaned up and kissed his cheek. "Can you put it on my bed? I'm doing my makeup right now and don't really want to get it everywhere."

"Sure," Mark said. "Are you nervous?"

"Yeah, but I keep reminding myself that today is just training," Alexandria said.

"I'm sure you'll be fine," Mark said. "I have to get ready for work, so I'll see you later."

"Thanks, Mark," Alexandria said. Mark smiled at her and then left the room. She was putting her shoes on when there was another knock. She opened it and Anna was standing there. She looked tired but stronger than Alexandria had seen her since she first arrived. "Hey, sweetheart."

"Did Mark give you your lunch?" Anna asked.

"Yeah," Alexandria said, smiling. "It was very sweet of him."

"I made you the dessert with him," Anna said.

"Aw, thanks," Alexandria said.

"Good luck today at work," Anna said.

"Thanks, Anna," Alexandria said. She hugged Anna, who then walked away. Alexandria smiled, grabbed her lunch and purse, and then left the house.

Alexandria sat in the break room at lunch. It was noon, and she was on a half-hour break. She had learned a lot, and her notebook was already half filled with notes. She got her lunch out of the fridge and smiled as she opened it: a ham and cheese sandwich, an apple, a can of soda, a small bag of pretzels, and two chocolate chip cookies. She grabbed her phone and called Mark.

"Hey, Lexi, how's it going?" he answered.

"Good. I get a half-hour-long break, and I just opened my lunch. Thanks so much," Alexandria said.

"Do you like it?" Mark asked.

"I love it. You got everything perfect," Alexandria said.

"I'm glad. I've seen what you've ate lately, but I did ask Elizabeth and Duncan for some help," Mark said.

"It's very sweet of you," Alexandria said. "How was work?"

"Good, boring," Mark answered.

"That's good. I better go and eat this. Thanks for everything, Mark," Alexandria said.

"No problem," Mark said, and they hung up.

"Hi," a thirty-year-old woman said, entering the break room. She had straight dirty-blond hair and hazel eyes. She was in a pair of black dress pants and a purple dress shirt.

"Hi," Alexandria said. "I'm Alexandria. I just started training here today."

"I'm Kimberly," the woman said. "Do you mind if I join you?"

"Not at all," Alexandria said. "Sorry, I had to call my ... friend, who made my lunch."

"That's sweet," Kimberly said. "My husband used to do that when we first were married and then we had a daughter and now he doesn't do it that often."

"Yeah, I'm not really sure what this guy is to me. We're friends, but we've been on a date and he's told me that he loves me. I'm not used to feeling this way about people, so I'm still working on some feelings and stuff," Alexandria explained.

"Yeah, that's always a tricky situation. I didn't really trust men for a long time until my husband came around and just stayed with me until I finally started to trust him," Kimberly said. "You're lucky to have someone who cares enough about you to do all that for you though."

"Yeah, I know. I'm actually very lucky," Alexandria said. "I just feel bad for not being able to repay the feelings yet because I'm still learning."

"Everything takes time, and you just have to learn to accept it," Kimberly advised.

"Yeah, I'm starting to learn that," Alexandria said, smiling. "Thanks, Kimberly."

"Anytime," Kimberly said, smiling.

*****

Mark was at the mall with Colton. Mark had wanted to get something for Alexandria, knowing the tough time that she was going through. Mark knew that Colton was getting closer to Alexandria, and so he wanted his advice.

"Do you know what kind of books Lexi reads?" Mark asked as they passed a bookstore.

"No idea," Colton said. "Honestly, I really don't know that much about her, Mark. The only thing I really know is how she feels toward things."

"Maybe I'll get her a devotional or something. She keeps saying that she needs some help with her faith," Mark said.

"Mark, just pick her something up and let's get the hell out of here. I hate malls," Colton grumbled, throwing his hands in his pockets.

Mark rolled his eyes. "Fine, fine. I'll get her a devotional and then we'll go home."

"Thanks," Colton said. Honestly, it was making him sick. He wished that he was the one buying these things for Alexandria instead of Mark. He normally didn't mind malls, but he hated that he was being dragged all around with Mark, trying to find something for Alexandria.

*****

Alexandria entered the house after she was done at work. It was getting close to five, so she knew everyone was probably in the living room watching television until dinner was ready.

"Hey, sweetheart," Elizabeth said as Alexandria entered the living room. "How was your first day of work?"

"It was great. It was mainly just training and learning their programing, so it wasn't too difficult. I'm really looking forward to it," Alexandria said.

"That's great," Mark said, smiling.

"I'm going to change into more comfortable clothes and go on my computer until it's dinnertime," Alexandria said.

"All right," Duncan said.

Alexandria went upstairs and pulled her e-mail up as she changed into a pair of yoga pants and a loose shirt. She was surprised when she had an e-mail from a fellow member of her church, a guy named David.

"Hey, Alexandria. Just wanted to see how you were doing. Haven't seen you in church in a while. Hope to see you on Sunday."

Alexandria smiled and pulled open a reply: "Hey, David! Yeah, it's been crazy. Joseph and Marie died, and so I moved back in with the people that I had lived with when I was younger. So I've been adjusting to that, and there's a little girl here that reminds me a lot of myself when I was younger and she's been really ill lately (pray for her please. Her name is Anna), and so I've been helping take care of her. I'm planning on being there on Sunday though and bringing my friend with me. How have you been lately?"

Alexandria was surprised that he had replied rather quickly.

"Prayer sent up for her and for you. I'm sorry for your loss, but at least you're at a happier place now. At least I hope it's a happier place. That's great that you'll be back! There's a small group for young adults starting soon if you two want to join. Eric has been wondering if you would want to join. I've been doing pretty well lately, still looking for a job right now though."

Alexandria immediately replied, glad to be speaking to someone from her old church.

"There are some job openings here in Denver. I applied to like ten different places before getting a job with an accounting firm here. It might be a little bit of a travel, but hey, it's money, right? Thanks for the prayers. It always means a lot. I can't wait to go back to church on Sunday. I didn't realize how much I missed it until I started to lose my faith recently."

"Yeah, it's always tough when that happens. But you're a strong woman, you'll pull through. And we're all here for you, Alexandria. Well, I gotta go. See you on Sunday!"

Alexandria smiled, and there was a knock on her door. She looked at the time and saw it was five thirty. She jumped up and opened her door to see Colton standing there.

"Sorry, I was talking to a guy from my church," Alexandria said.

"You're fine," Colton said. "Are you and Mark going on Sunday?"

"Yeah," Alexandria said.

As Alexandria and Colton walked into the foyer on their way to the living room, there was a knock on the door. The two looked to each other, and Colton opened the door. A thirty-seven-year-old woman that was about five feet, ten inches and had long brown hair stood there. She looked just like Alexandria, but older.

"Hi … my name is Alice Herondale. Is there an Alexandria living here?" the woman asked softly.

Alexandria stepped forward and then sucked in a breath. It was her mother standing there. "What … what are you doing here?"

"Alexandria," the woman said and stepped forward.

"Explain," Colton said, stepping in between the two women. He glared at the older woman in front of him. He could tell just by the way that Alexandria was acting that this was not a good friend that was visiting.

"Colton, Lexi, what's going on?" Duncan asked when he appeared.

Alexandria looked at Duncan, and his heart sank. He had never seen such pain and hurt in her eyes, except for when she had seen her father yet again. He knew there were only two people that could bring her barriers down that badly—her biological parents.

"My … mother is here," Alexandria said softly.

Chapter Twenty-Two

Colton whipped around and stared at Alexandria and then looked back at the woman in front of them. There was then no denying that there was a familial resemblance between the two women.

"What are you doing here?" he questioned. He was getting angry just seeing the woman standing in front of him, knowing what he had done to Alexandria.

"I wish to speak to my daughter," Alice said. "And you have no right to tell me that I cannot." She didn't understand what this man thought that he could do or say to her.

"Yes, I know," Colton said. "Alexandria, do you want to speak with your mother?"

"Please, Alexandria, let me explain," Alice said. She was pleading with her daughter; she wanted to talk about everything that had been going on.

"I've heard from Dr. Rizzoli and my father this week, why should I listen to you as well?" Alexandria spat.

"Your ... your father spoke to you?" Alice questioned.

"Yes. He came to the benefit and told me that it was *your* entire fault that I was left to live my entire life so far, wondering why I wasn't good enough for you two," Alexandria said. She stepped forward and made Colton stand back with the rest of the family that now stood behind them. Mark took a step forward, ready to help if Alexandria needed him to. Colton realized this and stepped back. It was not his job to protect Alexandria.

"I was sixteen, Alexandria!" Alice defended. "You will never understand the pain that I felt when I had to give you up!"

"I know that," Alexandria said. "I understand that I will never fully understand why you did what you did after giving birth to me."

"Then why are you so angry?" Alice said.

"The pains of being abandoned will never leave me," Alexandria said softly. "Especially because I was not only abandoned once by you but twice."

"If I could go back and take that day back, I would," Alice admitted. "I would take both of those days back and hold you in my arms for eternity. Your father told me about your past. If I had known that you weren't in a good home, I would have taken you away from them. I would have protected you from everything."

"Why not protect me before it even happened? Why not come and reclaim me as your daughter when you were done with school and married?" Alexandria retorted.

"We still weren't ready," Alice said. "And I wasn't ready to face you. I knew I couldn't be able to look in your eyes and not feel the guilt of abandoning you. I wouldn't be able to not burst into tears at the sight of you. It hurts me now to see you."

"Then why not save us both the pain and just not come?" Alexandria asked.

"Because you need to know that I'm dying," Alice said.

"Dr. Rizzoli already told me that you had some health problems," Alexandria said.

"What?" Elizabeth questioned from behind them.

"I have a heart condition. I'm going to die soon. I came to tell Alexandria myself that I was dying and to tell her that she is getting half of my money when I die and that she is the beneficiary on my life insurance," Alice said.

"What?" Alexandria said, staring at her biological mother in shock.

"Whether I raised you or not, you are still my firstborn daughter. And when we took the life insurance out, we figured that you deserved something after we abandoned you. We took it out right after we met you when you were in high school," Alice explained. "The life insurance is worth $100,000."

Alexandria fell to the ground. She could not believe what Alice was telling her. "You can't be serious. You just … you can't be serious. You have three other children that need you and need that money."

"They have their father who is making enough money to take care of them," Alice said.

"My father just lost his job," Alexandria said, shaking her head. "I won't take the money. No matter what, I'm not going to take the money."

"Why not?" Alice asked.

"Because it's pity money. It's money that isn't rightfully mine. I didn't know you! I don't know you at all! You're a complete stranger to me! Both you and my father are complete strangers to me! I shouldn't get anything from you two!" Alexandria said.

"It's $100,000 though, Alexandria," Alice said.

"I don't care. Money doesn't matter to me. What matters to me is that I have a family now. I've learned to work for my money, and I'm not about to just let you change that. I'm going to work to get where I want, not just be given the position or the money," Alexandria said. "So you can go and take your money and keep it and give it to the children that you love and have cared for their entire lives."

"Alexandria—" Alice debated.

"Get out," Alexandria demanded. "Get out of here now."

"Please—" Alice pleaded.

"Alice, I believe it's best if you leave," Elizabeth instructed.

"Alexandria … I always have and always will love you," Alice said. "I wish I had seen you grow up. I wish I had gotten to help you. Let me help you now."

"I won't accept it. I've gotten by the last twenty-one years without your help. I think I can last the rest of my life," Alexandria said. She looked up and glared at Alice.

"Of course," Alice said. She nodded and then walked away.

The group was silent for a moment, and Anna walked over to Alexandria and put her hand on her shoulder.

"Lexi," Anna said.

Alexandria looked at the girl beside her and broke. She couldn't handle all this happening any longer. She needed time to just stop. She wanted to go back to when she was young and was oblivious to her biological parents and when she was like little Anna and just running around, playing with the other children.

Mark bent down and hugged Alexandria while Anna rubbed her back. Everyone stood back in wonder, not sure what to say or do. When she finally stopped crying, she hugged Anna tightly.

"I'm sorry," Alexandria said.

"Why? You didn't do anything wrong," Anna said.

"Why didn't you take the money?" Colton asked.

Alexandria brushed the tears away before speaking. "I don't care about the money. I just care that I have everyone here with me. I've worked my butt off since I was old enough to work. I'm not about to change that because my mother feels guilty for leaving me."

Mark rubbed her back and she turned to him. "Let's get something to eat right now. I have something for you later."

Alexandria smiled. She kissed his cheek. "Thank you."

"Anything for you," Mark said, smiling.

They warmed up the food quickly before eating as it had gotten cold because of them leaving the dining room and taking a few minutes. When they were done, Mark went to his room quickly to grab his gift for Alexandria before joining everyone downstairs in the living room.

"It's not wrapped, but here," Mark said, handing her the devotional he had picked up for her earlier that day.

Alexandria smiled. "Thanks. I really need this. I need to get back into the swing of things and get closer to God again."

"Do you want to go to church with us on Sunday?" Elizabeth wondered.

"I'm going to the church I went to at home. There are a few friends that I've met there that I want to see again. Do you want to come, Mark?" Alexandria said, looking at Mark.

"Sure," Mark said, smiling.

"Sounds good," Alexandria said.

*****

Alexandria lay in bed late that night, not able to sleep. All that she could think about was that her mother had come here. She couldn't believe that she had actually turned down all the money that her mother was willing to give her.

There was a knock on her door. She was confused and opened it to see Colton standing there. She was shocked that he had two tall glasses milk and cookies in his hands. She smiled at him and let him enter.

"How did you know I was awake?" Alexandria asked as they sat on his bed.

"I just assumed with what had happened earlier today," Colton said, shrugging. He took a cookie and dunked it in the milk. Alexandria smiled.

"Thanks, Colton. I needed this," Alexandria said.

"Of course," Colton said. "So did you want to talk about your mother, or do you want to completely ignore the topic?"

"I would like to completely ignore the topic, but it's all I can think about. I can't believe that my parents wanted me to have all that money," Alexandria said.

"They feel bad for leaving you. I would take the money if I were you," Colton said.

"It just doesn't seem right to me to take it. They didn't want anything to do with me throughout my entire life. It just … It doesn't feel right," Alexandria said, shaking her head before eating another cookie.

"Yeah, I guess I get what you mean. I just can see what all you could do with that money for yourself and for all the rest of us," Colton said.

"Yeah, I know. But I just don't like taking money from people," Alexandria said. "I'd rather just earn the money myself and feel like I deserve the money."

"Yeah," Colton said, nodding. "So do you and Mark have a date coming up soon?"

"I don't know actually," Alexandria said. "As far as I know, we don't. But I'm not completely positive on that."

"I see," Colton said.

"So have any girls caught your eye lately?" Alexandria asked.

Of course she had to ask the one question Colton hoped that neither she nor Mark would ever ask him.

"There's one girl that I'm starting to like, but she's taken."

"Do I know her?"

Yes. "No."

"Do you want to tell me about her?"

No, because that means describing you. "There isn't much to say about her. She can be a little rough sometimes, but that's what makes me like her. And she has this side to her that it seems she doesn't really show anyone else but me. She's had a rough past too, and that's another reason why I like her. She isn't ashamed to admit that she's had a rough past, and she's learning how to be a better person because of it. She's just all around a great girl."

"She sounds really nice," Alexandria said.

Colton couldn't believe that he had just admitted all that to Alexandria. He hated himself for it. He wasn't supposed to be in love with her. He wasn't supposed to take her from Mark. He had promised Mark that he wouldn't do that.

"I need to go to bed," Colton said, standing up. "You can keep the cookies in here and eat some if you want. I just really need to sleep."

"All right," Alexandria said. Colton left the room. Alexandria couldn't help but wonder why he so suddenly needed to leave. Something had briefly passed through his eyes, and she hadn't been able to read it. She wasn't even sure if she wanted to know.

She ate a few more cookies and then lay down in bed, quickly falling asleep.

*****

Colton lay in bed for a long time that night. He needed to get away from Alexandria for a while. He couldn't continue to feel this way about her. He needed to get away from everything for a short while. He didn't know what to do. His door opened and he saw Anna enter his bedroom. He looked at her in confusion.

"Can I lie with you tonight, Colton? It's lonely in my room," Anna said. He nodded and helped her up onto his bed.

"What's up, Anna?" Colton asked.

"I couldn't sleep. I kept having nightmares," Anna said.

"What are your nightmares about?" Colton asked.

"I keep dreaming that Lexi's been kidnapped and that you're trying to save her," Anna said.

"Well, Alexandria is safe and sound in her own room," Colton said.

"Are you sure? Can we go check?" Anna asked.

"Sure, sweetheart," Colton said. They got out of bed, and he held her hand as they headed to Alexandria's bedroom. He opened the door slightly, and Anna looked in to see Alexandria sleeping soundly on her bed. "See, she's okay."

"Okay," Anna said. "I'm still scared though, Colton. I don't wanna lose her."

"I think she's going to be fine," Colton said as they walked back to his bedroom. "Alexandria is a strong woman. She can take a lot more than we think she can."

Colton sat down on his bed, and Anna jumped up beside him. "Colton, usually when I have dreams like this, they come true. It scares me so badly."

"I know, sweetheart," Colton said. It was the truth. Many times, when she had dreams like this, it did come true. He hoped desperately that she was wrong this time though. "But I'm sure that Alexandria will be okay. And she's got my number and Mark's number, just in case something does happens."

"All right," Anna said. Colton lay back down and Anna curled up into his arm. Anna was asleep within seconds.

Colton's door opened again, and he was surprised to see Alexandria opening the door.

"I thought it was you two that I saw," Alexandria said softly and sat down in the chair that was closest to his side of the bed.

"Still couldn't sleep?" Colton whispered.

"I had fallen asleep, but then I got woken up and a little freaked out," Alexandria said.

"Yeah, sorry about that," Colton said.

"Why is Anna up? Is something wrong?" Alexandria asked.

"She had a nightmare about you being kidnapped and that I was trying to save you," Colton said. "That is why we came into your room. She had to make sure that you were okay."

"That makes sense," Alexandria said, nodding. "She looks so peaceful."

"Yeah, it's nice," Colton said, playing with Anna's hair.

"I'm going back to bed. Good night, Colton," Alexandria said.

"Good night, Lexi," Colton said. Alexandria left, and Colton lay there for a while, staring at the young girl in his arms that reminded him so much of his little sister, it scared him. After a while, he had finally fallen asleep.

Chapter Twenty-Three

Colton was checking the mail. Everyone was either at school, at work, or in the drawing room. He was surprised to see a letter addressed to him in the pile. The handwriting seemed vaguely familiar, but he wasn't entirely sure where he had seen it before.

> Dearest Colton,
>
> I'm so glad the letter got to you safely. I miss you so much, son. I'm sure that you are a strong man and that Elizabeth and Duncan are proud of you as am I. I want to see you again. It has been far too long. Please meet me on Sunday at five at night at Java Café downtown. I will explain everything to you.
>
> Love,
> Your mother

Colton froze in his spot. He didn't know what to do. All he could think was that he had to talk to Alexandria about this. He needed her help. He wasn't sure if he wanted to meet with his mother or not. He knew that even if he did, he would need someone with him.

He pulled his phone out and dialed Alexandria's phone number. He was surprised when she picked up.

"What's up, Colton? Is something wrong?" Colton could hear the worry in her voice and vaguely wondered if she was worried about him.

"I got a letter from my mom again. Can I meet you after work?" Colton questioned.

"Uh, yeah, if you want to come and pick me up, we can walk back together," Alexandria suggested. She was slightly confused about this suggestion but knew that since it involved his mother, he wanted to talk to her privately.

"Thanks, Lexi," Colton said. "I'll explain everything to you when I pick you up."

"All right, I'll say a quick prayer for you," Alexandria said.

"Thanks," Colton said. "I'll see you later."

"See you later," Alexandria said, and they hung up.

Colton stared at the letter for a minute until Elizabeth entered the foyer. "Is something the matter, Colton?"

"Uh, no, Elizabeth, I just heard from someone I haven't heard from in a while," Colton said, shaking his head.

"Oh, okay," Elizabeth said. "What else is in the mail?"

"Here is the stuff for you and Duncan. Alexandria is the only other one with some mail," Colton stated as he quickly flipped through the mail.

"Does it say who it's from?" Elizabeth asked.

"No," Colton said. But he had a feeling about that handwriting, and so he decided that he would bring it with him later when he met her after she was done at work.

*****

Alexandria was confused when Colton had called her. She had thankfully been on her lunch break, but she hadn't been expecting any phone calls or anything. She had a feeling about what it was that Colton wanted to talk about. She just hoped that she was wrong. Throughout the rest of the day, she was focusing on the job training and wondering about Colton's phone call. She was glad when Colton was standing there outside of her job.

"Hey," Alexandria said. "What's up, Colton?"

He handed the two letters to Alexandria. She opened the one from his mother first. "Are you going to meet her?"

"I don't know," Colton said and ran a hand through his hair. "I just don't know! I want all my questions to be answered. But then again, I don't know any questions to ask!"

Alexandria smiled. "I'm sure it's going to be fine. It's a public place, so it's not like anything could happen. And if you really want, I can come with you." She wasn't sure what suddenly possessed her to offer to go with him, except for the fact that she had been through a very similar situation while she was alone.

"I … I don't want to take you away from Mark," Colton said. He was probably worrying his friend already about how much he trusted Alexandria, and he didn't want to push the limit any more than he already had.

"Mark will understand," Alexandria said, shaking her head. "This is about you and your family. I'm sure he will understand."

"Thanks, Lexi," Colton said, smiling. "I really will need someone else there, especially someone who understands what I'm feeling."

"Of course," Alexandria said. She then opened the letter that had her name.

Dear Alexandria,

I'm sorry for not speaking to you again since the party. Things have just been difficult with having lost my job and then also with your mother being so sick. She told me that you denied her the money that we had set aside for you. Are you sure that's such a wise idea? I'm sure you need the money and that Elizabeth and Duncan could use the money.

I am writing to tell you that I have to go out of state for a while. I'm not sure how long I'll be gone. I'll let you know when I'm back though, I promise. Stay safe.

Love,
Your father

"Somehow, it doesn't hurt this time," Alexandria said.

"What do you mean?" Colton said. Alexandria handed him the letter to read. "Yeah, I see what you mean. I mean, it's not like he's abandoning you for good though. He's just going out of state for a while."

"Yeah, but it's like you and your parents. I just can't trust that he really is going to come back and contact me when he gets back," Alexandria said.

"Yeah, I know what you mean," Colton said.

They just made small talk as they headed back to the house. Colton saw Mark enter the foyer as they entered and gave them a confused look.

"I got a letter from my mom today, Mark." Colton was going to be honest with his friend. There had been far too many secrets between the three of them recently, and he was done with most of them. The only thing he wanted to keep secret were the feelings he was avoiding for Alexandria.

"About what?" Mark asked, walking over to his best friend.

"She wants to meet me Sunday at Java Café," Colton said. "And I'm going. She said that she'll explain everything to me then."

"And I said I would go with him, if you don't mind, Mark," Alexandria said. "I know … I know what it's like to have to face your biological parents after they've abandoned you. I wish I hadn't been alone when I had done it a few years ago."

"Um, that's fine, I guess," Mark said. "I'm just surprised your mother actually contacted you again, Colton."

"Me too," Colton said. "And honestly, I'm really nervous about this."

"I'm sure it's going to be fine, Colton," Alexandria reassured. "I'm going to change really quickly before dinner, and then I'll meet you guys there."

"All right," they said.

"I'm sorry for telling her first again Mark," Colton said.

"I understand," Mark said. "Just be careful. I have a strange feeling about this."

"Yeah, I know. I do too," Colton said.

Chapter Twenty-Four

It was already Sunday morning. Alexandria and Mark were in church when Alexandria saw her friend David standing there. She grabbed Mark's hand and quickly ran over to David.

"David!"

The twenty-five-year-old man with short blond hair and blue eyes started grinning before he even turned around to see Alexandria standing there. He immediately hugged Alexandria tightly. "Hey, Alexandria! It's been too long."

"Yeah, it has been, David," Alexandria said. She released him and then smiled at Mark. "David, this is my friend Mark. Mark, this is my friend David."

"It's a pleasure to meet you," Mark said, shaking David's hand.

"You too," David said. "So are you coming to youth group tonight?"

"I don't know if I'll be able to make it. I have to meet with someone at five," Alexandria said. "I'll definitely go next week though."

"That's fine," David said, smiling. "You know that you're always welcome here."

"Yeah, I know," Alexandria said. "Well, we should probably go and sit down. See you later!"

"See you later," David said, and the two entered the sanctuary.

The service had been exactly what Alexandria had needed. It was about dealing with the cards that you were dealt and that, no matter what, God was with you. It had her in tears by the end of the service. It made her realize that God had given her a terrible hand, and yet, she was strong enough with His help to get through it all. She was reminded that although she had been given a rough start to live, she was given multiple chances and she always stood back up, stronger than ever before.

Mark had been moved by the service as well, and although he tried not to cry, as soon as he saw Alexandria start to break down, he shed a couple of tears as well. When the service was over, she hugged the minister tightly, having missed the church greatly.

It was around noon when they returned, and everyone but Colton was watching television. When both Alexandria and Mark realized that, they looked at each other and headed down to the gym in the basement. There, Colton was hitting the punching bag rather hard.

"Hey, you wanna spar?" Mark suggested.

Colton punched the punching bags a few more times and then stood there for a minute.

"Yeah."

The two of them started fighting, and Alexandria just watched them, fascinated by the way they moved together. They must have trained together a lot since they both started going here. Their movements were in perfect sync together. Alexandria could see Colton visibly relaxing as they sparred, and it made her glad.

When they were done, Mark had Colton on the ground and was on top of him. Mark held his hand out for Colton, who took it. Mark regretted it though as soon as he saw the glint in Colton's eyes. Colton then proceeded to pull him down to the ground.

"Dammit! I should have seen that coming," Mark cursed as he sat up. Both men stood up and Colton surprised both Alexandria and Mark by hugging him. "Okay, did not expect that. Who are you, and what did you do with Colton?"

"Sorry, I just … really needed that spar," Colton said.

"I figured," Mark said.

"It always amazes me that you two can work in such harmony together," Alexandria stated. "The way you two spar … it really is like a dance."

"That's what happens when you spar together for years. You learn the way the other one moves," Mark said.

Colton looked at Alexandria and surprised them by hugging her. She fit like a glove in his arms, and she felt extremely comfortable. It felt amazing to her. Mark couldn't help but feel a tinge of jealousy when he realized how perfect they looked together. He knew it then even if the other two didn't. They were meant to be together, and he was going to lose her. The other two just had to figure it out first. And until then, he would enjoy his time with Alexandria.

"You should probably shower before we go to meet your mother," Alexandria said as they separated. "And shave."

Colton laughed. "All right, I think I'm going to the living room afterward."

"Okay," Alexandria said, and Colton walked away.

Mark smiled over at Alexandria, and she walked over and hugged him, feeling awkward for having hugged Colton right in front of him.

"So do you want to go out to eat soon?" she asked.

"Sure," Mark said. "Do you want to go out tomorrow?"

"Sounds good," Alexandria said. She leaned up and kissed his cheek. "I'm going to the living room. You probably should shower also."

"Yeah, I'm going to," Mark said. "And, Lexi?"

"Yeah?" she responded.

"Thanks for being there for Colton. It's good to know that he actually trusts someone other than me with his secrets even though it kinda hurts that it happens to be you," Mark said.

"Well, I don't feel anything other than friendship for him, so you don't have to worry about anything like that," Alexandria said, smiling.

"I know," Mark said. He knew the truth at least, whether she did or not.

They both went upstairs then, and while Mark headed to his bedroom, Alexandria headed to the living room where everyone else was. She sat in the couch beside Elizabeth, who smiled when she sat down. Colton and Mark entered the room a short while later, and Alexandria couldn't remember the last time she felt content like this.

They all just watched television and talked until it was about four thirty, and Alexandria could see Colton constantly looking at the clock. She smiled at this fact, finding it rather cute.

"Alexandria, do you think we should leave now?" Colton asked.

"Probably," Alexandria replied.

"Where are you two going together?" Jessica replied.

"To meet with my mother," Colton said.

"Wait, what?" Elizabeth questioned.

"My mother wrote to me. She wants to meet with me and explain why she did what she did. I am having Alexandria come with me because she knows what it feels like to be abandoned," Colton said.

"Just ... be careful," Duncan said.

"We will be," Alexandria said. Apparently, she wasn't the only one having the bad feeling about all this.

They got into the car, and Alexandria drove downtown, not quite wanting to trust Colton to drive to the café. It was a couple of minutes before five, and they walked up to the café. Alexandria took Colton's hand and squeezed it tightly before they opened the door. As soon as they entered the café, Colton froze. Although it had been a few years, he could recognize his mother instantly; she had the same eyes that he had; it was impossible to miss them. He felt a million emotions going through his mind—happiness, fear, and so many that he wasn't sure of.

"Is that her?" Alexandria asked, pointing. Colton nodded. "You have her eyes."

Colton nodded again, and they walked over. The woman stood up. "Colton."

"Hi, Mother," Colton said. "This is my friend, Alexandria. Lexi, this is my mom ... Nicole."

"Hello," Nicole said, smiling. "It's nice to meet you, Alexandria."

"It's nice to meet you too," Alexandria said. They sat down.

"So ... what's going on?" Colton asked. "Lexi knows my past, so it's fine to talk in front of her."

"I ... I had to give you up to save you. We didn't know that we were going to be put under witness protection until after we had left you with Elizabeth and Duncan. We weren't allowed to talk to you at all until we knew for sure that the gang was gone. If I had known we were going to be under witness protection, I would have kept you and brought you with us," Nicole explained.

Colton just nodded. He couldn't believe what was happening. His mother actually sat in front of him. "What about the rest of the family? Where are Dad and Britt?"

"Dad … had a heart attack a couple years ago and died," Nicole said. "Britt … ran off after your dad died."

"Why didn't you tell me my dad died?" Colton exclaimed. He felt like he had just gotten a punch in the gut. He really had lost his father.

"Witness protection, Colton. They can't say anything to any-one from their previous life," Alexandria stated, putting a hand on Colton's shoulder.

"Did you at least try to find Britt again?" Colton asked.

"I did for a long time," Nicole said. "But when people want to hide in witness protection … they get hidden."

"Wow," Colton said. He was amazed at all that his mother was telling him.

They sat there in awkward silence until they ordered their cof-fees. They made small talk while they drank their coffee. When they were done, Colton told his mother that he needed to think about things some more before she contacted him again. As they left, the bad feeling continued to get worse for Alexandria. As soon as they stepped out of the café, Alexandria felt someone grab her arm. She twisted, and the face she saw scared her. It was one of the drug dealers her parents had dealt with. She started to scream, but he put a cloth over her nose and mouth, and she immediately felt sleepy. Colton had been so focused on trying to figure out what to do with his mother, he hadn't noticed her struggle until he heard her start to scream.

"Lexi!" Colton screamed. The man threw her into a van in front of the store.

"If you want her safe, you won't follow us or call the police. We have your phone number. We'll call you in a short while," the man said before shutting the door and driving off quickly.

Chapter Twenty-Five

Colton couldn't believe what was happening. He pulled his phone out and dialed Mark's cell phone number.

"What's up? How did it go?" Mark asked. The bad feeling that he had was just getting worse and worse, and he hoped that it was wrong.

"Lexi was kidnapped," Colton stated. "I'm heading back now and will explain everything then. Make sure everyone is in the living room still."

He hung up his phone before Mark could even say anything in response. Colton ran to the car until he realized that he didn't have the keys. Alexandria had taken them with her. He cursed and then ran back to the house, hoping his phone wouldn't go off before he got back. He suddenly wished he had gotten the license plate number of the van before he had called Mark.

He finally got back to the house and immediately went to the living room where everyone anxiously stood.

"What happened?" Mark questioned. Colton could tell that he had been pacing the floor.

"I don't even know. We had just gotten done having coffee with my mother when we got outside, and I got so wrapped up in my own world that I forgot about Lexi, and all of a sudden, I heard her screaming and then saw this one guy throwing her in a van and he said not to follow them and that they have my phone number and will call me in a short while," Colton explained. His words were speeding up so that they could barely understand what he was saying. "I can't believe I didn't pay attention to Lexi! I should have known with this bad feeling! Dammit!" He punched the wall, and everyone stared at him in shock. He never got this angry in front of them. Mark knew he got this mad, but he kept it down in the gym.

"Colton, calm down," Elizabeth said, standing up. "We're going to get her back."

"I just … This is my entire fault … I should have been paying attention to her. I shouldn't have asked her to come with me," Colton said. He ran a hand through his hair, trying to figure things out.

Mark surprised them all by punching Colton in the stomach, causing him to fall to the ground, out of breath.

"Mark!" Elizabeth shouted, appalled at what her adopted son had just done.

"No, I needed that," Colton said, smirking up at Mark. "Thanks, Mark."

"Anytime," Mark said and helped Colton up with a smile.

"Care to explain why that just happened to the rest of us?" Jessica said. No one else understood how being punched had helped Colton.

"It snapped me back into my mode to try to figure out what to do," Colton said. "Elizabeth, you know some of the police, correct?"

"Yes," Elizabeth answered with a nod.

"All right, can you call them and have the police track the phone numbers that call me? You know my cell phone number for them to use," Colton asked. Elizabeth nodded and stepped out of the room. "I don't know if there's anything else we need to do until they call me."

"Probably not," Mark said.

Colton looked at Anna and saw the tears falling down her face. Colton kneeled and hugged her tightly. "It's not your fault, sweetheart."

"I had the dream though," Anna said.

"But that doesn't mean that it's your fault. You weren't there. There's nothing you could have done, Anna," Colton said and tilted her head up. "I need you to be strong for me, okay, Anna? If you're strong, Anna, then I can be that much stronger to help get Lexi back for us."

Anna nodded. "You're calling her Lexi."

Colton hadn't realized he was making that slip around everyone. "Everyone else is calling her that, so I guess it rubbed off."

"We all know that's not it, Colton," Jessica said.

"Yeah, honestly, we all see it. You're just stupid," Collin stated. He rolled his eyes at the older boy.

"Whatever," Colton said. He had a feeling about what they were talking about, but he hoped that he was wrong. He couldn't believe that they were mentioning this in front of Mark, knowing their relationship.

"All right, my friend Alana is going to look in to tracking your phone number, Colton," Elizabeth said, entering the room again. "She said to just hang tight and they'll have cops going around our area to make sure there's nothing strange going on."

"Okay," Duncan said.

Colton's phone went off, and everyone stared at him as he pulled it out of his pocket. An idea struck him as well as he saw that the phone number was a blocked number. "Hello."

"Hello, Colton, this is a friend of Alexandria's. Here is the deal. Tonight, you're going to meet us at her old house around ten. You will knock three times on the front door. You're going to be by yourself and have no cops following you. You're going to have a duffel bag full of $1,000 as well as some clothes for you and some clothes for Alexandria for up to three days," a voice said.

"Why?" Colton inquired.

"If you were smart, you wouldn't ask why. You would just do it," the voice said and hung up the phone.

Colton ran a hand through his hair and then put his phone in his pocket. He could feel everyone staring at him. "They said that I need to meet them at her old house around ten and that I'm going to have a duffel bag with $1,000, along with some clothes for both of us for up to three days."

"Why would they want that?" Carlee asked.

"I don't know," Colton said. "It's strange that they only want a small amount of money."

"Yeah, it is," Elizabeth said. "I'm going to call Alana and then tell her what you just said."

"They said no cops following me," Colton said. "Oh! And have them track Lexi's phone. It may still be on."

"All right," Elizabeth said.

"I need her old house's address," Colton said.

"I don't think she moved within the last ten years. I'll go and get you the address," Duncan said.

"Thanks," Colton said.

"Do you want one of us girls to go and get her clothes?" Carlee asked.

"I'll handle it," Mark said. "Come on, Colton, let's get the clothes."

"Right," Colton said. The two men walked up the stairs, and Colton sat on Alexandria's bed while Mark started going through her drawers. "Mark."

"I know, Colton," Mark stated. "I've known since you first lay eyes on her. It was even more obvious when you hugged her today after we sparred. You two fit perfectly together."

"Then ... why ...," Colton said, staring at Mark.

"Because I wanted to be happy as well," Mark replied, shrugging. "It was kind of selfish. I just ... I wanted some time with her in a romantic sense before you got to her."

"I guess I don't blame you," Colton said. "I honestly did not expect to fall for her. And then we started to have these late-night conversations about anything in the world, and we both revealed more about ourselves then we intended to. I just ... I couldn't help it."

"Neither one of us could," Mark said. "For once ... I'm not angry for you getting her. You two deserve each other. You were right when you said that you two understand each other better than anyone else can because you were both abandoned."

"I'm glad," Colton said.

"All right, here's three days of clothes and underwear for her," Mark said, putting them on the bed. "You're going to get her back, Colton."

"I'm gonna try at least," Colton said.

"Don't go in there with a try attitude. Go in there with a 'you will do it' attitude," Mark said. "It's the only way to get her back."

"Colton! Mark! Get back down here!" Elizabeth shouted. The two of them ran out of the bedroom and ran down the stairs to the living room where Elizabeth was.

"What's up?" Colton asked.

"All right, the cops tracked the phone number and Alexandria's phone. They're both in her old house right now. They are going to wait until you go in there, Colton, to make sure that they're actually there, and then while you're in there, they're going to come in and get you two out of there safely."

Colton nodded. "Okay. I'm going to pack my things though, just in case something happens with it."

"All right," Elizabeth said.

"Colton," Duncan said. Colton turned and Duncan handed him a stack of bills and a slip of paper with an address. "Here is the money for her. And here is the address."

"Thank you," Colton said.

Duncan surprised them all by hugging Colton tightly. "Bring her back to us, Colton."

"I will," Colton said. "Don't worry, I'm going to bring her back to us."

"We know. You wouldn't be able to live with yourself if you didn't," Jessica said.

"Yeah, you have to save her! It will be like those fairy-tale stories when the prince saves the princess and they end up together!" Carlee said.

"Is it really that obvious to all of you?" Colton asked.

"You should have seen your face when you got back," Collin said, shaking his head. "The only way a guy like you gets that look is if you're in love. And you've actually been happy lately. You never were happy until she got here."

"All right," Colton said, sighing. "I'm heading upstairs now."

"All right," Elizabeth said.

Colton grabbed a duffel bag from his closet and filled it with some clothes and then went into Alexandria's room and grabbed the clothes that Mark had picked out. He sat down on her bed, recalling the many conversations that they had had on that very bed, talking about anything—Anna, their pasts, their futures, everything.

He didn't realize he was starting to cry until Anna had appeared in front of him and was hugging him tightly.

"In my nightmare, Colton, I remembered you carrying a bag exactly like this," Anna said. "Colton … you have to be very careful. In my nightmare, you were in the house, staring at another guy who had a gun in one hand and Lexi in the other. That's right before I woke up."

"I will be," Colton said. "And I'll bring her back to you, I promise."

"I know," Anna said. "Although it scares me with all this, I'm at peace about the ending. I know that God will take care of you and Lexi."

"Yes, He will," Colton said. Anna then left and Colton found himself kneeling and praying.

The next couple of hours were difficult for everyone. Colton went downstairs and stayed with the rest of the group, trying to keep his mind off what was going to happen. At nine thirty, he started to drive to Alexandria's old house with the duffel bag. Elizabeth said that the cops would not be following him. They would already be there, a safe distance away but close enough that if something happens they would be able to be there.

Colton pulled into the driveway beside the house, seeing the van pulled in there as well. He immediately parked directly behind it, knowing that that would at least hold them back a little. He took a deep breath before grabbing the duffel bag and locking the car and putting his keys in his pockets. His movements were meticulous; he was doing anything he could think of doing to hold these people back, even just a little bit. He stood in front of the door and knocked three times, just like they had said.

The door opened, and Colton stepped through. He could immediately smell the smoke and the dust from the past.

"I brought what you wanted me to," he stated.

"Come into the kitchen," a voice said. Colton walked into the kitchen that he could see from the doorway and saw Alexandria sitting at the kitchen table, her hands tied behind her chair and her legs tied to the legs of the chair.

"All right, what do you want now?" Colton asked.

"Do you know who we are, Colton?" the person said. It was a tall man about five feet, ten inches with graying brown hair and brown eyes. He looked familiar to Colton, but he wasn't sure why.

"No," Colton said, shaking his head.

"We're part of the gang that took your family," the man said, "We're also drug dealers. Alexandria's parents never finished paying us for what they owed us—the thousand that you happen to have in your duffel bag. And then, there's the fact that your family ran before we could get our payment from them. Your family owed us a lot more, which is why you two are here. Tomorrow, you're going to help us rob a bank."

"No way," Colton denied.

Another man stood behind Alexandria, and Colton had missed the gun that he held in his hand that he had just cocked. Colton immediately froze.

"All right, all right. Fine, I'll help you."

"Good boy," the man said. "For now, you two can go to sleep up in Alexandria's bedroom. We're going to have people outside the room to make sure that you don't try any funny business. So you two may go there."

The man untied Alexandria, and Colton and Alexandria headed to the bedroom. Colton couldn't believe all that was going on. When they shut the door behind them, he immediately hugged Alexandria tightly. "I'm so sorry, Lexi."

"It's not just you," Alexandria said.

"My family owes these people money," Colton said.

"And so does mine," Alexandria said.

"But mine is the reason why we're being kept here," Colton said. "I'm so sorry for everything, Lexi. When we get out of here, I'm going to make it up to you. I don't know how, but I'm going to."

"That's only if we get out," Alexandria said. "My parents were killed trying to satisfy these people. I don't expect that we'll get out alive."

"Yes, we will," Colton said and lowered his voice so that the people outside couldn't hear him. "The police know that we're here. They're going to help us."

Alexandria looked out to the window and saw that there, indeed, were cops heading toward the house. She looked back at Colton. "You have to listen to me. I've escaped from this window numerous times. There is a tree a short distance away. We have to jump to this tree and climb down. If we don't do this, then we're going to break a bone, if not worse. I'll do it first, and then you can copy exactly what I do."

Colton looked in her eyes. At that moment, all he wanted to do was kiss her. He didn't though and regretted just standing there when the door was opened and the man stood in the doorway with a gun.

"I thought we told you no cops, Colton!"

"I didn't call the cops!" Colton protested.

"Then why are there cops around?" he called.

"I don't know," Colton lied. He stood protectively in front of Alexandria.

"Alexandria, get over here before I shoot you both," the man said. Alexandria sadly obliged and stood beside him. The man wrapped his arm around her neck and held the gun up. "Colton, you are going to go down and tell the cops that there is a mistake and that everything is fine. If you don't, then I will shoot Alexandria."

"That's not going to happen," a voice said. Colton looked behind the man to see a detective standing there with a gun to the man's head. "Drop the gun and release Alexandria and I won't shoot you, Carl."

"Before you shoot me, I'll shoot him," Carl, the man, said. He aimed his gun at Colton.

"Please ... don't shoot him," Alexandria said. Colton could see the tears threatening to fall from her eyes.

"Carl, if you let go of Alexandria, you can have me and the money from Alexandria's debt. My family owes you more money. I know how to get in contact with my mother. We can give you back all your money," Colton said, stepping forward slightly.

Carl stared at him. But that second hesitation was all that Alexandria needed. She brought her hand up at the same time she brought her foot up. She hit the hand that had the gun, immediately causing him to let go of it as soon as she also kicked him in the balls. The gun fell to the ground, and he kneeled, letting go of her. The detective immediately grabbed his arms and pulled them back, causing him to scream out in pain.

Alexandria ran into Colton's arms, not even thinking about it. He immediately wrapped his arms around her, staring as the detective walked out with Carl in handcuffs. Two more cops came into the room, and one walked over to them while the other picked the gun up.

"Can you come down to the precinct with us to give us your statements?" the officer said.

"Yeah, can we call our parents first though?" Colton inquired.

"Yeah, sure, we'll meet you both downstairs," the officer said and walked away.

"Lexi, are you okay?" Colton wondered.

Alexandria nodded. "I … I was so scared that he was going to rape me again, like he had done a while ago. And this house just brings back too many memories. I need to get out of here."

"All right, why don't you go downstairs with the officer then and I'll call Duncan and Elizabeth?" Colton suggested.

"I want to stay with you," Alexandria said, shaking her head. Colton smiled.

"All right, give me two seconds then so that I can call them," Colton said, reaching into his pocket and grabbing his cell phone. He quickly dialed the house number.

"Hello," Elizabeth said. Her voice was anxious, and Colton knew they had all been sitting by the phone, waiting for a phone call.

"I got her. We're going to the precinct to give the police our statements and then we'll head home," Colton said.

"Oh, thank heavens! Thank you, Colton," Elizabeth said. He could just picture Elizabeth falling down into a chair, filled with relief.

"Of course, Elizabeth. I have to go though, so we'll see you in a little while," Colton said.

"See you soon," Elizabeth said, and they hung up.

"All right, Lexi, let's head downstairs," Colton said. Alexandria nodded, and the pair headed down the stairs and outside to where the police officers stood.

"Do you want to drive there, or do you want us to take you?" the officer asked.

Colton looked at Alexandria, who shrugged. "We'll drive. I'm in good enough shape to drive."

"All right, just follow us," the officer said. Colton nodded and got his keys out before unlocking the car and letting Alexandria into the passenger seat.

"Are you okay, Lexi?" Colton said after starting the car.

"Still recovering from the shock," Alexandria admitted. "It's getting better right now. Thanks for saving me, Colton."

"Of course, I was part of the reason why you were kidnapped," Colton said.

"Don't blame yourself, Colton. It was also because my adoptive parents were drug addicts," Alexandria said.

"Let's just not argue about this … please," Colton said. "I'm just so glad that you're okay."

"Me too," Alexandria said. "I … I was so scared."

"Me too," Colton admitted. "Especially when I saw you tied up … I was so scared that they were going to kill you."

"Let's not think about this please. I just want to get past this," Alexandria said.

"All right," Colton said. "I didn't get to thank you for meeting with my mother with me. Thanks."

"Of course," Alexandria said, smiling. "When I was first meeting with my biological parents, I would have wanted someone with me. I know what you were going through, and there's no reason for you to go through it alone."

Colton just smiled at her. He surprised her by reaching over and taking her hand in his gently. He drove like that until they were at the precinct. When they got there, Colton didn't leave Alexandria's side unless it was to go to the bathroom. They gave their statements to the police officers and then were free to go. All the people in the house had been found and were arrested for kidnapping and numerous other charges.

Chapter Twenty-Six

Colton drove to the house, and the two stayed in the car for a moment.

"Are you ready to go in?" Colton asked.

"I think so," Alexandria said. "Are you?"

"I think so," Colton said.

The two of them smiled at each other and then got out of the car and headed into the house. He somehow wasn't surprised when everyone was in the foyer waiting for them.

"Lexi!" they all shouted. Everyone immediately hugged her tightly, one at a time. Mark was last, and he held her tight for a while.

"I'm so glad that you're okay," Mark said into her ear.

"Me too," Alexandria said.

"So why did they kidnap you?" Jessica asked.

"My adoptive parents owed them money," Alexandria said. She was going to leave the part out about Colton's parents until he spoke.

"And apparently so did my parents," Colton said. "And they were going to make us both rob a bank tomorrow."

"Wow," Jessica said.

"I think I'm going to bed now," Alexandria said.

"All right, good night," Duncan said, hugging her tightly.

"I'm going to bed too," Colton said.

"All right," Elizabeth said.

The pair went upstairs, and Alexandria opened her door and then turned to Colton. He spoke before she could say anything. "I'm going to change into pajamas, and then I'm going to get us cookies and milk."

She smiled at him. "Thanks, Colton."

"Of course," Colton said.

Colton quickly changed into a pair of flannel bottoms and a T-shirt and then went downstairs to the kitchen, where Mark was getting something to drink.

"Question, Mark," Colton said as he got the cookies from the cupboard. "What are we going to do about Lexi?"

"What do you mean?" Mark asked.

"About our feelings. Honestly, I don't know how she feels about me," Colton said.

"I don't either," Mark said. "But I don't want to break up with her right after what happened today."

"Yeah, I know," Colton said. "I think I should tell her my feelings though."

"I do too," Mark said. "But don't expect the best reaction out of her."

"I know," Colton said. "I'm probably going to wait a couple of days though, with what just happened."

"Yeah, probably a good idea," Mark said.

Colton smiled at Mark, glad that they still had a good relationship, and grabbed the two glasses of milk he had just poured and the cookies and went back up to Alexandria's bedroom.

Alexandria was curled into a ball on her bed. Colton entered the bedroom and could see from his spot in the doorway, that instead of the tears falling. He shut the door behind him and put the two glasses of milk on the bedside table along with the cookies and then sat down beside her, laying a hand on her back as he spoke. "I wish I knew what to say, Lexi ... I'm here though."

Alexandria sat up and then laid her head on his shoulder. "All I can see is the nights that my adoptive parents would get high. And I keep seeing Carl raping me with Joseph and them both forcing me to do things to them."

"Don't worry, I'm not going to let them come near you ever again, Lexi," Colton said, rubbing her arm. "I promise you."

"Thanks, Colton," Alexandria said. "I just ... I still am really shaken up about all of it."

"It's understandable. If you want me to, I'll stay here with you until you fall asleep," Colton suggested.

"That would be nice," Alexandria said, nodding.

"Then come on, let's eat cookies and talk," Colton said.

Alexandria laughed and nodded. Colton handed her a glass of milk and then moved to face her while putting the cookies in between them.

"So what do you want to talk about?" Alexandria asked.

"Let's just randomly say topics. It can be about anything at all," Colton said. "Tell me your favorite memory."

"My favorite memory isn't really a single memory. When I was young, Duncan and I used to go out to dinner at least once a week together. It was always fun to get out for a day with him. He has always been like a father to me," Alexandria said.

"Oh, nice," Colton said.

"What about you? What's your favorite memory?" Alexandria asked.

"My favorite memory is from my thirteenth birthday. It was nice because it was just my family, and I remember it because my sister was just clinging to me. I miss my sister a lot," Colton said. "Any memory of her is a good memory to me."

"That's good that you had such a good relationship with her," Alexandria said.

"Okay, next thing. If you could go anywhere in the world, where would you go?"

"Oh gosh. I would probably go to … Italy. I've always been fascinated by the culture, and I love Italian food. What about you?"

"I would go to Germany. My family is from Germany, and I would love to know about my family heritage."

"All right, my turn to ask a question. What's your favorite holiday?"

"My favorite holiday is definitely Christmas. It's so nice around this time, and Elizabeth and Duncan always makes it so nice. What about you?"

"Mine is probably Thanksgiving. It was the one holiday that my adoptive parents weren't drunk or high for."

"That would make it a pretty good holiday. Besides food, water, and shelter, what could you not go one day without?"

"Music, plain and simple. There is no way I could ever go a day without listening to music. What about you?"

"Same here. I wouldn't be able to live without music. Okay, what's your one pet peeve?"

"My pet peeve is probably people judging me before they actually get to know me. What about you?"

"Hmm, that would probably be people in general," Alexandria laughed. "All right, no, it's people chewing with their mouth open. I hate it. It's so gross."

"All right, what ability or skill do you wish that you could have that you don't already have?"

"I would probably want people skills. I'm terrible with people usually."

Alexandria laughed again. "Yeah, I can definitely see that."

"What about you? What skill or ability do you wish you had?"

Alexandria bit her lip. "I probably would want the ability to make people happy. That's all that I've ever really wanted in my life."

"You are probably the most selfless person I know, Lexi."

"I'm not sure if that's a compliment or not."

"Definitely a compliment. On to my next questions though. If you could have three wishes granted, what would they be?"

"You are coming up with some difficult questions, Colton! Gosh. I would probably ask for world peace—cliché, yes, I know—a cure for lupus, and for drugs to have never been created."

"And yet again, not a single thing that would help yourself. All those would help other people."

"Well, the drugs thing is personal because if they had never been created, I wouldn't have been stuck with drug-addicted adoptive parents."

"Good point."

"All right, so what three wishes would you wish for?"

"A cure for lupus, just like you, to not worry about money again in my life, and for Elizabeth and Duncan to not have to worry about money again."

"See, you're not as bad as you think you are. Only one of those three wishes was about yourself."

Colton laughed. "All right, last question from me. What is your first thought when you wake up?"

"Before I came home, it was 'Great, I'm still living in this hell-hole,' but now that I'm home with everyone, it's 'I'm home and blessed.' What about you?"

"It depends on the day, and usually it's 'Okay, what trouble am I going to cause today?'"

Alexandria laughed and then yawned. She looked over and saw that it was nearing one in the morning. "Oh wow, it's already almost one! I have to work in the morning."

"I'm sure if you called them and told them that you had been kidnapped yesterday they wouldn't object to you staying home for a day to rest, which I personally think you need."

"Yeah, I think so too. I'll call first thing in the morning."

"Well, since I'm assuming that you're going to bed now, I'm going to take the cookies and our glasses back downstairs and then go to bed."

"Thanks, Colton," Alexandria said, smiling as she got underneath her covers. "It really means a lot to me that you would do everything that you did for me today."

"Lexi, I would do anything for you," Colton said and then walked out of the bedroom.

Alexandria lay in her bed and was soon fast asleep, exhausted from the day's events. But it was far from a restful sleep. Images kept passing her—images of her past. She woke up, screaming, with sweat covering her entire body. As soon as she woke up, all she could think of was getting to Colton. She needed to be with him. She needed to be wrapped in his arms. She needed to feel safe. She threw the blankets off herself and ran out of her bedroom and down the hallway to where Colton's bedroom was. She opened the door gently and saw that he was sleeping peacefully. She couldn't help but freeze. He looked so peaceful sleeping there. She wasn't sure she really wanted to disturb his sleep then.

And then he shot up in bed and looked wild-eyed directly at her. He stood up and hugged her tightly. "Thank goodness it was you, Lexi."

"Did I wake you up?" she asked softly.

"No, I was having a nightmare. It was …you getting shot by Carl," Colton said. "I was about to run to your room to make sure you were okay."

Alexandria smiled. "I just woke up from nightmares from my past."

"Do you want to stay in here for the night then?" Colton asked. "That way, neither one of us has to run to the other one."

"It may be a good idea," Alexandria said. "Just warning you though. I toss and turn a lot in my sleep."

"I do too," Colton said. "Come on, let's at least try and get comfortable. It's a good thing Elizabeth and Duncan gave us all double beds."

"Yeah, that's for sure," Alexandria said, laughing. She got into bed, and Colton lay down beside her. She curled up beside him, and he wrapped his arm over her, pulling her close. It was a cute image in his head seeing her wrapped up in a ball beside him, holding on to his body tightly.

Within minutes, they were both asleep peacefully.

Chapter Twenty-Seven

The next morning, Lockwood Accounting had tried calling Alexandria's cell phone when she didn't come into the office by nine. When she didn't answer, they called the house phone. Elizabeth explained what had happened, and they gave her until Wednesday off. Elizabeth found it strange that Alexandria hadn't woken up yet even on her days off she was awake before nine.

"What's up, love?" Duncan asked as he saw the worried expression on his wife's face.

"Lexi isn't awake. Even on her days off, she's awake by now," Elizabeth said.

"She had a rough day yesterday. She's probably still asleep. It's nothing to worry about," Duncan reassured.

"I'm going to check her room anyways," Elizabeth said. After the night before, she still was very nervous about where the young woman was.

Elizabeth felt fear go through her entire body when Alexandria wasn't in her own bed. And then it dawned on her that she probably couldn't sleep, and so she checked Colton's room. She had thought about checking Mark's room but then remembered that he had already left for work and would have told them if she was in his room. She walked to Colton's room and opened the door gently, hoping not to disturb the people in case they were sleeping.

She almost wanted to get her camera when she saw the way Colton and Alexandria were sleeping together. They both looked so peaceful, and Elizabeth didn't dare disturb them. She left just as softly as she had come in.

A few minutes later, Alexandria woke up. She smiled when she looked up to see Colton lying there, looking peaceful. Her eyes widened. She had realized that as soon as she was in bed with Colton, she had fallen asleep, and it was peaceful for once. She didn't toss and turn all night. She actually slept all the way through the night. She looked over at his clock to see it said nine fifteen in the morning. She jumped, realizing she had to call the Lockwoods about work.

Colton jolted awake when Alexandria jumped up in his arms. "Wh-what's up?"

"Sorry, Colton, I just realized that I need to call the Lockwoods about work today," Alexandria said. "You can go back to sleep. I'm going to see what everyone is up to after I call the Lockwoods."

"I'm going to change and then get some breakfast and hang out too," Colton said. "Good morning by the way."

Alexandria smiled. "Good morning. That was the first good night of sleep I had gotten in a long time. Thanks, Colton."

"Anytime, Lexi," Colton said.

Alexandria left the room and sighed when she got into her bedroom. She couldn't keep this from Mark. She couldn't stop her heart from racing when she was in Colton's arms, and she couldn't deny how safe she felt in his arms. She couldn't continue to lead Mark on like this. She had to break it off with him. She felt terrible, considering it was for Colton. But she couldn't let him think that she was going to fall in love with him when she had a feeling she was going to fall for Colton.

She picked her phone up and called Lockwood Accounting. "Hello, this is Carol from Lockwood Accounting."

"Hi, Carol. It's Alexandria," she said. "Um, I can explain why I'm not in the office."

"Did you speak with Elizabeth yet this morning? We tried calling you when you weren't here yet, but you didn't answer your cell phone. So we called the house phone, and Elizabeth told us what had happened yesterday. You have until Wednesday off," Carol explained.

"Oh, thank you so much, Carol. I promise, I will work late if you need me to this week," Alexandria said.

"Alexandria, don't worry about it! You couldn't have controlled what happened. So just take the days off and don't worry about it," Carol said laughing.

"All right, thank you again, Carol," Alexandria said.

"Of course, Alexandria, see you on Wednesday," Carol said.

"See you Wednesday," Alexandria said. She hung up the phone and then changed into a pair of jeans and a nice T-shirt before texting Mark: "I need to talk to you when you get home from work." She wasn't looking forward to the conversation, but it needed to happen.

She headed downstairs and saw Colton cooking in the kitchen. He smiled at her and spoke, "Do you want some scrambled eggs and toast? I made too much egg for myself this morning."

"Sure," Alexandria said, smiling. "I'll be back in a couple of minutes. Do you know where Elizabeth is?"

"I think she's in her office," Colton said.

"Thanks," Alexandria said. She headed to Elizabeth's office and knocked on the door before entering to find Elizabeth sitting at her desk. "Morning, Elizabeth."

"Good morning, Lexi," Elizabeth said. There was a shine in her eyes, and Alexandria had a feeling that she knew where she slept last night.

"You know where I was last night, don't you?" Alexandria said as she sat down in one of the chairs across from the older woman.

"I checked on you this morning when Carol called, saying that you hadn't called and that you weren't there. I had a moment of panic before I figured you were in one of the guys' bedrooms. I figured you had gone to Colton because he had been there with you yesterday," Elizabeth said. "I just happened to be right."

"Yeah, that's for sure," Alexandria said. "I'm going to break up with Mark today when he gets back from work."

"Why is that?" Elizabeth asked.

"I'm starting to have feelings for Colton, and I'm not feeling it really for Mark. I don't want to keep leading him on if Colton's the one making my heart race and such," Alexandria said.

"Yeah, that's probably a good idea," Elizabeth said. "Did you talk to the Lockwoods?"

"Yes, I called them after I went back in my room this morning, and they told me I have until Wednesday off. Thank you for telling them what happened," Alexandria said.

"Of course, Lexi," Elizabeth said.

"I'm going to eat breakfast, so I'll see you later," Alexandria said.

"Okay," Elizabeth said, smiling. "Oh! We're going to have another party on Friday because I do remember it being your birthday."

"I honestly forgot that my birthday is Friday," Alexandria said. "I've been so caught up with everything else."

"That's understandable with all that's been going on lately," Elizabeth said. "See you later, Lexi."

"See you later," Alexandria said and went back to the kitchen, where a warm plate of eggs and white toast sat waiting for her. "Thanks, Colton."

"No problem," Colton said, smiling.

"I'm going to break up with Mark," Alexandria stated.

"Why is that?" Colton asked.

"I've realized that he's not the one I want to be with right now, and so I just don't want to lead him on anymore," Alexandria said. "And I have enough on my plate right now as it is."

"Yeah, that's understandable," Colton said.

"I have today and tomorrow off work because of yesterday," Alexandria said.

"That will be nice," Colton said.

"Yeah, I'm looking forward to just relaxing," Alexandria said. "Although I would rather work and get this all off my mind."

"Yeah, I don't blame you," Colton said.

*****

Mark had gotten Alexandria's text message and had a feeling about what she wanted to talk about when he got home. When he had gone to bed the night before, he could hear Colton and Alexandria talking in her room. He knew he had definitely lost to Colton. He just hoped that Colton would make Alexandria happy.

"Hey, are you okay, Mark?" a sweet voice asked. He turned to see another worker, Laura, standing there. Laura had long blond hair and bright green eyes. She was beautiful, and Mark was surprised he hadn't realized how sweet she was.

"Yeah, I'm fine, Laura. Thanks," Mark said smiling.

"Of course, Mark," Laura said, smiling.

*****

Mark took his shoes off and smiled when he saw Alexandria enter from the living room.

"Oh, hey, I didn't realize you were getting home," Alexandria said, smiling.

"Yeah, I can talk right now if you want," Mark said.

"Let's go up to my room. I'm about to dance up in the ball-room, so I need to change clothes," Alexandria said.

"All right," Mark said. They were silent as they walked up to her bedroom.

"Um, I know we weren't really officially a couple or anything, but I just … I don't think we should be together like that at all anymore. I … honestly, I'm starting to like Colton. It started happening before I was kidnapped yesterday, so that has nothing to do with that. I'm—"

"I know, Lexi," Mark stated. She looked at him in confusion. "I knew when he hugged you after we sparred yesterday. I've known since you two first met that you were going to end up together, but I wanted some time with you myself. I'm not hurt about it since I've known since the beginning. And there's no way girls can resist Colton."

"I'm sorry, Mark," Alexandria said.

"Don't apologize about it, Lexi, just … be happy," Mark said. "That's all that I really care about—that you and Colton are happy."

"Thanks, Mark," Alexandria said smiling. Mark smiled back and then left the room. She changed her clothes and then headed up to the ballroom. She put her music player on and instantly started dancing, letting all her emotions out.

Colton had come up to the ballroom to tell Alexandria that dinner was almost ready and was entranced by her dancing. When she was done, he smiled.

"Lexi, dinner is ready."

"I was engulfed in my own world, wasn't I?" Alexandria asked, blushing.

"Only for a minute," Colton said. "It shows your passion, so it's fine. And I came just a few minutes earlier anyways, just in case."

"Thanks," Alexandria said, laughing. "I already talked to Mark."

"How did he take it?" Colton wondered.

"Pretty well," Alexandria said, shrugging. "Sometimes, he doesn't show all his emotions, and so I'm not entirely sure how he's really taking it all."

"Yeah, that's true," Colton said. "But let's go and eat dinner."

"Right," Alexandria said, smiling.

They sat down at the dinner table with everyone else, and Elizabeth stood up when everyone was there. "Hey everyone, I just want to say that we're having another dinner party on Friday. It is actually Lexi's birthday on Friday."

Colton's eyes widened. He had no idea what to get her for her birthday. He looked to Mark, who just smirked at his friend's reaction. Mark had never seen Colton react that way to hearing that a woman's birthday was coming up.

"Is there anything specific you want for your birthday, Lexi?" Carlee asked.

"Not really," Alexandria said. "I'm really just happy as long as we're all together."

"All right," Collin said.

*****

"What am I supposed to give her, Mark?" Colton asked as they began to punch the punching bags after dinner. "I mean, I don't want anything sappy, but I don't want something simple for her either."

Mark had to laugh at his friend's reaction. Colton was not used to being with only one person and actually caring about that person.

"What has she been talking to you about? She talks to you about more personal things than she does anyone else." It was a fact that he was used to by now. Although it had hurt him at first, it no longer bothered him.

"But nothing to really tell me what she would want for her birthday," Colton said.

"Get her something personal, something that shows that you put some thought into it," Mark said.

"What are you going to get her?" Colton asked.

"A new Bible. Her old one is getting beat up," Mark said.

"All right," Colton said.

*****

Monday and Tuesday night, Alexandria woke up in the middle of the night of nightmares from her past. She felt bad waking Colton up both nights since he had been sleeping peacefully, but each night, she knew the only way for her to sleep again was if she was with him. He groaned on Wednesday when her alarm went off but smiled as soon as he saw her in his arms. He had fallen for her—and hard. He didn't know what to do.

It was Wednesday now. Alexandria was heading into the office, glad to get back into the swing of things. She smiled when she saw Kimberly sitting in her office across the hall from her own office.

"Good morning, Kimberly," Alexandria said.

"Good morning, Alexandria. How are you feeling?" Kimberly asked.

"I'm feeling pretty good," Alexandria said.

"That's good," Kimberly said. "Oh, Carol wants to see you in her office."

"Okay," Alexandria said. She dropped her purse in her office and then went to her boss's office. She knocked before entering. "Hey, Carol. Kimberly told me you wanted to see me."

"I just wanted to see how you were doing," Carol asked.

"I'm doing well. The last couple of days off helped me recover a lot," Alexandria said.

"I'm glad," Carol said. "You didn't miss much at all here, just business as usual. You can go back to your office, and if you have any questions, Kimberly is right there and I'm here as well."

"All right, thanks, Carol," Alexandria said and then went into her own office.

*****

Mark had the day off, and Colton had begged him to go with him to the mall to help him pick something out for Alexandria. Mark had to chuckle at the fact that the exact same thing had happened only a week before, but the roles were reversed. The previous two nights, Alexandria had been talking to Colton about how much she actually didn't like her birthday. It brought back too many memories.

It was in the middle of a bigger store that the idea hit him. She had told him that sometimes writing things down helped her get past things. She had also admitted to him that she thought that his scent may be what was helping her sleep. It was a comfortable scent, and she had quickly become addicted to it almost.

"I figured it out!" he screamed. People looked over at the pair, and Mark just laughed.

"All right," Mark said. "What is it then?"

"She's been coming into my room the last couple of nights because she's woken up from nightmares. She told me that sometimes writing things down helped her get through it, and she also said that my scent helped her sleep," Colton said. "So a journal for her to write things down in and one of my old sweatshirts that I'll wear for a while to get the scent."

Mark shook his head. "Honestly, that's a really good idea."

"I know, right?" Colton said grinning. He then looked at all of the journals that were in front of him. "That's a lot of journals. How am I supposed to decide which one to buy her?"

Mark laughed again. "Just look at them and see if there's one that just screams her. You'll know it when you see it."

Sure enough, Colton scanned the journals and found one that had a flower on it that had a Bible verse on it, and he immediately grabbed it. "Found it!"

"All right, let's go. Lexi will be home from work soon," Mark said, looking at the time.

"Right," Colton said. He was proud of himself for thinking of what he had thought. He hoped that she would like her presents.

Colton had run up to hide the present in his room quickly before Alexandria got home that night. When he was heading downstairs, she had just gotten home.

"Hey, Colton," Alexandria said, smiling. She could feel her heart starting to race as soon as she saw it was him.

"Hey, Lexi," Colton said, smiling. "Hey, do you want to go out to eat Saturday, maybe to celebrate your birthday? I would say Friday on your birthday, but Elizabeth and Duncan kinda stole that chance from me."

Alexandria giggled. "Apparently, they have. I'd love to go out to eat with you."

"Fantastic," Colton said. "I'll tell you more tomorrow when I actually figure out where we're going."

"Sounds great. I'm going to change, and then I'll meet you in the living room, okay?" Alexandria replied.

"Okay," Colton said and walked to the living room, where everyone was sitting.

"So what are you going to do for Lexi's birthday?" Anna asked when Colton sat down beside her on the couch.

"I'm gonna take her out to eat on Saturday and give her the presents I got her," Colton said.

"Oh! What did you get her?" Anna asked energetically. Colton whispered them in her ear. "She's going to like those!"

"Who is going to like what?" Alexandria asked, walking into the living room.

"You're going to like what Colton got you!" Anna said happily.

There was a knock on the door, and after a moment, Bridget came in. "Colton, there's someone here to see you."

"All right," Colton said, standing. Alexandria had a bad feeling surge through her, and she stood up as well. "You have that feeling too?"

"Yeah," Alexandria said and followed him to the doorway between the living room and the foyer. She stopped there and allowed him to go to the door himself. It was his mother at the door, waiting to talk to him.

Chapter Twenty-Eight

"What are you doing here?" Colton questioned.

"I just wanted to see how you were doing," Nicole stated.

"No, you need to get the hell away—from me and this area. The gang found me. They kidnapped Lexi and they threatened me. They were going to make her and I help them rob a bank in order to pay off *your* debt," Colton seethed.

"I didn't know they would do that. They just told me to bring you to the café," Nicole said.

"What?" Colton shouted. His mother had given them up to be kidnapped.

"The gang found me a while ago when I was trying to find Britt. They threatened that they would kill me if we didn't have you come to the café," Nicole said.

"So you would rather risk your child's life than your own?" Colton spat.

Nicole was silent. It was enough of an answer that Colton needed. "Get out. You're not my mother. Get out."

"Colton—" Nicole protested.

"I believe it's best if you leave, Nicole," Alexandria said, walking over and standing beside Colton. "And I don't think it would be a good idea for you to return. I think you need to go back into hiding."

Nicole couldn't debate with the two and left. Colton slammed the door behind her and then walked to the gym. Alexandria followed him, debating about whether or not to get Mark to come as well. She decided against it, figuring Colton would want some alone time.

She got a few steps away from the bottom of the stairs when she slipped and fell on her bottom on the stairs. Colton turned and started laughing. She glared at him as she stood up and rubbed her butt. "I would say you're a jerk, but you're smiling right now, so I'll be nice."

"Even though you just called me a jerk anyways," Colton said.

"That was kinda the point in that," Alexandria said, smirking. "What do you want me to do to help you right now?"

"Stand behind this punching bag while I punch the shit out of it," Colton stated.

Alexandria nodded and braced herself behind the punching bag. He mumbled as he punched it with all the energy he had. When he finally couldn't take it any longer, he stopped punching and broke down, crying. Alexandria let go of the bag and wrapped her arms around him tightly, knowing that that was the one thing she could do for him. He clung to her tightly, letting all the tears fall.

"I'm so sorry about that, Colton," Alexandria said. "I wish I knew what to say about it all, but I don't. All I know is that you're going to be a better parent than your mother one day."

"If I have kids," Colton said. "Thanks, Lexi."

"I would do anything for you, Colton," Alexandria stated.

Colton looked at her lips and found that he wanted to kiss her that very moment. He was almost going to until he heard Anna's voice from upstairs. "Lexi! Colton! It's dinnertime!"

"We'll be right there!" Alexandria called. She smiled at Colton. "Do you want me to sleep in your bed tonight?"

Colton laughed. "It's up to you. I don't mind if you sleep with me, but I understand if you don't want to."

"Hey, I've been getting the best nights' sleep ever since I started sleeping in your bed," Alexandria said. Colton laughed, and they headed upstairs.

"Who was at the door, Colton?" Mark asked.

"Nicole, my mother. She told me that the gang had threatened that they would kill her if she didn't have me meet her at the café that night," Colton replied. "So she pretty much saved her own butt by sacrificing mine. I told her she was no longer welcome here and that she wasn't my mother."

"Colton!" Elizabeth exclaimed.

"It's the truth. I've gone the last few years without them, I can last the rest of my life. Especially when she tells me that it's her fault that Alexandria was kidnapped and that I was threatened," Colton said. "I don't need people like that in my life. I have all of you."

"Aw, Colton's getting sweet on us," Carlee cooed. Colton glared at her.

"It's all that time he's been spending with Lexi," Collin said, winking at the pair. Alexandria immediately blushed, and Colton moved his glare over to him.

"Enough," Duncan said. "Colton, you know that we are all always behind you no matter what you decide to do."

"Yes, I know," Colton said, smiling at Duncan.

*****

Colton was sparring with Mark. He had hoped that Alexandria would go and do something else for the short time while they sparred, and he was glad when she said she was going to check her e-mails and such.

"You okay?" Mark asked.

"Getting there," Colton admitted. "I … I had thought that life was going to be okay until my mother came back into it. I'm glad she's out of it now."

"Yeah," Mark said.

"I just wish I knew where my little sister was. I want to know if she's alive and safe," Colton said. "She's the only real family I have left apparently. At least, if Nicole wasn't lying to me about her and my father."

"Talk to Elizabeth's cop friend about possibly looking into it," Mark suggested.

"Yeah, I might," Colton said.

"Are you going to ask Lexi to be your girlfriend this weekend?" Mark inquired.

"I honestly haven't quite decided yet. I still am not completely positive that she wouldn't tell me no," Colton said.

"Colton, what did she tell you that she told me when we broke up?" Mark said.

"That she has enough on her plate as it is and that she realized you weren't the one she wanted to be with right now," Colton recalled after a moment. "Why?"

"Because you're an idiot. She broke up with me for you. She told me herself," Mark said. "She wants to be with you."

"I'm still scared," Colton said.

"Wow, the big manly Colton is actually afraid of something," Mark said. "Who would have ever thought that it would be a girl to make him scared?"

"Yeah, I know," Colton said, laughing. "But whatever, I'm just going to see what's happens on Saturday with the dinner. I don't even know where we're going."

*****

Alexandria was lying in bed, checking her e-mail when there was a knock on her door. Feeling lazy, she just called for the person to enter, not really caring who it was. She smiled when it was Elizabeth and Anna. "Hey, guys."

"Hey," they said, smiling. Elizabeth revealed a dress bag from her back, and Alexandria sat up in confusion.

"What's that?" Alexandria asked.

"I realized today that we never got you a dress for the party on Friday. So Anna and I went shopping earlier today for a dress for you. The party is just semiformal, so it's not like it's as fancy as the previous one. But here," Elizabeth said, laying the dress on Alexandria's bed.

Alexandria opened the dress bag and was amazed at the beauty. It was a simple dress, but that was the way Alexandria liked things—simple. It was a strapless chiffon dress with ruched bodice. It had an A-line silhouette and was floor length. The bodice was white, and the skirt on the dress that had a rope along it was all a deep purple. It was beautiful, and Alexandria loved it.

"This is gorgeous. Thank you so much."

"Of course, Lexi," Elizabeth said, smiling. "So how was work been going?"

"It's been going pretty good. There isn't too much to say about it," Alexandria said, shrugging. "Um, Elizabeth, did you … did you invite my biological parents?"

"I did not invite your mother. I invited your father but haven't heard from him," Elizabeth said. "I thought it would be best since you seemed to have been done with your mother."

"Yeah, I appreciate it. And my father probably won't make it. He told me he had to go out of state for a while but would let me know when he returned," Alexandria explained.

"Oh, okay," Elizabeth said, smiling.

That night, Alexandria had started to go to sleep when her door opened. She was confused until she saw Colton entering her room. She sat up completely. "What's up, Colton?"

"I couldn't sleep. Do you mind if I sleep in your bed with you for once?" Colton asked.

"Not at all," Alexandria said, smiling. She pulled the covers back, and he lay down in bed beside her. "How are you holding up?"

"I'm doing okay. I just want to know if Britt is safe or not right now," Colton answered. "I'm scared that the gang is going to get to her."

"You probably should talk to Elizabeth's cop friend and see if they can look in to it," Alexandria said. "I think that's really your only option right now."

"Yeah, I think you're right," Colton said, sighing.

"It will work out. I'm praying for it and for God to protect your sister," Alexandria said.

"Thanks, Lexi," Colton said. He closed his eyes and, within a few minutes, was asleep. Alexandria fell asleep only a few minutes later.

Chapter Twenty-Nine

It was already Friday. Alexandria went to work as usual and quickly ran home to get ready. The party was going to start at seven, and so Alexandria didn't have much time to get ready. When she entered the house, she could hear laughter coming from the living room. She went in there to see that everyone was already in there. "Hey, everyone."

"Happy birthday!" they all shouted. She smiled. It was nice to feel like she was wanted somewhere, that she really was loved.

"Thanks, guys," Alexandria said, smiling. "I'm gonna go and shower and get ready for the party."

"Sounds good," Elizabeth said. "When you're done, you can open your presents as long as there is time."

"You guys really didn't have to get me anything," Alexandria said and then saw the stack of presents in the center of the room. "Thanks though. I'll be back in a short while."

"All right," Duncan said, smiling.

Alexandria took a quick shower, changed into her dress, and then did her makeup. She was done around six and was grateful that she didn't take long. She was surprised when she opened her door to see Colton standing there. "Hey, Colton."

"Hey, Lexi," Colton said. "You look gorgeous."

"Thanks," Alexandria said, blushing. "Is everyone still in the living room?"

"Yeah, I was just checking to see if you were almost done so that we have enough time. I'm going to give you my presents tomorrow when we go out to dinner," Colton said.

"Sounds good. Do I get any hints as to where we're going?" Alexandria asked.

"Nope," Colton said, smirking.

"You're evil," Alexandria said, glaring at him.

"Yeah, I know," Colton said, laughing.

They went to the living room, and Alexandria was glad that everyone was there. They had apparently all changed while they were waiting for her because the men were all in black dress pants and a colored shirt. Duncan was in a white shirt with a pink tie, Collin was in a blue shirt, and Mark was in a red shirt. It was then that Alexandria realized that Colton wasn't wearing his dress clothes. Carlee was in a simple teal-colored spaghetti-strap knee-length dress that had a belt under the bust with a small jewel on it. Jessica had on a red strapless knee-length dress with two-layered skirt with a black belt around the waist. Elizabeth had on a knee-length short-sleeved pink dress with a deep V. Anna had on a knee-length spaghetti strap dress that had a small bow on it.

"So what are you waiting for? Open your presents!" Carlee said happily.

Alexandria laughed and sat down and opened all her presents. Carlee and Collin had gotten her new dance clothes, Mark had gotten her a new Bible, Jessica had gotten her a gift card for a store that Alexandria liked, Anna had gotten her a drawing that she had done herself of the two of them together, and Elizabeth and Duncan had gotten her a gift card to another one of her favorite stores.

"Where's your present, Colton?" Jessica teased.

"She's getting it tomorrow after I take her out to dinner," Colton said.

"Oh la la," Carlee said.

"No, it's not like that," Colton said. Alexandria couldn't mistake the blush on his cheeks and found it adorable.

"Uh-huh, sure," Collin said rolling his eyes.

"Whatever, I have to go and get changed anyways," Colton said, waving the comment off.

"Do you know where he's taking you tomorrow?" Carlee asked.

"No idea. I just know its semiformal," Alexandria said, shrugging.

"I'm sure it will be a good restaurant. He's not one to pick bad ones," Mark said.

"Yeah, that's for sure. I'm sure you will have a good time," Elizabeth said, smiling.

"Yeah," Alexandria said, smiling. There was a knock on the door, and Bridget then returned with a woman and Alexandria sucked in a breath. She had the same eyes that Colton had and the same black hair. There was no question that this was Colton's little sister although she looked to be about eighteen now. Alexandria stood up, and everyone stared at her in confusion.

"This is Brittany. She is looking for Colton," Bridget said.

"He just went to change. If you would like, you can sit down," Alexandria said, motioning to one of the chairs. "He won't be very long."

"Thank you," Brittany said, sitting down on the couch.

"Lexi, I think we should go and let Colton know someone is here to see him," Mark said.

"Yes," Alexandria said. "We'll be right back, Brittany."

"All right," Brittany said, and Alexandria saw her playing with the seam of her shirt. Alexandria couldn't help it when she knelt down beside the woman and spoke.

"Don't worry, he's missed you," she whispered. She saw Brittany's face turn from surprise to relief in a matter of moments.

Alexandria and Mark practically ran up the stairs to Colton's room as Alexandria said, "I can't believe it's her."

"I know," Mark said. "I really wasn't sure if she was still alive or not to be honest with you."

"Me neither," Alexandria said. They were in front of his door, and she started pounding on the door. "Colton! Open the door! There's someone here to see you!"

"Would you give me five minutes?" Colton shouted from inside.

"No, we won't! You'll find out when you see who is here!" Mark called.

This intrigued Colton, and he opened the door. He was currently in his black pants and had on a white muscle shirt and a purple shirt the same shade as Alexandria's dress in hand. "Who is here to see me? If it's my mother, I'm going to kill both of you."

"It's not," Alexandria said. She was trying not to stare at his chest and his strong arms, and so she focused only on his eyes. "You'll be happy to see this person."

"Fine," Colton said. He threw his shirt on over his undershirt and closed his door with a sigh. He had an odd feeling about who it was that was waiting for him, and he wasn't sure if he was really looking forward to this.

"You'll be happy about this, trust us," Mark said. Part of him wanted to shout and tell his best friend who was waiting, but he also wanted to see Colton's face when he saw his sister for the first time in years.

"Yeah, yeah, you two are just lucky I was pretty much ready," Colton said as he buttoned his shirt as he walked.

He was buttoning the last button when he entered the living room. Brittany immediately stood up, and Colton froze. He stared for a good minute, and Brittany fidgeted.

"Would you two say something? We're all wondering what is going on!" Jessica said.

"Jessica, don't be so rude to our guest!" Elizabeth scolded. Jessica rolled her eyes.

"Britt … is … is that really you?" Colton said.

"Yeah, big brother," Brittany said. "I've been going by Chelsea now, but I'm always going to be Britt to you, aren't I?"

"I only know you as Britt. I was never told your new name or anything," Colton said shaking his head. He walked up to his sister and then hugged her tightly. "I missed you so much. I didn't think I would ever see you again."

"I missed you too," Brittany said. "I can't stay here very long. I came to give you my new address and phone number. I don't have anything to do with Mother any longer and Dad died. I'm safe from the gang and from anything that can hurt me. I heard that the gang had kidnapped your friend and tried to get you to help them rob a bank, and so I had to see you. I'm sorry I didn't find you earlier. I … I thought you had died. Mother and Father said that you had just run away. They didn't tell me that you were the one that had been left alone. I'm so sorry, Colton. I wish I had known the truth."

"It's okay," Colton said. "Are you sure you can't stay? We're having a party to celebrate Lexi's birthday, and you're more than welcome."

"No, I really have to go. My taxi is waiting for me outside," Brittany said. "I just had to see you again before I moved yet again. I miss you, big brother."

"I miss you too, little sis. Take care of yourself and let me know if you need anything," Colton said.

"Will do," Brittany said. She hugged her brother once more and then walked out of the house.

"I thought your little sister died," Collin said.

"My family didn't die in a car accident like I have told you all. They left me here so that Elizabeth and Duncan could take care of me because my family was being threatened by the gang that kidnapped Lexi," Colton explained. "My mother had told me that my sister had run away and she didn't know where she was."

"Wow," Carlee said.

"So aren't you glad we disturbed you changing?" Mark asked, patting his best friend's shoulder.

"Yes, thank you," Colton said and hugged Mark.

Alexandria just smiled at him, and Colton hugged her tightly. He finally realized then that this was where he belonged. He didn't belong running around like he had done in the past. He belonged with this family right in this room. He finally felt like he had a true family.

"Come on, people are probably going to be coming soon," Elizabeth said.

"Right," Colton said.

*****

It was already time for dancing. The dinner had been fabulous as usual. Alexandria was so happy to be having a good time with her friends and family.

"Hey, Lexi, Colton," Elizabeth called from on the small stage where the orchestra was.

The two looked at each other in confusion and then went up to the stage.

"What's up?" Colton asked.

"Why don't you two start us out with a dance like last time?" Elizabeth suggested.

The two looked at each other and started grinning. "Sounds great," Alexandria replied.

"All right, everyone," Elizabeth said when the orchestra was set up. "I know most of you were here the last time we had a party like this, and so we're going to have Colton and Lexi start us off with a dance!"

Everyone started clapping and immediately went to the sides, knowing how they were last time. The pair looked at each other, and the orchestra started playing a fast-paced song. Colton bowed and held his hand out for Alexandria, who laughed and curtsied before putting her hand in his. He immediately twirled her around, making her skirt fill out around her. They immediately started dancing with lots of energy, doing stunts that Alexandria usually only did with dancers who had been dancing for years before. At the end of the song, both of them were breathing very heavily, and their hearts were racing. It was difficult for Colton to avoid kissing Alexandria. Everyone started clapping, and they both bowed and then went to the sides.

"I'll grab us some drinks if you want to find the rest of the family," Colton said. Alexandria nodded and found the rest of their group and hugged them all.

"You two never cease to amaze us with your dancing," Elizabeth said.

"Yeah, Colton always shocks me. Most of those dance moves I would only be able to do with someone who has danced for most of their lives," Alexandria admitted. "And yet he can do them so easily. It always amazes me."

"How is it you two manage to always be together in step? Like, there's no doubt in your steps and neither one of you is ever off," Carlee said.

"I really don't know," Alexandria said, shrugging. "I usually let him lead and just follow whatever he's doing. It just somehow ends up working."

"Yeah, because that was all completely improvised, right?" Mark questioned.

"Yeah," Colton said and handed Alexandria a bottle of water. "I just started dancing and she started following."

"And yet it happened to be perfect," Duncan said. "You two are quite a pair."

"I'll take that as a compliment," Alexandria said, laughing.

"Yes, it is," Duncan said.

"Hey, Anna," Colton said, kneeling to the young girl.

"Yeah, Colton?" Anna asked. She didn't like these parties most of the time because there wasn't really that many people around her age there.

"Why don't you and I dance together?" Colton asked.

"Sure!" Anna said happily.

"Hey, Colton, do you mind if I dance with Lexi?" Mark asked as Colton headed onto the dance floor with Anna.

"Yeah, it's all up to her," Colton answered.

"Sure," Alexandria said. The two went on the dance floor behind Colton and Anna, and Alexandria smiled. "You didn't have to ask Colton's permission. We're not dating."

"Yeah, but with how much he likes you, I couldn't just ask you to dance. It's a guy thing," Mark said, shaking his head.

"Does he really like me that much?" Alexandria asked.

"He is head over heels for you," Mark said. "I was with him when he picked out your birthday present. He was like freaking out because he had no idea what to get you. It was actually really funny. He likes you a lot more than you think, Lexi."

"I'm glad," Alexandria said, blushing. "I'm sorry things didn't work out, Mark."

"I had a feeling they probably wouldn't from the start, but I figured I would give it a shot anyways," Mark said. "And seeing how happy you two are even before you're actually dating makes me realize that you two deserve to be together."

"I'm glad you think that way," Alexandria said.

"And there's a girl from work that I'm starting to talk to more," Mark said. "She's really nice and really beautiful. I wish I had the guts to invite her tonight."

"That's good that you may have found someone," Alexandria said. "Invite her just to hang out with us someday!"

Mark laughed. "Sure."

Alexandria looked to where Colton and Anna were. It made her heart soar seeing the two together. Anna was on top of Colton's feet, and they were swaying together. Alexandria couldn't help but find it the cutest thing ever.

Mark smiled when he saw the smile on Alexandria's face. There was no doubt that she and Colton belonged together. Even if they were young, there was no doubt that this pair needed to be together. And there was no way that anyone could stand in their way or should stand in their way.

The song ended, and Mark, Alexandria, Colton, and Anna walked over to the group yet again. Throughout the night, Colton and Alexandria would dance together, and everyone was just having a good time.

Chapter Thirty

It was about one that morning. Colton had been awake in bed, thinking about his sister. He was so happy that she was alive. He almost couldn't believe that she really was alive and that he could talk to her almost anytime that he wanted to now that he had her phone number and address. He somehow wasn't surprised when his door opened and Alexandria entered. He pulled the blankets back, and she lay down beside him.

"I really need to learn to sleep in my own bed," Alexandria said.

"I don't mind," Colton said, shrugging. "I like our late-night conversations."

"I like them too," Alexandria said, smiling. "They help me relax, and I'm able to vent about anything that's on my mind with you."

"Yeah, same here," Colton said. "I honestly can't believe my sister showed up here."

"Yeah, I know. That's great, though, that you're able to talk to her again," Alexandria said.

"Yeah, it's great," Colton said.

"So do I get any hints about my birthday presents or anything?" Alexandria asked, looking up at him through full eyelashes.

"Nope," Colton said, laughing.

Alexandria smiled. She loved his laugher and loved that she could feel it since she was resting her head on his shoulder. "I'm really glad that we got to know each other on a better level then when we first met, Colton."

"Me too, Lexi," Colton said, "I'm really glad."

Alexandria surprised them both by leaning up and kissing his cheek. "Can't I get just one hint about my presents and where we're going for dinner?"

"No, Lexi," Colton said, laughing.

"Come on! Please!" Alexandria pouted. She was making it really hard for Colton to resist her and not kiss her yet.

"Not yet, Lexi," Colton said and moved a hair behind her ear. "It's going to be a surprise. You're going to like it though. I can promise you that."

"All right," Alexandria said, sighing. She lay her head back down on his shoulder.

"Good night, Lexi," Colton said.

"Good night, Colton," Alexandria said. Colton surprised them by kissing her forehead. It was then that Alexandria realized that Mark had been right about Colton, and she was hoping that they would start to date soon.

They just lay like that for a few minutes, enjoying each other's companies, until they both drifted into a deep sleep. The next morning, Alexandria was glad when she didn't hear an alarm going off. She had been woken up by Colton moving around and saw him leaving the room when she was fully awake. She stretched and then sat up fully, wondering what it was that had caused him to leave the room. She was about to go into the hallway to see what was wrong when he reentered the bedroom.

"Um, our dinner may have to be put on hold," Colton said.

"What do you mean?" Alexandria asked. She could tell something was wrong.

"Anna woke up with a really high fever," Colton said. "They don't know what's going on, but they are taking her to the hospital just in case it's something serious. They don't want to take any chance with her and with the lupus and what has happened recently."

"I'll go and get changed, and we can head to the hospital," Alexandria said.

"All right," Colton said. Alexandria hugged him tightly and then kissed his cheek before leaving the room and heading to her own.

She quickly changed into a T-shirt and a pair of jeans and then went back to Colton's bedroom, where he was wearing a pair of jeans and a black T-shirt. Mark was in the room as well, wearing a pair of jeans and a blue T-shirt.

"I'm driving," Mark said. Alexandria nodded, and they headed to the car.

The three were at the hospital quickly, and everyone else was waiting in the waiting room. The three took the only empty seats around them, and Alexandria stared at her wrist for a moment before praying.

"Alexandria?" a familiar voice said. Alexandria looked up to see David standing there, looking at her in confusion.

"Hey, David, what are you doing here?" Alexandria said, standing up and walking over to him.

"I'm visiting members of the church," David said. "What are you doing here?"

"My sister woke up with a really high fever, and she gets very ill very easily, so we're just being very careful," Alexandria said. "David, this is my family."

"You have a large family," David said, his eyes widening.

Alexandria laughed. "I told you about my past that I was abandoned. We've all been left in the care of Elizabeth and Duncan here. I'm not *really* related to any of them, but they're all related to one another. It's really confusing."

David laughed. "I can tell."

"Yeah, these are Jessica, Carlee, Collin, Elizabeth, Duncan, Mark, and Colton," Alexandria introduced. "Everyone, this is my friend from church, David."

"Hi," they all said.

"Rhodes family," a doctor said. Everyone stood up, and Colton immediately walked over to Alexandria, not even thinking about it.

"Yes?" Elizabeth said, walking up to the doctor with Duncan.

"It's her lupus coming back," the doctor said. "We've given her some of the usual medicine, and she should be okay to go home now."

"It was actually a short hospital trip?" Jessica questioned.

"Yes, it was," the doctor said, laughing. "I'll have a nurse bring Anna down to you guys."

"Thank you," Duncan said and the doctor walked away.

"It's pretty bad that we're getting so used to everything being blamed on her lupus that we're grateful when they say that's all that it is," Colton said.

"It's easier than having something else be wrong with her," Alexandria said.

"Yeah, that's true," Colton said. He turned to see Anna walking down with the nurse, looking as strong as ever. "Hey, sweetheart."

"She's a little weak right now," the nurse said.

"Do you want me to carry you then, Anna?" Colton asked. Anna responded by holding her arms up. Colton laughed and reached down and picked her up, carrying her with ease.

"We'll take her home and meet you guys at the house," Mark said, shaking his head.

"Thanks," Elizabeth said.

"Of course," Colton said.

Anna sat down in the back with Alexandria, who sang softly to the songs on the radio. It was a relaxing trip back, and when they got back, Anna was immediately put to bed to rest. The rest of the group went to the living room to watch television. Mark, Alexandria, and Colton sat on the couch together, and Colton couldn't help but put his arm over the back of the couch.

"So are we still going to dinner tonight?" Alexandria asked, looking to Colton.

"I think so. If you don't mind, I'll keep my phone on sound just in case something happens," Colton said.

"Yeah, that's fine," Alexandria said, smiling.

"All right, thanks," Colton said.

Chapter Thirty-One

The rest of the day, everyone just hung out and let Anna sleep. Alexandria went upstairs during the afternoon and checked her e-mail and took a quick shower and changed into a semiformal dress that she had in her closet. It was a little black dress. It had small straps, a sweetheart neckline, and a skirt that puffed out slightly with the lining and ended a little above her knee. There was also a bow around the waist.

"That's a nice dress," Carlee said from the doorway. Alexandria had forgotten that she had opened her door because it seemed too closed off in her bedroom.

"Thanks," Alexandria said. "I'm hoping that Colton will like it."

"I'm sure he will," Carlee said. "I don't think you could do anything that wouldn't please him though. He is head over heels for you, girl."

Alexandria bit her lip. "That's what Mark was saying earlier."

"Mark knows Colton the best, so I'm sure he's right," Carlee said. "You should have seen his face, though, when he got back after you had been kidnapped. There is no denying that he really cares about you."

"Yeah, that's true," Alexandria said.

"Do you know how you're going to do your hair?" Carlee asked.

"I'm thinking about just leaving it natural," Alexandria said.

"Yeah, your hair is so curly naturally that I think you're fine," Carlee said.

"Yeah, that's what I'm thinking," Alexandria said.

The two were quiet for a minute, and it was a comfortable silence until Carlee broke it. "Do you really consider us all family to you, Lexi?"

"Yeah, of course," Alexandria said. "You all really are like siblings to me."

"I'm glad," Carlee said, smiling. "You're like a sibling to all of us."

"I'm glad," Alexandria said.

Mark appeared in the doorway and knocked on the doorframe. "Hey."

"Hey," Alexandria and Carlee said.

"What's up?" Alexandria asked.

"I've been sent to ask what color you're wearing," Mark said.

"Black," Alexandria said.

"All right, I'll tell him that. Oh, and tomorrow Laura's coming over to the house to hang out," Mark said and walked away with a grin on his face.

"Get your butt back here, Mark!" Alexandria shouted. Mark laughed and continued to walk. Alexandria ran out to the hallway in her robe. "Mark!"

"Yes?" Mark said, turning around.

"So her name is Laura?" Alexandria questioned.

"Yeah, you'll meet her tomorrow, Lexi," Mark said. "She's really nice and she's Christian also."

"Awesome," Alexandria said, grinning.

"See you later," Mark said, shaking his head and walking away.

"Not gonna lie, your reaction to that was hilarious," Carlee said, laughing as Alexandria entered the bedroom again.

Alexandria laughed. "Yeah, I don't tend to think about things before I do them."

"It's a good thing though," Carlee said. "Well, I better let you finish getting ready. See you later, Lexi. Have fun with Colton."

"Thanks," Alexandria said. "Can you shut the door behind you?"

"Sure," Carlee said and shut the door as she walked out of the bedroom.

Alexandria changed into a pair of tan tights and then put on the dress. She did her makeup and brushed her hair out, happy with the way it looked. She looked at the clock and saw that she had a few minutes left before they would be leaving. She turned her laptop on and saw that David had messaged her: "Hey, it was nice to see you and meet your family today. Hope your sister is feeling better. See you tomorrow?"

"My sister is resting right now. Yeah, I'm planning on going to church. See you then!"

"See you then, Lexi."

There was a knock on her door, and she opened it to reveal Anna. "Sweetie, shouldn't you be resting?" she said, kneeling to Anna's eyelevel.

"I wanted to say bye before you and Colton went out," Anna said. "Have a good time with each other. I'm really glad that you and Colton are together now."

"Well, it's not official that we're together yet," Alexandria corrected.

"Well, hopefully soon," Anna said and smiled. "Have a good time."

"Thanks, Anna. Do you want me to walk you back to your room?" Alexandria asked.

"Sure," Anna said, smiling. "Will you carry me actually?"

"Of course," Alexandria said. She picked up Anna with ease and headed down the hallway toward Anna's room. "Did you know that your room actually used to be my room?"

"Really?" Anna asked.

"Yeah," Alexandria said nodding.

Just as they passed Colton's bedroom, he walked out of it. "Oh, hey, ladies."

"I'll be just a second. I have to drop her in her room and then grab my purse," Alexandria said.

"All right," Colton said, smiling. He waited for Alexandria to put Anna down and kiss her forehead before they went back to Alexandria's room.

"All right, I'm all set," Alexandria said, smiling.

"You look beautiful, by the way," Colton said. He wore a pair of black dress pants and a white shirt. It was simple, but it looked great on him.

"Thanks, you look really nice too," Alexandria said.

"I'll give you my presents when we get back. I'm thinking we can go to the restaurant and probably just walk around and hang out for the rest of the night," Colton said.

"Sounds great," Alexandria said.

Colton just smiled and they got into the car with him driving. Alexandria couldn't help but make the comment. "Is it a good idea to let you drive?"

Colton laughed. "Yeah, I'm actually a good driver. Mark just likes to exaggerate."

"All right, if you say so," Alexandria said, smiling.

They made small talk until Colton pulled in front of a little Italian restaurant. Alexandria had heard of the restaurant and had once gone there with Duncan. It was a really nice restaurant, and Alexandria loved the food there when she was a child.

"I hope you like Italian," Colton said smiling.

"One of my favorites," Alexandria said, returning his smile.

They made small talk as they ate their dinner. Alexandria was amazed that no matter how much time they spent together, they would just continue to talk. They rarely ran out of things to say to each other. It was nice. When they were done eating dinner and had paid for the check, they decided to go for a walk around the park that was nearby. Because it was getting to be June, it was still really light out.

"This is such a beautiful park," Alexandria said.

"Yeah, it is," Colton said. He wanted to have the courage to ask her to be his girlfriend, but every time he started to think about it, he choked. What if she didn't want to be with him? What if what everyone was telling him was a lie?

Alexandria couldn't help but want to ask Colton if what everyone was saying was true: that he was head over heels for her. But every time she thought about asking him, she couldn't think of the words or the right way to bring it up.

Alexandria had a bad feeling come over her as they entered a part of the park. There was no one around them, but she couldn't help the bad feeling. She froze where she stood, and Colton looked at her in confusion.

"We should go back. I have a bad feeling," Alexandria said. Moments later, Colton's phone went off.

"Hey, Mark," Colton said. Alexandria's entire body tensed. Alexandria couldn't hear what Mark was saying to Colton. "Okay, we'll head there right now. Thanks, Mark." With that, he hung up and looked to Alexandria. "Anna is throwing up blood. They're taking her to the hospital right now."

"All right," Alexandria said. "That would explain the bad feeling."

"Yeah," Colton said. "When we get back from the hospital, I'll give you your presents."

"All right," Alexandria said.

*****

The ride was silent as they drove to the hospital. Alexandria just wished that this would stop already. Anna had been so happy lately, so lively. Why was it whenever she seemed at her healthiest, she came spiraling down? When they arrived in the hospital, everyone was in the waiting room talking to a doctor.

"Is it the lupus acting up?" Colton asked.

"We're doing some tests to make sure, but that's what we think it is," the doctor said. "We're going to keep her overnight to keep an eye on her."

"All right," Alexandria said. She felt beaten up; she just wanted this all to be done already. She was surprised when her cell phone went off; she was even more shocked when she saw that it was Dr. Rizzoli's phone number. "Excuse me for a minute." She stepped outside of the hospital and answered, "Hello."

"Hey, are you all at your house?" Dr. Rizzoli asked.

"We're actually at the hospital right now. Anna's lupus is acting up again," Alexandria said.

"Okay, I'm going to head over there right now. I need to talk to you," Dr. Rizzoli stated.

"Okay, I'll be in the waiting room," Alexandria said. "See you soon."

"See you soon," Dr. Rizzoli said, and they hung up.

Colton looked at her in confusion when she reentered the hospital waiting room, and she just shook her head as the doctor was explaining the test to Elizabeth and Duncan.

"You all may go and see her, but only in a couple of people at a time," the doctor said.

"All right, can you show us to the room?" Elizabeth asked. "Duncan and I will come first."

"Follow me," the doctor said.

"Who was on the phone?" Colton asked. Usually she didn't like to leave the hospital if something was said about Anna, so he was confused by her leaving.

"Dr. Rizzoli. He said he has something to talk to me about. I have a feeling about what it is," Alexandria said.

"What do you think it is?" Colton wondered.

"I think that my mother died," Alexandria said.

"Are you sure?" Colton inquired.

"Yeah, I'm not too hurt by it. I never really got to know her, so it doesn't matter," Alexandria said, shrugging.

"Hey, everyone," Dr. Rizzoli said, walking over to the group. "So what happened with Anna?"

"She woke up this morning with a really high fever and then, later on, was throwing up blood. The doctors think that it's just the lupus," Mark explained.

"Yeah, it probably is," Dr. Rizzoli said. "I wish that there was a cure for it already."

"Yeah, I think we all do," Colton said, smiling at Alexandria as he recalled the night when they stayed up and they admitted that if they had three wishes that would be granted, they both wanted a cure for lupus. Alexandria returned his smile.

"So did my mother die?" Alexandria stated. Straightforward and to the point, it was the way she liked to handle bad news. She didn't want to beat around the bush about this stuff.

Dr. Rizzoli was surprised at this and nodded. "Yes, the calling hours are Sunday from five to eight at night, and the funeral is Monday at five at the Methodist Church in town. Your father wants you to be there. Your siblings ... don't really care."

"I don't plan on going," Alexandria said. "I didn't know her. She wasn't my mother. Elizabeth is more of a mother to me than she was."

"Lexi—" Colton said.

"No," Alexandria said, "I don't care. I feel nothing toward my mother except anger. She abandoned me when I was a baby, and she let me to be abused by my adoptive parents."

"It's understood," Dr. Rizzoli said. He smiled at her. "I honestly had a feeling that would be your reaction, but James wanted me to try to convince you to come anyways."

Alexandria laughed. "You know me better than my own biological father. It's the truth though. I don't consider them family. And I would just get too strange of looks since no one would know me but my father."

"That is true," Dr. Rizzoli said, nodding. "I mainly just came to tell you that and to see how you all were doing."

"We're all pretty healthy besides Anna," Alexandria said. "Thank you, Dr. Rizzoli."

"Of course," Dr. Rizzoli said. He smiled at the group and left.

"Are you okay?" Colton asked.

"Like I said, I didn't know her," Alexandria said. "I may have looked just like my mother, but I didn't know her at all. And I really don't know what I would do when I got there. Am I supposed to be a grieving daughter when I didn't know her?"

"That's true," Colton said.

Chapter Thirty-Two

They went in to visit with Anna in pairs. Collin and Carlee went in next, then Mark and Jessica, and then Colton and Alexandria. Alexandria was surprised when she felt Colton's fingers interlace with her own as they walked in. She smiled weakly at him, unsure if she was ready to face what was inside the room. Colton squeezed her hand, and suddenly she felt reassured. She felt like she could face just about anything if he was beside her. Her smile widened, and he opened the door.

The sight wasn't as bad as Alexandria had expected. Anna was sitting up at the moment, propped up by a couple of pillows. Her face was pale, and her eyes weren't shining as much as Alexandria would have liked.

"Hey, sweetheart," Colton said as he and Alexandria sat on either side of Anna.

"Hey," Anna said, attempting a weak smile, "I'm sorry I took you guys away."

"It's okay, Anna," Colton said. "You know both of us would drop everything to make sure you were okay."

"Yeah, but …," Anna said, and then began coughing. It was a terrible sound to Alexandria. It sounded like hacking and like she was choking, and Alexandria just wanted to hold Anna and make the coughing stop. A nurse came in and gave her a glass of water, but it didn't help and Anna coughed up blood on the sheet.

Alexandria couldn't handle it at that point and had to leave. She had to get out of the hospital. She said goodbye quickly and ran out of the room, unable to live with the sight of Anna, so young and full of life, coughing up blood and seeming like an elderly woman.

Colton was right behind her after kissing Anna's head quickly. When he saw Alexandria standing at the end of the hallway, he didn't hesitate to wrap his arms around her and hold her tightly. They both started crying then, unable to bear the fact that Anna could die at such a young age and that she was in such pain right now.

"I'm sorry, I just … I couldn't handle it anymore," Alexandria said when they were done crying.

"I couldn't either," Colton said, brushing away her tears. "But she'll pull through. She always does somehow."

"Yeah, I know," Alexandria said and flipped her wrist over to see what she had tattooed there. "Hope and faith. I just have to keep remembering that."

"Can I go to church with you tomorrow?" Colton asked. Alexandria looked up at him in shock. "I want to start going again. And obviously it means a lot to you, and I want to be involved with what's important to you."

"Thanks, Colton," Alexandria said. "Yeah, I'd love it if you came with me. Come on, let's get going to the group before they worry that something happened."

"Right," Colton agreed. They both went out to the waiting room, where everyone was sitting. "All right, we're all set."

"What took you guys so long?" Jessica asked.

"Anna started having a coughing fit," Alexandria stated. "And I just … I couldn't handle seeing it."

"And neither could I," Colton admitted. "So we had to recompose ourselves."

"Uh-huh, sure," Carlee said, smirking as she rolled her eyes.

"It's the truth!" Alexandria said, blushing.

"Mhm, whatever you guys say," Collin said.

Alexandria just rolled her eyes. Mark smiled at the two. "If you two want to continue your date, you can. I've got the other car."

"Okay, thanks," Colton said, smiling. Mark nodded, and the group all left to their cars. Elizabeth and Duncan drove with Collin and Carlee, and Mark took Jessica home. Colton and Alexandria got in the car, and Colton started driving. "There's somewhere I want to show you before we go back home."

"All right," Alexandria said.

Colton drove for a short while until he stopped in front of a fountain in the middle of town. It had started to get dark, and so the fountain was lit up by the sunset behind itself. Alexandria couldn't believe how gorgeous it was.

"Wow," Alexandria said.

"Yeah," Colton said. "This is one of my favorite places in town. Anna was actually the one to show me. I had just gotten my license, and she had wanted to take a walk in the park on one of her healthier days at that time. So I drove us to this park, and we walked around and she showed me this fountain. It had been right around sunset even though she probably should have been in bed resting."

Alexandria walked up to the fountain and found the edge to be dry, so she sat down. Colton followed right after her. "I'm glad Anna was at least able to enjoy last night before she got sick."

"I wonder if it's not because of last night that she got sick, what with being up so late and having so much sugar and everything," Alexandria reasoned.

"That could be it," Colton said. "But I don't know. I'm sure she'll be feeling better soon. This stuff never stays for very long with her."

"I keep seeing the image of her coughing in my head," Alexandria said, shaking her head.

"Me too," Colton stated. He reached out and took Alexandria's hand. "Hey, Lexi."

"Yeah," Alexandria responded, turning to face him fully.

"I know we haven't really been on any dates or anything … but I really like you. I … I'm not good with my emotions, and yet with you I know everything is certain. I just … I want to be with you. I want you to be my girl," Colton said. There, he had finally done it.

Alexandria stared at Colton, not really believing what he had said. "Are you serious?"

"I'm very serious," Colton stated. "I want us to be in an actual relationship. We practically act like it as it is."

Alexandria laughed. "Yeah, that's true. Sorry about that reaction, I just couldn't believe that you actually wanted to be in a relationship with me. But yes, Colton, I would love to be your girlfriend."

"I was getting a little concerned there. I had talked to Mark and Carlee, making sure that you really did like me as more than just friends before I took the plunge," Colton said. "They both said that you did, but I still was scared."

"That's kinda funny because I talked to Mark and Carlee also about how you felt about me," Alexandria said.

"That is funny," Colton said, smiling. "But come on, let's get home."

"Sounds good," Alexandria said, smiling. They stood up and Colton held her hand as they walked back to the car. Alexandria's phone went off as she got into the car. She didn't recognize the phone number as she answered it.

"Hello?"

"Hey, Alexandria, it's James … your father," a deep voice said.

"Oh, hey," Alexandria said. She was shocked that he was calling her.

"Are you coming to your mother's funeral?" he asked.

"No," Alexandria answered simply, "I don't feel like I should go there. I don't know anyone there, and I would get some strange looks from everyone."

"Your mother would have wanted you to be there," James said.

"She wanted to keep me too, but she decided against that," Alexandria spat. Colton instantly knew who she was talking to when he heard her tone of voice with that.

"Alexandria!" James shouted. He was appalled at what his daughter had just said to him.

"What? It's the truth! Am I sad that she's dead? Yeah, kinda, but I didn't know her. I'm tired of people asking me if I'm going to be there and if I'm okay. I didn't know her, and that's the end of it," Alexandria said. "Therefore, I'm not going to her funeral. It would be like going to a great-aunt's funeral that I had met maybe once in my entire life."

"I understand," James said. "But I do want to meet up with you afterward, just for a coffee or something."

"All right," Alexandria said. "When and where?"

"I can just stop by after the funeral, and we can stay at the house there," James suggested.

"That works. I'll see you then," Alexandria said.

"See you then," James said, and they hung up.

"Sorry about that, it was my biological father," Alexandria stated.

"I'm assuming he asked if you were going to the funeral with the talk of your mother," Colton said.

"Yup, and you heard my reaction. He's going to stop by after the funeral, though, to talk to me," Alexandria said.

"That will be nice," Colton said.

"Yeah, as long as he doesn't ask about how I feel about my mother," Alexandria said.

"That's true," Colton said. "So do you want to go and get your presents now?"

"Sure," Alexandria said, smiling.

They made small talk as Colton drove back to the house. The house was rather quiet but not necessarily in a bad way—just in a content way. Alexandria smiled as she entered with Colton and then saw Carlee and Collin were talking at the top of the staircase.

"Did you finally get the guts, Colton?" Collin said.

"Collin!" Carlee said, smacking her twin brother.

Colton laughed and surprised everyone. At that moment, everyone entered the foyer, shocked at hearing Colton's laugh throughout the house.

"Yeah, Collin, I did," Colton said and took Alexandria's hand lightly, making her blush madly.

"Finally!" Carlee shouted. This just caused Alexandria to join Colton in laughing.

"It's so strange to hear you actually laughing, Colton," Jessica said.

"Yeah, well, you better get used to it," Colton said. "I have a feeling I'm going to be happy for a while now."

"I'm glad," Alexandria said, squeezing his hand. They looked at Mark, who walked over and shook Colton's hand and then hugged Alexandria.

"Make sure you two stay happy. And, Colton, if you break her heart, I'm going to kill you," Mark said.

Colton smiled. "I'll deserve it."

"Can we just not talk about that happening?" Alexandria said. "I'd rather not have anyone killed on my behalf."

"All right," Mark said, laughing.

"Thanks," Alexandria said. "Oh, my biological father will be here Monday after the funeral. I'm not going to the funeral, but he wants to talk to me about something, so he's just going to come over here."

"Okay," Elizabeth said. "Duncan and I are going to bed. Good night, everyone."

"Good night," everyone said, and Elizabeth and Duncan went upstairs.

"Do you want any of us there with you, Lexi?" Mark asked. He knew that Alexandria was always nervous about meeting with her biological father.

"No, I should be okay. I would actually prefer to be alone with him, just in case he wants to say something about my past," Alexandria said.

"All right," Mark said.

"Well, I still have to give her her birthday presents," Colton said and started tugging her toward the stairwell.

"Can I change into something more comfortable first?" Alexandria asked.

"I suppose," Colton said. Alexandria smiled. She had not felt this happy since she was young. She liked it. She had missed all this.

"Thanks," Alexandria said, "I'll be in your room in just a few minutes, okay?"

"All right," Colton said. Alexandria ran to her room and changed into a pair of yoga pants and a loose T-shirt and then went into Colton's room.

"So what are my presents?" Alexandria asked. She jumped on his bed where he was sitting with a box in his lap.

Colton chuckled. "Here you go."

Alexandria happily opened the presents. "I have been thinking about getting a journal! I just haven't had the chance to go shopping! And oh, this smells just like you! Hey, maybe this will be the way to make me be able to sleep without sleeping in your bed!"

"I like it when you're sleeping beside me though," Colton said, pouting slightly.

Alexandria laughed. "I like sleeping with you, so it's probably not going to change that."

"Good," Colton said. He couldn't help it when he leaned forward and kissed her lightly.

Alexandria smiled and leaned her head against his. "Colton?"

"Yeah?" Colton said.

"I'm actually happy. Like, really happy. It's been so long since I've been this happy," Alexandria said. "I ... I really am glad that we're dating."

"Me too," Colton said, smiling. "I'm really happy too. I really don't remember when I was ever this happy."

"I'm glad that you're happy now," Alexandria said, smiling.

Chapter Thirty-Three

It was Sunday. Colton and Alexandria woke up early and were in the foyer at the church, waiting to go inside for service.

"Lexi!" David shouted. Alexandria turned around and saw David walking toward them.

"Hey, David," Alexandria said, smiling. "David, you met Colton yesterday. Colton, this is my friend, David."

"It's nice to meet you," Colton said, shaking David's hand.

"You too," David said. "So how is your sister doing?"

"She got sent to the hospital last night again," Alexandria said. "It's best to keep her in your prayers all the time. She has some serious health issues."

"Will do," David said. "Hey, there's a Young Adult group starting up here. It's Monday nights from seven to nine. You two are more than welcome to join."

"We can't make it tomorrow night, but maybe in the future," Alexandria said.

"Yeah, it's right here in the church. We may be changing places, depending on how many people we get and that. I'll let you know if we change places," David said.

"Fantastic, thanks," Alexandria said.

"I'm going to run to the bathroom," Colton whispered in Alexandria's ear. He kissed her forehead and then went to the bathroom.

"Is ... he your boyfriend?" David asked.

"Yeah, we just started dating yesterday," Alexandria said. "We both live in the House of Hope. Everyone there except for me has been adopted by Elizabeth and Duncan."

"Oh wow. I thought you had wanted to be adopted by them," David said, recalling a conversation with her a few months before.

"I had. But I also didn't want to have an issue if I wanted to be in a relationship with Colton before. And I've always been a Rhodes at heart," Alexandria said. "And that's all that really matters."

"True. Have you heard anything from your biological parents?" David wondered.

"Yeah, my biological mother just died recently. I'm not really that depressed about it or anything, so don't worry about it. And my father is trying to have a relationship with me, but I'm not sure if I really want to anymore," Alexandria said. "I did at first, but now he's barely tried to contact me and just some other things have happened that have made me realize that I don't really need him."

"You seem a lot happier now than you have in the past," David stated.

"I am," Alexandria said, smiling. She saw Colton exit the bathroom, and her eyes softened, knowing that he was part of the reason why she was happy. "I have a family now. I have people that care about me."

"I'm glad," David said. "Well, I'll see you later."

"See you later, David," Alexandria said. Colton walked over to her, and then they went into the sanctuary with the other church members.

*****

The rest of Sunday was spent relaxing and enjoying the time with everyone. Sunday night, Alexandria just went right into Colton's room and didn't bother trying to sleep in her own bed. Ever since she had been kidnapped, she wanted to be with someone at night, and that person was typically Colton. Anna was brought home Sunday but was put on bed rest for the next couple of days.

Monday morning, Alexandria had gone to work. After she was back from work, she was getting nervous. Her father was supposed to be coming over that night, and she wasn't sure why she was nervous about seeing him. Alexandria was helping Elizabeth cook dinner when Colton appeared in the kitchen.

"Lexi, your father is here," Colton said. Bridget entered then with her father.

"Oh, hi," Alexandria said.

"I can help Elizabeth finish dinner if you want to go upstairs to the ballroom," Colton said.

"Thanks, Colton," Alexandria said. She washed her shaking hands, and he kissed her head before she walked upstairs.

"I thought you were seeing Mark, not Colton," James said.

"I was. But then I was kidnapped last week and realized that Colton is the one that I wanted to be with," Alexandria said.

"Wait, you were kidnapped?" James questioned.

"Yes. Colton's parents were being threatened by a gang, and that was why they left him here. The same gang that was after them was after my adoptive parents. In order for us to repay our parents' debts, they kidnapped me and threatened Colton and were going to make us rob a bank for them. It didn't work though, and they were all arrested," Alexandria explained.

"Are you sure it's a good idea to be with Colton then?" James inquired.

"He was the one that saved me," Alexandria stated.

"Oh, okay," James said nodding. "So … how have you been?"

"A lot happier than I have been in the past," Alexandria said, smiling. "I've found my home finally."

"I'd like for you to live with me," James blurted out. "I got a place in Connecticut and a new job. I want you to come with me. Please, Alexandria, I want to make up for the years I haven't been there."

Alexandria looked at him in shock and confusion. He wanted her to drop everything that she had worked so hard at getting just to go and live with her?

"If you had offered this to me a month ago, I would have taken you up on the offer. But I can't now. I belong here with the Rhodes. I'm finally happy for once in my life, Father. I'm not going to give that up to start over again. I've started over far too many times in my life now. I have a good job here. I have a great boyfriend. Everyone here is my family. I can't just leave them. And Anna needs me here. I need to stay here, Father. I'm sorry."

James looked at her and smiled. "I should have known. Here is my contact number and my new address. I hope that you are happy, Alexandria. I think of you every day."

"Thanks, Father. I'll keep in touch," Alexandria said, smiling.

"I should probably go. I'll talk to you later," James said.

"Talk to you later," Alexandria said.

She hugged James tightly, and he left the ballroom. When he was gone, she took a few deep breaths and then started to dance, trying to let all the emotions out. She wasn't surprised when she was turning and saw Colton standing at the doorway.

"Is dinner ready?" she asked as she continued to dance.

"Yes," Colton said. "And your father left. He didn't tell us what he wanted."

"I didn't think he would," Alexandria said. She finished her dance and then walked over to him.

"Why not?" Colton asked.

"I'm going to announce what he wanted when we're at dinner," Alexandria said. She kissed his cheek. "Come on, let's get some food."

"Is everything okay?" Colton wondered.

"Yes, everything is fine," Alexandria said, smiling.

"All right," Colton said. They walked down to the dining room, and Alexandria was glad that they were the last ones to be there.

"So may we ask what your father wanted?" Elizabeth asked as the two sat down.

"My father asked me to go and live with him in Connecticut," Alexandria stated.

"What?" they all exclaimed. Colton stood up, appalled that she had not told him before.

"Calm down, I'm not going," Alexandria said, waving at Colton to sit down.

"Why didn't you tell me when I went to get you?" Colton asked.

"Because I thought it was obvious that I would not be going with him," Alexandria said. "You guys are all my family. I've restarted my life too many times already. I'm not about to do it again, not when I finally feel like I got it right."

"So … you're staying here with us?" Anna questioned.

"Of course, sweetheart. I wasn't about to leave you," Alexandria said, smiling at the younger girl. "Colton, you can sit down. I'm really not leaving."

Colton sat back down. He didn't want Alexandria to leave him—ever. He suddenly couldn't see himself without her. He hadn't realized just how much he cared for her.

"It's funny. When you first got here, you didn't want to stay for very long," Duncan said.

"When I first got here, I didn't think that I would be pulled in so easily by everyone here. I had hoped that I would only stay here for a couple of weeks. I hadn't expected to feel at home again," Alexandria said.

"So you're really not leaving," Carlee said.

"Not for a very long time," Alexandria said.

"Good," Elizabeth said, smiling.

They then made small talk as they ate dinner. When they were done, Alexandria went back up to the ballroom, and Colton followed after her.

"Please don't ever scare me like that again," Colton said before she began to dance.

"I figured it was obvious, Colton. I'm sorry that I scared you. I thought that the fact that I love you and the fact that I love everyone else like a family would be enough to reassure you that I wasn't about to leave," Alexandria said.

"You … you love me," Colton questioned. It was so strange for him to have been told that he was loved by someone who wasn't family.

"Yes, Colton, I love you. I can't explain my feelings for you in any other way. I can't sleep unless I'm with you. The thought of not being with you breaks my heart. I can't imagine not being with you," Alexandria said.

Colton grabbed her roughly and kissed her passionately. She was confused at first but kissed him back just as passionately. When they broke for air, he put his forehead against hers. "I love you too. When you were kidnapped … I thought my life was over. When I just thought that you would be gone, I thought my life was over. I never want to feel that way again."

"You shouldn't have to feel that way again," Alexandria said, smiling, "'Cause you're gonna be stuck with me for a long time."

"Good," Colton said.

Epilogue

It was five years later. Alexandria was in what was now hers and Colton's bedroom. A lot had happened in five years. Alexandria and Colton got married two years before. Colton went back to college for finance and was now working in the investment banking industry. Anna was still fighting the lupus but was getting stronger and stronger every day. Carlee was now pursuing her dream in dance. Collin was going to college for computer science. Jessica was a senior in high school now, about to graduate. Mark had begun dating Laura from work and, that night, was about to propose.

Alexandria was sitting in her vanity chair, rubbing her ever-growing belly. She was four months pregnant. Colton had argued with her for the previous three years while they were dating about having a child. Finally, Alexandria had convinced him about having a child while Anna was in the hospital.

"Hey, Lexi," Mark said, knocking on the bedroom door before entering.

"Hey, Mark. Getting nervous?" Alexandria said with a smile as she turned to the doorway.

"Oh, yeah. Now I understand Colton's nerves when he proposed to you," Mark said.

"Even though you have nothing to worry about and neither did he," Alexandria said, waving her hand.

"So have you opened the envelope to see if it's a girl or a boy?" Mark asked.

"I'm waiting for Colton to get back from work," Alexandria said. Colton had been unable to get the day off to be with her for the appointment where the doctor would tell them if it was a boy or a girl, and she refused to know until he knew as well.

"Are you getting antsy to open it?" Mark wondered.

"Very much so. I actually had Anna hide it as soon as I got it so that I wouldn't be tempted to open it until Colton got home," Alexandria said. Mark laughed.

"That was probably a good idea," Mark said.

"Yeah, that's what I kinda figured," Alexandria said.

"Hey, can I peek at your sonogram picture, Lexi?" Anna asked, appearing in the doorway.

"You just can't tell me," Alexandria said.

"You know that as soon as I see it I'm going to run over to you and tell you though!" Anna pouted.

"Then I guess you don't open it," Alexandria said, shrugging.

"I wanna know!" Anna said.

"Try actually being pregnant and wanting to know!" Alexandria responded.

"Good point," Anna said, laughing.

"What are you all laughing about?" Carlee asked.

"Carlee!" they all shouted. Carlee wasn't supposed to come home for another few weeks, even just for a weekend visit.

"Way to forget about me," Collin said, appearing behind his sister.

"We just didn't see you, Collin!" Alexandria said. "What are you guys doing here? You aren't supposed to be home for another few weeks."

"Elizabeth told us that you were going to find out the sex of the baby today, so we had to come home to find out!" Carlee said.

"Thanks, guys," Alexandria said, smiling. She stood up and hugged both of them.

"Of course," Collin said.

"So? What is it?" Carlee asked.

"We're waiting for Colton to get home. I had Anna hide it so that I'm not tempted to open it," Alexandria said. "He couldn't get today off from work. They have a huge merger going on this week-end that they have to make sure that they have everything for."

"Ugh, I wanna know so badly!" Carlee complained.

"Try being me," Alexandria said, rubbing her stomach. Her phone went off on her bedside table, and she grinned when it was Colton: "You haven't looked yet, right, love?"

"I made Anna hide it from me as soon as I got home. Carlee and Collin are here to find out as well. When will you be home?"

The front door opened, and everyone looked around at one another. Jessica, Elizabeth, and Duncan were in the kitchen cooking, and the rest of them were all in the bedroom, except for Colton. Alexandria's phone went off: "Right now, where are you?"

"I'm in our room, Colton!" Alexandria shouted. Hurried foot-steps were heard, and Colton was standing in the hallway.

"All right, all right, I'd like to get to my wife please," Colton said. Everyone moved aside, and Colton entered the bedroom. He hugged and kissed Alexandria.

"Anna, can we have the sonogram please?" Alexandria asked.

"Yeah, be right back!" Anna said and ran off.

"She's having a healthy day, huh?" Colton observed.

"Very healthy," Alexandria said, nodding.

"Here you go!" Anna said, handing it to the pair.

"Do you want us all gone while you two open it?" Mark asked.

"Please," the pair said, nodding.

"We'll go and get Elizabeth, Duncan, and Jess," Collin said.

"But ... but," Carlee said.

"Carlee, let them find out on their own," Collin said. He was about to grab her collar and pull her away when she willingly turned around.

"Come on, Anna, let's let the lovebirds be alone," Mark said.

"Thanks, guys," Alexandria said. Mark shut the door behind him after they were all gone.

"So what are you hoping our baby is?" Colton asked as they sat down on the bed together.

"Honestly, a girl," Alexandria said, "But as long as our baby is healthy, I don't care."

"Me too," Colton said. "All right, one, two, three."

Alexandria pulled the sonogram out, and they both grinned when they saw the sonogram. He kissed her deeply.

"We have our own little girl," he said.

"She is going to be daddy's little princess, isn't she?" Alexandria said.

"You know it," Colton said. "Come on, let's tell everyone."

Alexandria nodded, and they got off the bed and went to the door, only to see everyone standing there patiently, including Elizabeth, Duncan, and Jessica.

"So? So? So?" Carlee and Anna said.

"We're going to have a girl," Colton announced.

"Ah!" they all squealed. Everyone immediately hugged Colton and Alexandria tightly.

"Ah! I gotta go! I'm gonna be late!" Mark exclaimed when he saw the time after hugging the pair. "Love you, two. Congrats!"

"Good luck, man," Colton said.

"He doesn't need luck! She's going to say yes!" Alexandria said, rolling her eyes.

"And how do you know?" Colton asked when Mark was out of earshot.

"I asked her awhile ago," Alexandria said. "I was talking about being pregnant and she was worried that Mark was never going to propose."

"You didn't tell her that he was planning on it, right?" Colton said.

"Of course not," Alexandria said, rolling her eyes.

"Good," Colton said.

"Come on, let's go eat dinner," Elizabeth said.

"It smells delicious," Alexandria said, smiling.

"Thanks," Jessica said. She had recently found that she loved cooking and was always helping Elizabeth in the kitchen now.

Colton hugged Alexandria tightly. "I love you, Lexi."

"I love you too, Colton," Alexandria said.

About the Author

Elizabeth Woodruff has been writing for as long as she can remember. There is rarely a time when she does not have a notebook with her to write down the ideas that come into her mind suddenly. During college, Elizabeth was a member of Active Minds, which promotes dismantling the stigma around mental illnesses. Currently, Elizabeth is a small-group leader at her church and helps teenage mothers. Elizabeth tries to help people facing difficult times and facing mental illnesses as much as she can. Elizabeth lives in Rochester, New York, with her husband and son.

CPSIA information can be obtained
at www.ICGtesting.com
Printed in the USA
BVHW081812031218
534638BV00006B/336/P